MW01137676

The Honourable Lucas Kincaid

EMMA MELBOURNE

Copyright © 2024 by Emma Melbourne

All rights reserved.

Cover by Erin Dameron-Hill, www.edhprofessionals.com

This book was created without the use of AI.

No part of this book may be reproduced in any form or by any electronic or mechanical means, including information storage and retrieval systems, without written permission from the author, except for the use of brief quotations in a book review.

One

Mayfair, London
February, 1818

Lucas Kincaid strode purposefully through his London townhouse in search of his ward, Miss Felicity Taylor. He found the young lady in the entrance hall, preparing to go out.

Felicity paused in the act of tying her bonnet and surveyed her guardian through clever brown eyes. She was tall for a lady, with a straight nose and a determined chin, and although she wasn't a classic beauty, she made the most of her looks. That morning, she was stylishly dressed in a pink merino coat trimmed with a high lace collar. A matching bonnet complemented her dark hair, and kidskin gloves and half boots completed the ensemble. The overall effect was charming, but nonetheless, Kincaid frowned.

"Are you going out, Felicity?" he asked abruptly.

"You can see that I am."

"Where are you going?"

Felicity smiled. "The fact that you're my guardian doesn't give you the right to know where I'm going, Mr. Kincaid."

Kincaid was fairly sure that it did, but he wisely decided not to argue the point. After seven years as Felicity's guardian, he had learned to pick his battles. "I came to ask if you wanted to ride in Hyde Park with me. There's something I want to discuss with you."

Felicity's expression told him she was tempted by the invitation, but she shook her head. "I would love to, but Miss Flint and I are off to the modiste."

Kincaid realized he had neglected to acknowledge Felicity's companion, who was waiting by the door in a sensible brown cloak and boots. As a middle-aged lady of few words, Miss Theodora Flint was easy to overlook, but Kincaid always felt guilty when he did.

"Good morning, Miss Flint," he said, giving her a warm smile. "You're looking very well today."

"Thank you," Miss Flint replied.

Kincaid turned back to Felicity. "Perhaps we could ride tomorrow. I won't ask you to delay such an important errand as a trip to the modiste."

"It is an important errand, Mr. Kincaid," Felicity replied earnestly. "If you recall, I'll be making my *ton* debut next month. Besides evening gowns, I'll need dancing slippers, boots, hats, and gloves." Her eyes sparkled with devilment. "Not to mention new stockings and petticoats."

A faint blush spread across Kincaid's cheeks at the mention of her underclothes. "It's a wonder you haven't outrun your allowance," he said critically.

"Yes, I often think so," Felicity agreed. "Especially since I have such a tight-fisted guardian, who doesn't seem to understand that money is meant to be spent."

"I would be a poor guardian if I let you squander your fortune on fripperies before you came of age."

"Really, Mr. Kincaid, that's rather harsh," Felicity protested. "I don't think the money is entirely wasted. I thought this coat was quite becoming."

Kincaid cast his eye down Felicity's figure and quickly glanced away.

"It's very nice," he said stiffly.

Felicity laughed. "If that's your reaction, I certainly need to buy new clothes."

"I'm hardly a connoisseur of ladies' fashions," Kincaid retorted.

"That may be, but I am determined to have a new coat as well as new evening gowns. Think of it as an investment; if I'm not properly turned out, I'll never find a husband to take over the responsibility of managing my fortune."

"I doubt you'll have difficulty finding a husband, Felicity."

"Maybe not, but it wouldn't do to leave it to chance. And I'm hoping to find a man who appreciates me for more than my money."

"Perhaps you'll find a man who loves your dresses as well." Kincaid hadn't meant to be cruel, and he regretted the words as soon as they were spoken. To his relief, Felicity grinned.

"I certainly hope to do so," she agreed. "So you'll understand the importance of the trip to the modiste."

"All your clothes are beautiful, Felicity," Kincaid assured her. "There's no need to replace them."

"But I might enjoy doing so," Felicity said, with a gleam of mischief in her eyes. "And you don't need to worry that I'll ask for an advance on my next quarter's allowance. If you remember, you agreed to increase my allowance when I come of age."

When Kincaid didn't reply immediately, Felicity began to plead her case. "Don't tell me you forgot? You promised to let me have the entire income from my fortune when I turn twenty-one next month. And don't say I'm still too young, since you were little more than a schoolboy when you were put in charge of the money."

"I was twenty-four, Felicity," Kincaid replied. "Hardly a schoolboy."

"Perhaps not," Felicity conceded. "But you seemed a great deal younger than you do now." At thirty-one, Lucas Kincaid was a man in his prime, and there was certainly nothing of the schoolboy in his square jaw and broad shoulders.

Kincaid chuckled. "How am I to take that, I wonder?"

"Any way you like, I suppose," Felicity replied with a shrug. "But you intend to keep your promise, don't you? You'll let me have the income from my fortune?"

"I will." Since Felicity's fortune was large, the income it generated would be more than triple the amount she had been receiving as an allowance. Although Kincaid hated the idea of Felicity spending so much money on gowns and hats, he thought she had a right to do so if she chose. He would never admit it to Felicity, but he thought it was unfair that she wouldn't gain control of her fortune when she came of age. Instead, Kincaid would remain in control of her fortune until Felicity married, when the money would pass to her husband.

"And you don't think Mr. Battersby will object?" Felicity asked.

The corner of Kincaid's mouth lifted. "I don't think so." Mr. Battersby had been her father's solicitor, and was nominally a trustee of her fortune along with Kincaid. Battersby had supposedly been sharp in his youth, but age had dulled his faculties, and he no longer questioned Kincaid's decisions.

Felicity smiled. "Excellent. So I will soon have plenty of money, and I'm sure the shopkeepers will be happy to take credit for a few weeks."

Kincaid's eyes narrowed. "Are you in debt, Felicity?"

"I am not, Mr. Kincaid."

Some of the tension left his face. "And you will let me know if you need money?"

"So you can read me a lecture on economy?"

"I wouldn't lecture you," he began, but her skeptical look made him pause. "Well, I might, but I'd also pay your debts."

"How very noble of you."

"Hardly noble, Felicity," Kincaid said with a laugh. "I'd use your money to pay them."

"You're right," Felicity agreed. "If you were truly noble, you would have found a way around this horrid trust so that I could control my own money."

"I'm certainly not as noble as that," he replied lightly. "But I want you to promise that you'll come to me if you're ever in trouble. I don't want to learn that you've tried to borrow money, or tried to pawn something."

Felicity nodded. "All right."

"Promise me, Felicity," Kincaid insisted.

"I promise, Mr. Kincaid," she said easily. "Now, I confess, you've piqued my interest. What did you want to talk to me about?"

"It's nothing urgent. We can discuss it tomorrow."

"Perhaps we could go riding when I return?"

"I can't," Kincaid said, looking regretful. "I'm boxing with Langley and Ashingham at Jackson's."

"It still seems strange to think of Mr. Oliver as Lord Ashingham," Felicity mused. When she and Kincaid had first met Lord Oliver St. Clair, the Marquess of Ashingham, he had been working as a land agent under the name of Mr. Oliver.

"Just take care you don't call him Mr. Oliver in company."

"I doubt he would mind," Felicity said with a mischievous grin. "I always thought Mr. Oliver had a soft spot for me, you know. It's a pity that he was already in love with Isabelle when we met, or I might be the Marchioness of Ashingham."

Although Felicity's tone was teasing, Kincaid didn't look amused. "Oliver might not mind if you called him by his Christian name, but I hate to think of the gossip you would stir up if anyone else heard you."

"All right," Felicity agreed with a nod. "I will only call him Mr. Oliver when we are alone together."

Kincaid let out a sigh of frustration. "I know you enjoy teasing me, Felicity, but I wish you wouldn't. Once you're in the habit of saying outrageous things, you may find it hard to guard your tongue when you're in company."

"Sensible advice, Mr. Kincaid," she murmured. "So you're going to Jackson's?"

"Yes."

"You should be careful," Felicity said, feigning a look of concern. "Lord Langley and Mr. Oliver both look quite athletic. I know they're your friends, but you might do better to spar with men whose skills more closely match your own."

Kincaid rolled his eyes. "I think I can hold my own against Langley or Oliver."

"I hope so," Felicity said dubiously. "But there's no shame in retiring if the contest is uneven."

"Your concern is touching," Kincaid said dryly.

"Well, if you injure yourself boxing, you won't be able to ride with me tomorrow morning," Felicity said practically. "I'll have to go with one of the grooms, and they always get anxious when I want to gallop."

"I can see how that would frustrate you, Felicity," Kincaid said, fighting to hide a smile. "I'll do my best to avoid an injury."

"I suppose that's all I can ask."

"Is the trip to the modiste all you have planned for the afternoon?"

Felicity met his gaze. "Are you concerned I'm planning a secret assignation with an ineligible gentleman?"

Kincaid chuckled. "I doubt you would tell me if you were."

Felicity pretended to consider the question. "You're right. I likely wouldn't tell you. But I'm not planning any mischief, so you needn't look so worried."

After Felicity departed with Miss Flint, Kincaid stood in the entrance hall for a moment, lost in thought. He knew Felicity considered him a strict guardian, but he thought he had good reason to be. Not only was Felicity an heiress, her fortune had been left with an unusual condition: if she married without Kincaid's consent before she came of age, the bulk of her fortune would go to her mother's second cousin, Mr. Martin Nethercott.

Felicity's father had been trying to protect her from fortune hunters, but Kincaid thought he had chosen a foolish way to do so. If a fortune hunter found a way to compromise Felicity, Kincaid would be forced to consent to her marriage to preserve her reputation. And if an enterprising gentleman took Felicity to Scotland, where an underage girl could be married without her guardian's consent, Kincaid would have to pretend he had given his blessing. The alternative would be to see her fortune go to Martin Nethercott, and Kincaid would be damned before he let her money go to her cousin.

As Kincaid was considering this problem, Felicity and Miss Flint arrived at the Oxford Street shop of Madame Sylvie, London's most fashionable modiste. An assistant greeted Felicity deferentially before hurrying to the back of the shop to inform Madame Sylvie that Miss Taylor had come.

Madame Sylvie emerged from a back room and greeted Felicity warmly. She was an attractive woman of forty-three, with auburn hair and intelligent brown eyes. Unlike many of London's fashionable dressmakers, who assumed a French name to appear more sophisticated, Madame Sylvie was actually French. Her only deception was in the use of the word Madame; she had never been married, but she thought Madame Sylvie had more gravitas than Mademoiselle.

Sylvie had fled to England twenty-five years earlier, after her aristocratic parents were killed in the French Revolution. Alone and destitute, she had worked as a dressmaker's apprentice for several years before she acquired the means to start her own establishment. Success had come quickly, and Sylvie was now one of the finest modistes in London.

"Felicity, my dear," Sylvie said, enfolding her in a hug. "That dress is charming. Take off your coat so that I can see it better."

Felicity obediently removed the coat, and Sylvie narrowed her eyes as she studied the muslin walking dress. "Did I make it for you?"

"Yes, two years ago, but I altered the skirt a bit," Felicity admitted. "It flares out a little more, and I added the flounce at the bottom." Felicity liked to sew, and she frequently altered old gowns to keep up with the trends. She didn't own nearly as many gowns as Mr. Kincaid thought she did, and it amused her to keep him wondering how she could afford to dress so well on the allowance he made her.

But despite her skill with alterations, Felicity wouldn't have been able to dress nearly as well as she did if Sylvie hadn't insisted on sewing her gowns for free. Felicity's parents had given Sylvie a loan to start her business, and although the loan had been repaid, the modiste still felt as though she was in their debt.

Felicity's mother had befriended Sylvie twenty years earlier, when Sylvie was an overworked apprentice with dismal prospects. Under normal circumstances, an apprentice wouldn't have been allowed near an important customer like the Honourable Caroline Taylor, but Sylvie's employer had fallen ill and Sylvie had been given her chance. Felicity's mother had recognized Sylvie's genius and persuaded her husband to invest in a modiste's shop, and had remained a loyal customer for the rest of her life. Some of Felicity's earliest memories were of visiting the modiste, and a trip to Sylvie's shop always made her feel closer to her mother.

"Turn around," Sylvie instructed, and Felicity spun in a slow circle so the modiste could examine her gown.

"You are talented, my dear," Sylvie said. "I don't think I could have done better."

Felicity knew the value of the compliment, for Sylvie never gave false praise. Her honesty had served her well in her business, since her customers knew they could trust her to tell them if a colour or style didn't flatter them. "Thank you, Sylvie. I'm quite pleased with it."

Sylvie nodded. "You should be. I'm fortunate you don't need to earn your living, or you might set yourself up as my competition."

Felicity pretended to consider it. "I think I would rather be your partner."

"You have only to say the word, my dear," Sylvie said with a laugh. "If you tire of going to balls, you can come and make gowns with me. And speaking of balls, the satin has arrived for your ball gown."

Felicity and Miss Flint followed Sylvie through a door at the back of the shop that led to a private workroom. Two of the walls were fitted with shelves that held bolts of colourful fabric, and a large table took up most of the remaining space.

After Miss Flint was comfortably ensconced in a chair in the corner, Sylvie carefully laid a bolt of red satin on the table.

"You will look magnificent," the modiste said. "But the red is unconventional for a debutante. You are sure?"

"Yes," Felicity said, running a hand reverently over the fabric. It was smooth and supple, and the poppy red colour was exactly as she had imagined it. "I want something bold, Sylvie."

"And you don't think Lady Brentwood will make a fuss about the colour?" Sylvie asked, referring to Kincaid's mother, the Dowager Countess of Brentwood. "She will be chaperoning you, will she not?"

"Yes, she is coming to town to chaperone me, but she's not the type to fuss. Mr. Kincaid might protest, of course, but he's not a connoisseur of ladies' fashions," Felicity said with an impish smile. "He told me so just this afternoon, and if he complains about the dress, I will remind him of it."

Sylvie gave Felicity a penetrating look. She had heard a great deal about Mr. Kincaid, and would have been interested in meeting Felicity's guardian. "Most men aren't interested in ladies' fashions until they are interested in a lady," she remarked.

Felicity laughed. "Well, if Mr. Kincaid's ever been interested in a lady, he's certainly kept it a secret from me." She ran a hand over the satin again. "You'll help me with the cutting, won't you, Sylvie?"

"Of course." Sylvie turned back to the shelf to fetch

the muslin pattern pieces they had made on Felicity's last visit, which would serve as a guide to cut the satin.

"You're sure you want to sew it yourself?" Madame Sylvie asked dubiously, after they had finished cutting the satin. "Satin is a difficult fabric, and it will take hours. I could have my seamstresses do it."

Felicity shook her head. "I'll have plenty of time to sew it myself, since the ball isn't for another month." Although she had sewn several morning dresses, she had never made an evening gown, and she knew she was taking a risk. But Felicity was anxious about her Season, and she wanted a project to occupy her mind in the weeks leading up to her debut.

Sylvie carefully folded the satin pieces and placed them in a box. "Good luck, my dear," she said as she handed the box to Felicity.

"Of course, if it doesn't go well, I'll be back to beg you to make me something else," Felicity told her with a laugh.

"And for you, I would do it," Sylvie admitted. "But I'm warning you, Felicity, I wouldn't be pleased."

"Then I suppose I'll have to get it right," Felicity said cheerfully. She walked over to rouse Miss Flint, who had fallen asleep in the corner, and took leave of the modiste with a smile of thanks.

Two

Kincaid made his way to his study, where he propped his feet up on his desk and debated what to do about the letter he had received that morning. His mother, the Dowager Countess of Brentwood, had written to tell him she would no longer be able to chaperone Felicity for the Season. Kincaid's older brother Archie, the Earl of Brentwood, still needed their mother at his Sussex estate.

Kincaid supposed his mother's decision was an understandable one. Archie's wife Elizabeth had given birth to twins the month before, and the doctor had been afraid she wouldn't survive the confinement. Fortunately, both Elizabeth and the babies had lived, and they were now thought to be out of danger. But Elizabeth still wasn't well enough to resume the management of the house, and Kincaid's mother had moved from the Dower House to the main residence to support the family.

But Kincaid also knew his brother employed a very capable housekeeper at Brentwood, who ran the house with very little direction. In fact, the house would probably run better without the countess's interference, since Elizabeth was famous for her inability to make up her mind. He had no doubt that a similarly capable nursemaid had been hired to care for the twins, so he didn't see why his mother's presence was essential.

Even if his mother was needed at Brentwood, Kincaid thought Felicity's need was greater. Really, his own need was greater, since he felt woefully unprepared for the challenge of launching a young lady into society. Since he had no sisters, he had never watched a young lady try to navigate the marriage mart, and he had trusted that his mother would manage Felicity's debut. Although Felicity wasn't related to the Kincaids by blood, she was the daughter of his mother's dearest friend, and his mother had known her since her infancy.

But his mother had made her decision, and he had nothing to gain from dwelling on it. Someone else would have to act as Felicity's chaperone, and Kincaid frowned as he considered the possibilities. His mother had written that Felicity's cousin, Lady Delphinia Nethercott, might take her place, but Kincaid had reservations about that idea. Miss Flint was an option, but she had little influence in society and even less influence over Felicity's behaviour.

Felicity had a tendency to be outspoken, and Kincaid knew society could be cruel to young ladies who didn't conform to its rules. Her debut would already be unconventional, as she was several years older than the average debutante. Kincaid had hoped she could come out under the aegis of a lady with some standing in society, but unfortunately, he couldn't think of anyone suitable for the role.

The problem was that Felicity had very few relatives. Her maternal grandfather had been a viscount, but he had died without sons and the title had passed to a distant cousin. Kincaid had never met the current viscount, and as far as he knew, the man had never shown any interest in Felicity or her affairs. Furthermore, the viscount was unmarried, so there was no viscountess to act as a chaperone.

He was reading his mother's letter again when he was interrupted by his butler, who announced that Lady Delphinia and her son, Mr. Martin Nethercott, had called.

Kincaid ran a hand through his dark hair and cursed in frustration. He had hoped that his mother hadn't written to the Nethercotts about Felicity's need for a chaperone, but the timing of their call suggested otherwise.

"Shall I tell them you're not receiving callers this morning, sir?" his butler asked.

"I'll see them, Wainwright," Kincaid said, rising to his feet with a sigh of resignation. He walked reluctantly to the drawing room, where he found his callers examining a painting.

Although Lady Delphinia was approaching her fiftieth birthday, she could have passed for a much younger woman. Her blonde hair had barely faded and she had retained her sylph-like figure, which was currently displayed to advantage in a lavender gown. She gave the appearance of a fragile beauty, but Kincaid suspected she was stronger than she looked.

Martin Nethercott had inherited his mother's fair hair and blue eyes, but his figure was athletic rather than delicate. He was the same age as Kincaid, but although they had been at Oxford together, the two men had never been friends.

Nethercott turned when he heard Kincaid approach. "Ah," he drawled. "The Honourable Lucas Kincaid."

As the younger son of an earl, Kincaid could style himself as 'The Honourable,' but the courtesy title was rarely used in speech. Martin Nethercott was the only person who addressed him that way, and when he did, it was always in a mocking tone.

Kincaid bowed. "Lady Delphinia, Mr. Nethercott," he said politely. "I'm afraid you've just missed Felicity."

"Poor, dear Felicity," Lady Delphinia said vaguely.

Kincaid didn't know how to reply to that, so he simply nodded.

"That's a lovely painting," Lady Delphinia remarked, gesturing to the landscape on the wall. "A Gainsborough?"

"Yes."

"Does it belong to Felicity?" she asked innocently.

"I inherited it from my father," Kincaid replied curtly.

This intelligence seemed to dampen Lady Delphinia's interest in the Gainsborough. She walked to the sofa and seated herself with a little sigh, as though the effort of crossing the room had exhausted her. Nethercott seated himself next to her with far less drama, and Kincaid took the chair opposite them.

"Shall I ring for tea?" Kincaid asked politely.

"Oh, no," Lady Delphinia demurred. "We can't stay long. But I received a letter from your mother this morning, and I knew I had to call. I was very sorry to hear about your brother's wife."

"Thank you," Kincaid replied. "But I understand Lady Brentwood is recovering."

"We ladies make such sacrifices for our children," Lady Delphinia murmured.

Kincaid would have been interested to hear what sacrifices Lady Delphinia had made for her son, but he merely nodded.

"Your dear mother explained that she won't be able to chaperone Felicity this Season," Lady Delphinia continued.

Kincaid nodded. "She is unable to leave Brentwood right now."

"She asked if I could take her place," Lady Delphinia said with a sigh. "It will require a great deal of exertion, but I don't see how I can refuse." She smiled sweetly at Kincaid. "I know my duty to my family."

"I appreciate your offer, Lady Delphinia," Kincaid replied. "But I'll need to discuss it with Felicity first."

Lady Delphinia's eyes widened in surprise. "I don't think there is anything to discuss. Your mother requested that I take her place, and I am willing to do so."

"You forget, Lady Delphinia, that my mother is not Felicity's guardian," Kincaid said evenly. "I am."

Lady Delphinia laughed, a tinkling sound that Kincaid found particularly unpleasant. "But surely you're not suggesting you could serve as Felicity's chaperone, Mr. Kincaid."

Kincaid forced himself to smile. "Certainly not. But Miss Flint could do it."

Lady Delphinia wrinkled her brow. "Miss Flint? I don't believe I am acquainted—"

"Felicity's companion," Kincaid explained.

"Ah yes," Lady Delphinia said. "I had forgotten her name. But given Felicity's unfortunate circumstances, the choice of her chaperone will be particularly important."

"What circumstances are those?" Kincaid asked coolly.

Lady Delphinia laughed again. "Well, Felicity says the strangest things," she said. "Those of us who know her understand she doesn't mean any harm, but I'm afraid she will offend people if she doesn't learn to guard her tongue."

Although Kincaid shared this concern, he would never admit it to Lady Delphinia. "I can't imagine what you mean."

"Well, that's hardly surprising, is it?" Lady Delphinia asked. "It's not the sort of thing a young gentleman would understand."

It was a thinly veiled hint that Kincaid wasn't a fit guardian for Felicity, and he fought to hide his irritation. When Lady Delphinia had first learned that Kincaid had been appointed Felicity's guardian, she made no secret of her feelings on the subject, and she had been reminding him of them ever since. Kincaid would never forget Lady Delphinia's performance at the reading of the Taylors' will; when she heard that Kincaid was to be Felicity's guardian, she had sweetly told Mr. Battersby that he must have made a mistake.

Lady Delphinia had gone on to point out that Kincaid was merely Felicity's mother's godson, not even a blood relative. The very idea of him as guardian was outrageous, and if Felicity's father had indeed willed it so, he must not have been of sound mind. Lady Delphinia had no doubt that Mr. Battersby would find a way to overturn the will and appoint her as Felicity's guardian, and her son as trustee of the fortune.

Although Lady Delphinia hadn't raised her voice, Battersby had recognized a formidable adversary, and had nervously explained that he couldn't overturn the will. The only way the arrangement could be changed was if Kincaid declined the responsibility.

If Lady Delphinia had been shocked to learn that Kincaid was to be Felicity's guardian, Kincaid had been equally surprised. At twenty-four, he had been preparing to enter the church, and hadn't felt qualified to take on the responsibilities of a fourteen-year-old orphan and her immense fortune. If anyone from his family were to be named Felicity's guardian, he thought his older brother, the Earl of Brentwood, would have been the logical choice. He had been on the verge of telling Battersby he couldn't do it when his gaze fell on Felicity.

Felicity had barely survived the fever that claimed her parents' lives, and it had left her pale and gaunt. But despite her youth, her grief, and her recent illness, she had sat through the reading of her parents' will with a straight spine. She had seemed to sense Kincaid's eyes upon her, and met his gaze with a questioning look. In the end, the look in her eye, combined with an instinctive distrust of the Nethercotts, had made his decision. He had taken on the responsibility of Felicity and her fortune, and in doing so, let himself in for seven years of criticism from Lady Delphinia.

"I've often thought it a shame that Felicity has so little female guidance," Lady Delphinia continued.

Kincaid dragged his mind back to the present and

forced himself to smile at her. Seven years later, he still had an instinctive distrust of the Nethercotts.

"Felicity has had governesses," he pointed out. "And my mother has visited frequently. Felicity has Miss Flint too, of course."

Lady Delphinia gave her tinkling little laugh. "Of course. But given the irregularity of Felicity's background . . ."

"What's wrong with Felicity's background?" Kincaid asked. Although his words were polite, there was steel in his tone.

"Well, her father's circumstances . . ." Lady Delphinia allowed her voice to trail off, as though it pained her to speak the words.

Kincaid feigned ignorance. "What circumstances?"

"His father—Felicity's grandfather—was in trade," Nethercott put in.

"Ah," Kincaid said. "I don't see what's irregular about that. Many people are."

"I suppose that if Felicity wished to marry a tradesman, there would be nothing irregular about it," Lady Delphinia conceded. "But it's certainly not common among people like us. And then there is her age; she will be twenty-one, will she not?"

"She will," Kincaid confirmed.

"So she will be several years older than the other debutantes," Lady Delphinia pointed out. "People may wonder if there was a reason her debut was delayed."

"There was," Kincaid replied. "She wanted to wait until she was old enough to marry without my consent."

Lady Delphinia looked skeptical. "I can understand why she might not want to be bound by your judgment," she said thoughtfully. "But dear Felicity will be compared to young ladies in their first bloom of youth."

"I trust there are still some men who would prefer to marry a young lady rather than a child," Kincaid remarked.

"I was married at seventeen," Lady Delphinia murmured.

"How interesting," Kincaid replied, with perfect truth. Since Lady Delphinia was an earl's daughter with a high opinion of herself, Kincaid would have expected her to hold out for a man with a title and fortune. Instead, she had married an untitled gentleman of modest fortune while still in her first bloom of youth. Either she had fallen madly in love with Mr. Nethercott, or a scandal had forced the issue.

"Yes," Lady Delphinia said with a nod. "Although I suppose I was fortunate that we married as quickly as we did."

"Oh?" Kincaid asked curiously. "Why is that?" If a scandal had in fact forced her into a hasty marriage, he couldn't imagine that Lady Delphinia would tell him about it.

"Because my dear husband died so young, of course," she replied. "I was only twenty-one when poor Albert passed. But I try to be grateful for the time we had together."

"Indeed," Kincaid replied.

"I just hope dear Felicity hasn't left it too late," Lady Delphinia remarked. "I'll do what I can for her, of course, and I would like to host a ball in honour of her debut. It should be held here, since your house is far more suitable than mine, but I will take care of the planning."

"I suppose all I'll have to do is settle the bills," Kincaid said dryly.

Lady Delphinia looked at him in surprise. "Well, of course. Given that the ball is for Felicity, it only makes sense for the expenses to come out of her fortune. And I will need several new gowns, if I am to act as her chaperone. I do want to be a credit to dear Felicity."

"There's no need to get ahead of yourself, Lady Delphinia," Kincaid said pleasantly. "The Countess of Langley is already planning to give a ball for Felicity. I expect you'll receive an invitation soon." He could have added that, unlike Lady Delphinia, the earl and countess hadn't expected either Kincaid or Felicity to pay for it.

Lady Delphinia looked aggrieved. "I wasn't aware that Felicity was acquainted with Lady Langley."

Kincaid smiled. "I am friends with Lord Langley, and Felicity accompanied me on a visit to his estate last summer."

"I see," Lady Delphinia said slowly. "You don't think that a ball for Felicity should be hosted by one of her relatives?"

"I don't see that it matters. Lady Langley's support will be very helpful to Felicity."

"I can't recall if the Countess of Langley has ever thrown a ball," Lady Delphinia mused.

"If she hasn't, it will only add to the attraction," Kincaid remarked. "Everyone will want to attend the Countess of Langley's first ball."

"That may be," Lady Delphinia conceded. "But the ball is meant to honour Felicity, and we wouldn't want Lady Langley to upstage her."

"I don't think there's any fear of that," Kincaid said.

"Lady Langley is far too generous to let that happen." He didn't add that he doubted anyone could upstage Felicity when she exerted herself to be charming.

"Well," Lady Delphinia remarked. "It is unfortunate that Felicity isn't here. The other purpose of my visit was to invite her to live with me."

"Live with you!" Kincaid exclaimed. "But she lives here."

Lady Delphinia pursed her lips. "But you must see that it's hardly suitable for Felicity to live alone with an unmarried gentleman."

"But I'm her guardian, and she is chaperoned by Miss Flint," Kincaid sputtered. "Surely no one could think there was any impropriety between us."

"And no one ever heard of a guardian taking advantage of his ward," Nethercott remarked sardonically.

"But I—Felicity—the suggestion is preposterous!" Kincaid stammered.

Lady Delphinia shrugged her shoulders delicately. "If your mother was living with you, I'm sure no one would think twice about it. But Miss Flint—well, one tends to forget about her, and those who remember may question her efficacy as a chaperone. Rumours can spread quickly, I'm afraid."

Kincaid was silent as he thought about it, and Lady Delphinia pressed her advantage. "I'll call tomorrow to discuss it with Felicity," she said. "I would enjoy her company, and I could give her some of the feminine guidance she's been lacking."

"No," Kincaid said abruptly.

"But surely, you will leave the decision to Felicity?" Lady Delphinia asked. "After all, when she comes of age next month, you won't be able to dictate where she lives."

"Certainly, the decision will be Felicity's," Kincaid agreed. "But I will discuss it with her myself."

Lady Delphinia was forced to be satisfied with this.

"Your life will change a great deal when Felicity marries," Nethercott commented. "Have you given any thought to what you will do?"

"I don't expect that much will change," Kincaid lied.

"Surely some things will change," Lady Delphinia said, looking at him skeptically. "I don't imagine you'll spend your summers at Fairleigh Manor after Felicity's husband takes over its management."

Fairleigh Manor was an estate in Hampshire that Felicity had inherited from her parents. It wasn't large, and its rents only accounted for a fraction of Felicity's income, but the house and surrounding park were beautiful. After her parents' deaths, Felicity had spent most of her time at Fairleigh with a governess, and Kincaid had visited often.

"I suppose I'll have to occupy myself with the management of my own affairs," Kincaid replied. "Perhaps I'll buy my own country house."

Lady Delphinia raised an elegant eyebrow. Her implication was clear; she didn't believe Kincaid had the resources to buy his own country house. She was wrong, but Kincaid knew it was pointless to try to convince her of it. Shortly after he came of age, he had inherited his London townhouse and a comfortable independence from a widowed aunt. After ten years of careful investments, he was now in a position to afford a house in the country if he made economies in other areas. He hadn't thought of doing so until Lady Delphinia mentioned Fairleigh Manor, but the idea was appealing.

"If I recall, before you were named Felicity's guardian, you were planning to become a vicar," Lady Delphinia said thoughtfully. "Perhaps you could still enter the church."

"I suppose we'll have to see," Kincaid said smoothly. He had no intention of becoming a vicar, but he didn't think it was necessary to tell Lady Delphinia so. "I apologize, Lady Delphinia, Mr. Nethercott, but I have an engagement elsewhere," he said, standing to ring for the butler. "Wainwright will show you out."

"Do let me know when you've spoken to Felicity," Lady Delphinia said, as Wainwright appeared in the doorway. "I will need to order new evening gowns if I am to be her chaperone."

"Of course."

As soon as Kincaid heard the front door close behind the Nethercotts, he punched the back of an armchair in an effort to relieve his frustration. The chair was less forgiving than he expected, and the hit left his knuckles stinging.

He was shaking out his hand when he noticed Wainwright had returned, and was watching him from the doorway with a concerned expression.

"Everything all right, sir?" Wainwright asked.

"Perfectly fine, Wainwright," he lied.

Three

Kincaid decided to walk to Jackson's Boxing Saloon, in the hope that the fresh air would clear his head. As he made his way down Bond Street, his path was blocked by a group of young ladies who had just emerged from a milliner's shop. He was stepping into the street to go around them when one of the ladies acknowledged him with a curtsy.

"Mr. Kincaid," the lady said with a shy smile.

Kincaid stopped and bowed politely as he tried to recall the lady's name. Her features were pleasant but unremarkable, and she was dressed rather severely in a dark blue cloak and bonnet. She looked vaguely familiar, and Kincaid thought he had danced with her during the previous Season.

"Miss Harris," he tried, and he was relieved when the lady's smile broadened. "I hope you are well?"

"Very well, thank you. I don't believe you've met my younger sisters?" Miss Harris asked, gesturing to the young ladies standing next to her.

"I'm afraid I haven't had the pleasure."

"Then allow me to introduce Mary, Sophronia, and Charlotte," Miss Harris said. "Louisa is still inside with Mama, but the shop was so crowded that we stepped outside."

"It's a pleasure to meet you all." Kincaid vaguely remembered Miss Harris saying something about younger sisters, but he hadn't expected her to have quite so many.

Sophronia giggled in the way that young girls often do in the presence of an eligible gentleman, but her eldest sister silenced her with a look. Kincaid looked at Miss Harris with growing respect.

"Mary and Sophronia are closest to me in age, and they have both come out this year," Miss Harris explained.

Sophronia giggled again. "But we haven't seen you at any of the balls, Mr. Kincaid," she said boldly. "I'd have remembered you."

"I'm afraid I haven't been to many balls yet this Season," Kincaid admitted. "But I hope to remedy that soon, and I hope to have the opportunity to dance with you. And with your sisters, of course."

"You may dance with Mary, but Jane hardly ever dances now," Sophronia said, giving her eldest sister a pitying look. She lowered her voice to a conspiratorial whisper. "Jane's too busy scolding Mary and me. She doesn't think Mama is a strict enough chaperone, so she tries to take on the role herself."

Miss Jane Harris blushed with embarrassment, and the colour in her cheeks softened her features. Kincaid met her eye sympathetically.

"I think you're fortunate to have a sister who cares about you," he told Sophronia. "And I hope to dance with Miss Jane Harris, too."

Sophronia pouted. "Just as long as you dance with me first," she said flirtatiously. "Don't forget!"

Kincaid was finally able to take his leave of the Misses Harris, and by the time he reached Jackson's Saloon, those young ladies were far from his mind. His thoughts kept returning to the problem of Felicity and the Nethercotts, and the question of who could act as her chaperone instead of Lady Delphinia.

He found Lord Langley sparring with Lord Oliver St. Clair, the Marquess of Ashingham. They stopped their bout to greet Kincaid, and Langley's eyes narrowed with concern when he saw his friend's expression.

"Something wrong, Lucas?" Langley asked. "You're looking awfully miserable."

Kincaid sighed. "I've just spent an hour with Lady Delphinia Nethercott and her son."

"Why would you do that?" Langley asked with a frown.

"It wasn't by choice!" Kincaid retorted. "They're Felicity's cousins, you know. They came to call while Felicity was at the modiste's, so I had to endure them alone."

"You need to find a butler who knows how to deal with unwanted visitors," Langley remarked. "I don't have one myself, but I've heard that such people exist." He turned to Oliver. "Are you acquainted with Lady Delphinia?"

Oliver shook his head. "I haven't had the pleasure."

"I'm not sure I'd call it a pleasure," Langley said dryly. "She's about as much fun as our mother-in-law."

Since Oliver had married Langley's wife's sister, the two men had the dubious privilege of sharing a mother-in-law.

"They're Felicity's only family, so I could hardly turn them away," Kincaid muttered. "But I'd love to go a round in here with Martin Nethercott."

"I'll take you on in his place," Oliver offered.

Kincaid had never boxed with Oliver before, but he was impressed by his skill. "You're good at this," he remarked.

Oliver grinned. "I've been practising with my wife."

Kincaid looked at him in confusion. "I don't know what that means."

"He means he taught his wife to box," Langley explained with a chuckle. "Do you remember when Isabelle hit Lord Braden at the Maidstone Assembly last summer?"

"Of course," Kincaid replied. He was unlikely to forget the sight of Isabelle hitting the lecherous baron, who had been pestering one of her friends.

"Oliver had been giving her clandestine boxing lessons all summer," Langley explained.

"They weren't clandestine," Oliver protested. "We just didn't tell anyone about them."

"I'm glad you didn't tell Felicity," Kincaid said with a laugh. "She would have wanted to learn, and I'm sure she would have done me an injury."

"How is Miss Taylor?" Langley asked. "Excited to make her debut?"

"I think so," Kincaid replied. "She drags poor Miss Flint to the modiste at least once a week. At this rate, she'll be able to wear a different gown every day." He sighed. "Felicity doesn't seem to understand that although her fortune is large, it isn't infinite."

Oliver frowned. "I thought you controlled her fortune?"

"I do, and I make her an allowance," Kincaid explained. "And I'm constantly amazed that she doesn't run through it, buying so many gowns from Madame Sylvie's. I've never been myself, but I understand she's expensive."

"She's the most expensive modiste in London," Langley confirmed. "But unquestionably the best. Miss Taylor has good taste."

"She does," Kincaid agreed. "The problem is that she has no notion of economy. I live in constant fear of learning that Felicity has run up debts."

"Surely the modiste wouldn't allow Felicity to run up a debt that was too great for you to settle?" Langley asked.

"Probably not," Kincaid admitted. "And I sometimes think it would be good for Felicity to outrun her allowance, so she would be forced to ask me to pay her bills. The embarrassment might teach her a lesson, and she would do well to learn it before she marries."

Oliver shrugged. "She might deal better with her husband than she does with you."

"She'll likely marry a man she's able to manipulate," Kincaid muttered. "And he might allow her to run through her fortune."

Oliver gave him a penetrating look. "But that wouldn't be your problem, would it?"

"I suppose not," Kincaid admitted. "But I've been Felicity's guardian for seven years, and it's strange to think of someone else taking over the responsibility."

"You could try keeping a diary," Langley suggested. "Writing your problems down might help you make sense of them."

Kincaid stared at him. "A *diary*? I've never known a man who kept a diary."

"I keep one," Langley said matter-of-factly.

Kincaid looked at his friend in disbelief. "What do you write about?"

"Anything, really," Langley replied. "When I first met Amelia, I wrote about how frustrating I found her. But now that I'm married to her, she reads the diary, so I mainly use it to communicate with her."

"You can't just talk to her?" Kincaid asked.

"Oh, I do," Langley told him. "But the diary is a good way for me to share opinions that I know Amelia won't like."

"Like what?"

Langley shrugged. "Last week I wrote that I was afraid our son's character would be spoiled if we continued to overindulge him."

"But Julian's still a baby," Oliver pointed out. "Could his character really be spoiled by overindulgence?"

"Well, Amelia certainly doesn't think so," Langley replied. "And if I tried to talk to her about it, she would want to debate the point. But since I wrote it in my diary, she won't try to discuss it with me, since she doesn't want to admit she reads it."

"But doesn't Amelia know that you know she reads it?" Kincaid asked.

"Oh, she suspects that I know," Langley said with a smile. "But she isn't sure."

"I see," said Kincaid, in the tone of a man who didn't

see at all. He turned to Oliver. "Do you communicate with Isabelle that way?"

Oliver shook his head. "It sounds awfully complicated. But Isabelle and I write each other letters."

Kincaid's brow furrowed. "But you and Isabelle are hardly ever apart."

"That's true," Oliver agreed. "But I find it's often easier to express myself on paper." He grinned. "And Isabelle writes such excellent letters. I often read them several times."

Kincaid reflected that marriage had done strange things to his friends. "Perhaps I'll try keeping a diary," he said with a sigh. "My mother wrote to tell me she won't be able to chaperone Felicity for the Season, and suggested that Lady Delphinia take her place."

Langley frowned. "Why can't your mother do it?"

"She's at Brentwood with my brother's family. Archie's wife had twins last month and still hasn't recovered her strength, so my mother's been helping to run their household."

"So Lady Delphinia will be her chaperone?" Oliver asked.

"I don't know," Kincaid admitted. "I still have to discuss it with Felicity."

"You don't seem happy about the prospect," Langley remarked.

"I've never liked Lady Delphinia," Kincaid confessed. "But she's Felicity's only female relative, so she may be the best option."

Oliver looked thoughtful. "Do you think Isabelle could do it? She and Felicity are friends, and she might be better than Lady Delphinia."

"Thank you, Oliver, but I don't think it would work," Kincaid replied. "Isabelle's younger than Felicity, and I don't want to draw attention to the fact that Felicity's twenty-one." He didn't add that he was hoping to find a mature lady who might influence Felicity to behave more conventionally.

"What about Amelia?" Langley suggested. "I think she's a year older than Felicity."

"I would hate to ask it of her," Kincaid said diplomatically. "I'm sure she's busy with your son." Although Langley's wife might be able to influence Felicity, he wasn't confident that her influence would be entirely positive. Amelia had some unconventional ideas of her own, and he feared she might encourage Felicity's eccentricities.

"I could always ask my mother," Langley offered. "She's in London for the Season, and she's been conspiring with Amelia to spoil my son. This would give her thoughts another direction."

"Thank you, Robert," Kincaid said. "But I wouldn't want to put your mother to the trouble."

"I don't think she would mind," Langley replied. "She's always liked a challenge."

Kincaid almost said yes. Langley's mother, the Dowager Countess of Langley, was both well-respected in society and intelligent enough to see through Felicity's tricks. In many ways, she seemed like an ideal choice, but Kincaid hadn't enjoyed hearing Langley describe Felicity as a challenge. While he would never deny that Felicity was a challenging girl, she was his challenge, and he didn't like hearing another man refer to her as such.

"It's a kind offer," he finally replied. "I'll speak to Felicity about it."

~

Kincaid was unusually quiet as he and Felicity rode through Hyde Park the following morning. He knew he should tell her about Lady Delphinia's suggestion that Felicity live with her for the Season, but he dreaded the possibility that Felicity would say yes.

"Why were you glaring at that gentleman?" Felicity inquired casually, as they passed a man riding an Arabian horse.

"I wasn't glaring at anyone, Felicity," Kincaid protested.

"You were," she insisted.

Kincaid sighed. "I didn't like the way he was looking at you."

"How exactly was he looking at me?"

Kincaid thought about his answer. "As though he would like to become better acquainted with you."

Felicity chuckled. "What a dangerous character," she said lightly. "But I have very little interest in becoming acquainted with him. He has a terrible seat on a horse."

"Is that the most important consideration for you, Felicity?" Kincaid asked with a laugh. "A gentleman's seat on a horse?"

Felicity chewed her lower lip thoughtfully. "Perhaps not the most important, but it's certainly a factor, Mr. Kincaid. I don't think I could spend my life with a man who wasn't at home in the saddle."

"No?"

"No," Felicity confirmed. "It's unfortunate that most courting takes place at balls. I have very little interest in a man's ability to dance, but I am very concerned about his ability to ride."

"I see."

"I hope we can continue to ride in Hyde Park after I make my debut," Felicity remarked. "I would like to have the opportunity to observe the riding abilities of potential suitors."

"It's never hard to persuade me to go riding, Felicity," Kincaid told her. He enjoyed riding as much as she did. "Have any gentlemen caught your eye today?"

Felicity shook her head. "Do you know, Mr. Kincaid, I haven't seen a single gentleman who rides as well as you do."

Kincaid feigned a look of surprise. "A compliment, Felicity?"

Felicity nodded. "I admit, Mr. Kincaid, that you ride very well."

"You should warn me the next time you mean to praise me," he teased. "So I don't fall off my horse from the shock."

"That would be very disappointing," Felicity agreed. "It would mean I had misjudged your abilities, and you know how much I hate to be wrong."

Kincaid didn't reply, as his attention had turned to a curricle that was coming towards them at too fast a pace for the park. Both he and Felicity watched with interest as the vehicle swerved around a pedestrian and narrowly avoided a tree. The driver didn't seem perturbed by the near miss, and continued towards them at a spanking pace.

As the curricle drew closer, Felicity recognized the driver. "I think that's Adrian Stone," she remarked.

Adrian was Lord Langley's younger brother and a notoriously reckless driver.

Kincaid squinted at the driver and groaned inwardly. "It is."

With some difficulty, Adrian brought his curricle to a stop beside Felicity and Kincaid.

"Good afternoon, Miss Taylor!" Adrian said, looking very pleased to see her. He was an attractive young man, with fair hair and cherubic features that made him look younger than his twenty-two years. "Afternoon, Mr. Kincaid."

"Good afternoon, Mr. Stone," Felicity said politely. "That's a very dashing vehicle."

Adrian looked gratified. "It's kind of you to say so, Miss Taylor. I was just thinking that you're riding a very fine horse."

"I quite agree with you," Felicity said with a smile, bending over to pat her mare's neck. "I've had Sugarplum since she was a filly. She's ten now, but still very spirited."

Adrian nodded. "You know, I was just thinking about you, Miss Taylor."

"Oh?" Felicity asked curiously.

"Yes," Adrian continued. "My brother mentioned you were making your debut next month. He said that Amelia's going to throw you a ball."

"Yes, she is," Felicity confirmed. "It's very kind of her."

"Well, it shouldn't be a great hardship," Adrian said, casting an eye down Felicity's figure. "You're an attractive girl, and you're not boring. It's not as though Amelia's been asked to launch an antidote with no conversation."

Felicity's lips quirked with amusement. "You're very kind, Mr. Stone."

"We shouldn't keep the horses standing, Felicity," Kincaid put in crisply.

"Oh, of course," Adrian agreed. "But it's always a pleasure to see you, Miss Taylor. I don't suppose you'd like to come for a drive with me one day?"

"I would like that very much," Felicity replied with a smile.

"Sometime later this week, perhaps?"

"Felicity will be very busy," Kincaid said in a discouraging tone.

"But not too busy to drive with a friend," Felicity countered. "I think I would enjoy that very much."

Adrian looked as though he wished to prolong the conversation, but his horses had evidently grown tired of it, and they started down the path without waiting for a signal from their driver.

"I don't think you should drive with him, Felicity," Kincaid muttered.

Felicity raised her eyebrows in surprise. "Why not? Adrian Stone is perfectly respectable, and you've been friends with his family for years. There's nothing improper about driving with a gentleman in an open carriage."

Kincaid cudgelled his brain for a reason to forbid it, and settled on the obvious. "Adrian's a terrible driver."

"Yes, he didn't look particularly skilled," Felicity acknowledged. "But he has a very nice curricle, and I hope he will let me drive it. Perhaps I'll ask him to teach me to drive."

Kincaid snorted. "Felicity, you drive better than he does."

She smiled mischievously. "I think I drive better than

most men, Mr. Kincaid, but that's to be expected, since you taught me. Maybe I'll teach Adrian."

"I don't like the idea," Kincaid grumbled.

"I daresay I have many ideas that you don't like," Felicity replied. "And while we're on the subject of ideas you don't like, I'm still hoping to buy myself a phaeton and pair. Have you given it any more thought?"

Felicity had been talking about buying a phaeton and pair for over a year, and Kincaid was tempted to let her do it. She was an excellent driver, and he frequently allowed her to take the reins when they drove together. He didn't think she would come to harm driving herself around London, but he worried about what it would do to her reputation. He didn't know of any other young ladies who drove themselves around town in a phaeton.

"I'm thinking about it," he told Felicity.

Felicity's face brightened. "Really?"

Kincaid chuckled at her expression of surprise. "Yes, really."

"And when might I expect your decision?"

"Don't push your luck, Felicity."

"All right," Felicity agreed with a shrug. "What did you want to talk to me about yesterday?"

Kincaid sighed. "My mother won't be able to come to London to act as your chaperone this Season, since Archie and his family still need her at Brentwood. Elizabeth is recovering, but she's still very weak."

Felicity's face fell for a moment, but she composed herself quickly. "I understand completely, and I'm pleased to hear that Elizabeth is getting better. I suppose Miss Flint could act as my chaperone."

"That's certainly one possibility," Kincaid agreed. "But

there are others. Lord Langley suggested that his mother might do it."

"That's very kind of him," Felicity said slowly.

"But you don't like the idea?" Kincaid asked, studying her expression carefully.

"I've never met Lord Langley's mother," she explained. "So if she agreed to chaperone me, it would be only because her son is friends with you."

"That wouldn't be so unusual."

"I suppose not," Felicity agreed. "But Lady Langley might feel as though she couldn't say no. It was different when it was your mother, since she was my mother's dearest friend, and I've known her all my life. But Lady Langley—it would feel like an imposition."

Kincaid nodded. "Lady Delphinia and Mr. Nethercott called yesterday, and Lady Delphinia offered to act as your chaperone."

Felicity looked thoughtful. "Did she seem to really want to do it? She wasn't just offering because she thought it was her duty?"

"I've always found it hard to guess what Lady Delphinia is thinking," Kincaid answered carefully. "But she spoke as though it was a settled thing. I told her I'd discuss it with you, and the decision would ultimately be yours."

"I see."

"She also suggested that you live with her," Kincaid said reluctantly. He hadn't wanted to tell her that part, but he knew Lady Delphinia was likely to bring it up with Felicity herself.

"Live with her!" Felicity exclaimed. "But I live with you. And Miss Flint, of course."

"I know. But Lady Delphinia thought that if she was going to be your chaperone, it would be more convenient for you to live with her." Kincaid didn't mention Lady Delphinia's suggestion that Felicity's presence in his bachelor household would give rise to gossip.

"I suppose there's something to be said for that," Felicity said thoughtfully. "What do you think I should do?"

"I think it should be your decision," Kincaid said, fighting to keep his expression neutral.

"I know you've never liked Lady Delphinia," Felicity began.

"I don't dislike Lady Delphinia," Kincaid protested.

Felicity's lips twitched. "You're a terrible liar, Mr. Kincaid," she teased. "It's one of the things I like best about you."

"I don't know what you mean," he muttered.

"And for the most part, I share your opinion of my cousins, and I've never felt particularly close to them. But the fact that Lady Delphinia came to call, and offered to do it—I think that says something, don't you?"

"Oh, quite likely."

"And there's something appealing about the thought of being brought out by a relative, even if Lady Delphinia is only a second cousin. Since my parents died, I feel as though I have so little family, you know?"

"I know," Kincaid said, resolving to be kinder to Lady Delphinia.

"Can I think about it?"

"Of course."

Four

When they returned home, Felicity went upstairs to work on her ball gown and Kincaid made his way to his study. He was trying to read a report on a shipping company in which he hoped to invest, but he found he was unable to focus. His mind kept returning to the unpleasant prospect of Felicity driving with Adrian Stone, and he wondered if he should have forbidden her from doing so.

"Mr. Martin Nethercott has called, sir," Wainwright announced apologetically. "Shall I show him in here?"

"I suppose," Kincaid said grudgingly. Turning Nethercott away would only delay the inevitable.

Nethercott strolled into the study and moved a chair so he could sit facing Kincaid.

"Have a seat, Nethercott," Kincaid said sarcastically.

"Thank you, I will," Nethercott replied easily. "You don't look pleased to see me, Mr. Kincaid. Not going to offer me a drink?"

"No," Kincaid replied unapologetically. "What do you want, Nethercott?"

"A hundred pounds should do it."

"No," Kincaid said simply.

Nethercott still looked amused. "It's a pittance compared to the size of Felicity's fortune—"

"That's how large fortunes are lost, you know. People think the money is inexhaustible, until one day they wake up and it's gone."

"A lecture on economy, Mr. Kincaid?" Nethercott asked with a smirk. "Or is that philosophy? I've never liked either subject."

Kincaid gritted his teeth and didn't reply.

"In any case," Nethercott continued, "Felicity's fortune is so large that a hundred pounds would hardly be missed."

"I would miss it."

Nethercott cast an appraising eye down Kincaid's clothing. "That's a very nice coat," he remarked. "Did Weston make it for you?"

"What does that have to do with anything?" Kincaid asked irritably. His coat had, in fact, been made by Weston.

Nethercott shrugged. "I'm simply pointing out that your position as Felicity's guardian has served you well. I understand Weston is a very expensive tailor."

"I'm not the one asking for money," Kincaid retorted.

"No, you never had to ask for it, did you?" Nethercott mused. "You had a fortune simply given to you."

"The fortune is Felicity's," Kincaid said tersely. "I'm only a trustee."

Nethercott nodded. "But as you've pointed out, you would miss the money. Or rather, you would miss a hundred pounds of it, if you gave it to me."

A muscle ticked in Kincaid's jaw. "I simply meant I would know it was missing. I've tried to take care of Felicity's money, and I can't justify giving you any more of it."

"Oh, I'm sure you've been entirely honourable," Nethercott drawled. "The Honourable Lucas Kincaid."

"The title is rarely used in speech," Kincaid said, hating himself for letting Nethercott get under his skin. "There's no need to address me that way."

"Is that right?" Nethercott asked easily. "I've learned a great deal from you today. I suppose you're generous with your knowledge, if not with your money."

"It's Felicity's money."

"That's never stopped you from sharing it with me before. Does Felicity know about the past loans you've made to me?"

"Loans, Nethercott?" Kincaid asked. "Are you planning to repay them?"

Nethercott didn't look ashamed. "Gifts, then. I wonder if Mr. Battersby knows about them? How did you list them in the books? Loans to Miss Taylor's indigent relatives?"

"No."

Nethercott raised an eyebrow. "Probably wise, since there's no proof you gave the money to me. Much better to pretend it was used for Felicity's expenses." He leaned back in his chair and crossed his legs at the ankles. "If I asked Mr. Battersby to review the accounts, I wonder what he would find?"

"He wouldn't find anything," Kincaid said crisply.

Nethercott's eyes widened. "How interesting," he murmured. "The money you've given me hasn't been Felicity's, has it? It's been your own."

Kincaid stared down at his desk and didn't reply, but his silence was answer enough.

"You really are honourable," Nethercott said in a tone of surprise. "I suppose I should thank you for your generosity."

"You can thank me by leaving my house and never speaking of the matter again."

"I'm afraid I can't do that," Nethercott said apologetically. "You see, Mr. Kincaid, I am in debt."

"That's hardly a surprise," Kincaid said dryly. Debt seemed to be a chronic condition for Mr. Nethercott.

"I suppose not," Nethercott agreed. "My mother has expensive tastes, and I've never been able to say no to a lady. It wouldn't be gentlemanly, you know."

"No," Kincaid said. "Far more gentlemanly to give the lady what she wants and then blame her for your financial difficulties."

Nethercott didn't seem insulted by the sarcasm. "Precisely. I knew you would understand. Just as I knew you would understand why I would rather not approach Felicity about the matter."

"Your inability to manage your finances has nothing to do with Felicity!"

Nethercott gave him a pained look. "There's no need to be insulting, Mr. Kincaid," he said. "No gentleman of refined tastes could manage on the money my father left me."

"You have my sympathy," Kincaid said sardonically. "But I still don't see how this concerns Felicity."

"But it does, because I am her cousin," Nethercott replied. "I could tell her that I'm being hounded by some dangerous men, and if I don't give them a hundred pounds, they'll break my legs."

"You mean you're in debt to a moneylender who would like you to honour the terms of your agreement."

"It amounts to the same thing," Nethercott said. "I'm sure Felicity would hate to learn that her cousin was badly beaten for want of a hundred pounds."

"Second cousin once removed," Kincaid corrected.

"You're right," Nethercott said thoughtfully. "Although my mother and I are her closest relatives, I suppose the blood relationship isn't very close. I'm looking forward to seeing more of my second cousin once removed."

Kincaid's eyes narrowed. "What do you mean?"

Nethercott smiled. "Since my mother will be Felicity's chaperone, it will be quite natural for me to accompany them to balls. And if Felicity accepts my mother's invitation to live with her, I'll see her almost every day. I visit my mother often, you know."

"The question of Felicity's chaperone hasn't been decided yet," Kincaid said brusquely. "Felicity is still thinking about what she wants to do."

"I forgot, you're considering having her come out under the aegis of Miss Flint," Nethercott said. "I suppose you won't have to worry about Felicity being outshone by her chaperone."

"Miss Flint is perfectly respectable."

"Oh, of course," Nethercott agreed. "No one could question her respectability. It's just that—well—no one has heard of the Flints."

"I don't see how that matters," Kincaid replied evenly. "Miss Flint is not seeking a husband for herself. She will be a perfectly acceptable chaperone for Felicity."

"If you think so," Nethercott said skeptically. "But I'm afraid we've strayed from the point. I need a hundred pounds."

"You have strayed from the point!" Kincaid retorted. "You've asked me for money and I've said no. We have nothing further to discuss."

Instead of standing to leave, Nethercott leaned back farther in his chair. "Do you know, Kincaid, I never thought Felicity would reach her twenty-first birthday unmarried," he said. "I expected you to make your move months ago."

"I don't know what you're talking about," Kincaid said, although he feared he did.

Nethercott smirked. "I suppose waiting until she's of age makes the thing look better. You can pretend Felicity had a choice in the matter."

"If you're referring to Felicity's marriage, she will certainly have a choice in the matter," Kincaid replied stiffly. "When she turns twenty-one, she will keep her fortune regardless of whom she marries."

"Well, her husband will keep it," Nethercott corrected. "But things have worked out quite well for you, with your mother unable to come to town. You have Felicity living with you, without a proper chaperone—"

"She has Miss Flint!" Kincaid exclaimed.

"But no one remembers Miss Flint," Nethercott said with a nasty smile. "And I'm sure Felicity's suitors will wonder if your relationship with her has been entirely chaste."

"It has," Kincaid said, through gritted teeth. "Hell, Nethercott, she's my ward!"

Nethercott nodded. "So convenient for you. If any

gentlemen are willing to overlook the possibility of impropriety—"

"There has been no impropriety," Kincaid interjected.

"You can glare at them when they come to call," Nethercott continued, as though Kincaid hadn't spoken. "I'm sure your expression would scare off all but the most determined of suitors."

"If I give you the money, will you leave?" Kincaid bit out.

"Of course. You're not the only man with a sense of honour."

Kincaid unlocked the bottom drawer of his desk and extracted a roll of banknotes. After quickly flipping through them, he handed Nethercott the lot. "Sixty pounds. It's all I have. Take it and go."

"I'm obliged to you," Nethercott said pleasantly, placing the notes in his pocket. "Good day, Mr. Kincaid."

"Sir John Smith-Lyon and his family have gone to the south of France," Kincaid announced at breakfast three days later. Miss Flint had yet to emerge from her bedchamber, so he and Felicity were alone at the table.

"Oh?" Felicity replied politely. Since she wasn't acquainted with the Smith-Lyons, she had no great interest in their travel plans.

"And I've decided to move into their house for the Season," Kincaid continued.

This caught Felicity's attention. "Move into their house?" she repeated in amazement.

"Yes, 29 Bentley Street." Kincaid's own house was at 23

Bentley. "It's only three houses away from this one, and I've arranged to let it for the next four months."

"And will we all move?" Felicity asked curiously.

"Oh, no," Kincaid told her. "You and Miss Flint will stay here."

"And the staff?"

"I'll take my valet, of course, but the rest of the servants will remain with you. The Smith-Lyons have left most of their staff behind, so I won't have to hire anyone."

Felicity stared at him in confusion. "But why? If it's because of the pianoforte, Mr. Kincaid, I promise I'll never play it again."

The corner of Kincaid's mouth quirked up. Felicity had no ear for music, and no great interest in it either. But Mr. Kincaid owned an excellent pianoforte, and several times a month Felicity amused herself by trying to play.

"I think you're improving, Felicity," he lied manfully. "In any case, it has nothing to do with the pianoforte."

"Well, what has it to do with, then?"

"This house is rather crowded," Kincaid began. "And since my mother is unable to come, I thought it made sense for me to move out."

Felicity frowned. "But this house doesn't seem crowded at all," she protested. "And it will be even less so now that your mother isn't coming."

Kincaid sighed. Since he hadn't prepared a better excuse, he decided to tell her the truth. "I'm afraid people might think it's improper for you to live in the same house as me," he admitted. "You're a young lady now, and people might say . . ." he let the sentence trail off awkwardly.

Felicity met his eye. "What might people say?"

"They might say it's improper," Kincaid managed miserably.

"Surely no one would think you were capable of impropriety, Mr. Kincaid." Felicity's dark eyes held a roguish gleam. "Not with me, at least."

"What do you mean?" Kincaid asked, frowning. "Do you think I'm capable of impropriety with other ladies?"

"Well, I've often wondered," Felicity admitted. "I'd like to think you were capable of improper behaviour. A man who wasn't would be very dull."

"Felicity!"

"Oh, I don't mean that I hope you engage in improper behaviour," she assured him. "There is a great deal of difference between being capable of doing something and actually doing it."

"I don't think you know what you're talking about," Kincaid retorted.

"I certainly don't know as much as I would like to," she agreed. "But since you've raised the subject, do you engage in improper behaviour?"

"I wouldn't tell you if I did."

"I suppose I shouldn't be surprised," Felicity said with a nod. "But if that's the case, it seems unfair of you to say I don't know what I'm talking about. How can I know if you don't tell me?"

"Felicity, even I don't know what you're talking about."

Felicity sighed. "No, I can see that you don't. When did you decide to move down the street?"

"Yesterday." It had all happened rather quickly; Kincaid had seen the Smith-Lyons' servants loading a great quantity of luggage into two travelling coaches and walked over to investigate. A maid had confided that Lady Smith-Lyon could no longer endure the English weather, so the family was moving to the south of France for four months. Sir John himself had emerged next, wearing a harassed expression, and had quickly agreed to let his house to Kincaid during his absence.

"I don't see how moving down the street will help," Felicity said thoughtfully.

Kincaid's brow furrowed. "We won't be sharing a roof." After Mr. Nethercott's unpleasant visit, he had considered moving into his brother's London house, but the Smith-Lyons' place seemed like a far better option. It was close enough to keep an eye on Felicity and convenient to his horses, which were stabled in the mews behind Bentley Street.

"No, we won't be sharing a roof," Felicity agreed. "But right now, I'm a young lady living in her guardian's home, under the chaperonage of Miss Flint. If you move out, people might think we have something to hide." Her eyes sparkled with mischief. "It might appear as though you've set me up as your mistress."

Kincaid flinched. "It isn't a joke, Felicity!" he railed. "You laugh about it, but a rumour like that could finish you in polite society. You shouldn't even know about such things."

"If you recall, I spent a year at Miss Archer's Ladies' Seminary when I was seventeen," Felicity pointed out. "What did you think I would learn there?"

Kincaid certainly hadn't expected Miss Archer's curriculum to include instruction on extramarital relationships. "I hoped you might learn how to conduct yourself in society. As well as dancing, watercolours, perhaps the pianoforte ..."

"Well, we both know I didn't learn the pianoforte," Felicity joked. "But there were lessons in deportment, along with dancing and watercolours. And I also met several young ladies from France, who explained that many of the things we consider shameful are quite normal there. For example, did you know—"

"You don't need to give me examples," Kincaid interrupted, looking alarmed.

"No, I imagine you've heard it all already."

"That's not what I meant!"

"Oh, come now, Mr. Kincaid," Felicity said playfully. "Don't tell me that when you were at Oxford, you and your friends never spoke about anything other than your studies? I'm sure your conversations were far more salacious than mine ever were."

Kincaid was wise enough not to say that things were different for young men than for young ladies. "We spent a great deal of time discussing our studies," he said evasively.

Felicity looked at him skeptically. "That doesn't answer my question."

"I don't recall any—er—salacious conversations."

"I can tell when you're lying, you know," Felicity said conversationally.

"Yes, so you've told me."

"You get a vertical line between your eyebrows," she continued. "It's likely because you're a fundamentally honest person, and you have to concentrate very hard when you lie."

Kincaid sighed and sipped his coffee. "I'm planning to move tomorrow."

Felicity frowned. "Would it be easier if I moved in with Lady Delphinia? It would save you the expense of letting another house, and people are far less likely to suspect an illicit liaison if I'm living there."

"No," Kincaid said quickly. "The expense is insignificant, and I've already made the arrangements. If you would prefer to live with Lady Delphinia, you may do so, of course. Sugarplum can stay here, if Lady Delphinia doesn't have room in her stables—"

"No," Felicity interrupted. "I would like to stay here."

Kincaid tried to hide his relief. "All right."

"If you're sure it isn't too much trouble," she continued. "I don't want to force you out of your home."

"You're not forcing me to do anything, Felicity," he replied. "But if you are feeling grateful, you might repay me by forgetting you know anything about mistresses and illicit liaisons. If you speak about such things in society, people will get the wrong idea about you."

"I won't talk this way in society, Mr. Kincaid," Felicity assured him. "I don't speak like this to anyone but you."

This caught Kincaid off guard, and it took him a minute to collect his thoughts. "I'm pleased to hear it," he finally said. "But you shouldn't speak this way with me, either. You might fall into the habit, and forget to guard your tongue with other people."

"Of course, Mr. Kincaid," Felicity said agreeably. "What should we talk about this morning? So many subjects could be troublesome."

"I'm sure you'll think of something."

"I suppose I could tell you about the bonnets I saw in

the milliner's window yesterday," Felicity said thoughtfully. "They were made of straw, with a very high poke. I almost bought one, but they were trimmed with different coloured ribbons, and I couldn't decide between the primrose ribbon and the lavender. What do you think?"

"I don't think either colour would flatter me."

Miss Flint appeared in the doorway, and Felicity greeted her cheerfully. "Morning, Theodora," she said. "I'm glad you're here, for I need an opinion about a bonnet, and Mr. Kincaid is unable to give me a sensible answer."

Kincaid shook his head and applied himself to his breakfast.

Five

The following morning, Felicity received a note from Adrian Stone inviting her to drive with him that afternoon. She sent back an affirmative reply, and at two o'clock, he arrived at 23 Bentley St. in his curricle. Felicity didn't keep him waiting, and they set off several minutes later. As they drove down the street, Felicity had the good fortune to see Mr. Kincaid descending the front steps of 29 Bentley. She waved to him cheerfully, and he stared back at her in alarm.

"I suppose Mr. Kincaid has been visiting the neighbours?" Adrian asked.

"Actually, Mr. Kincaid has moved into 29 Bentley," Felicity explained.

"Why would he do that?"

"I think he found his own house too crowded."

"If he finds his house crowded, he should see my lodging house," Adrian replied scornfully. "Did the two of you have an argument?"

"I think Mr. Kincaid was concerned there would be gossip about us," Felicity confessed.

Adrian frowned. "What sort of gossip?"

"The usual kind," Felicity said. "Speculation that we're in an improper relationship."

"No one who has spent any time with you and Mr. Kincaid would think there could be impropriety between you," Adrian scoffed.

Felicity grinned. "Quite likely not, but not everyone has spent time with us."

"I suppose that's true," Adrian admitted. "Must be expensive, though. I don't know how Kincaid manages it —I can barely afford my rooms, but here he is, renting a second house on Bentley Street."

Felicity had wondered about that herself. She knew Mr. Kincaid had inherited his house and some money from his aunt, but she didn't think it was a large fortune. If he had asked her opinion, she would have told him not to move, since she was confident that Miss Flint's chaperonage would be enough to silence all but the most spiteful of gossips. But she knew it would be useless to argue the point with her guardian, the same way it would be useless to suggest that he use her money to pay the rent for the second house.

"It will probably only be for a short time," Felicity told Adrian lightly.

"Of course," Adrian agreed. "No doubt you'll be married soon. Are you looking forward to your ball?"

"Of course," Felicity said quickly. She was both excited and nervous about making her debut, although she wasn't going to tell Adrian about her nerves. But after all, the purpose of a Season was to find a husband, and of all the decisions she would make in her life, her choice of husband was probably the most important. The man she married would have authority over both her person and her fortune, and the wrong choice would lead to misery. At the very least, she needed to find a man she could respect, and who would respect her in return.

There would be men who thought she was already past her prime, and others who believed that as the granddaughter of a tradesman, her bloodlines weren't pure enough. Their rejection might sting a little—she was human, after all—but Felicity knew there would be men who could see past her age and her ancestors. She didn't doubt that she would find a good man, but she was afraid of giving her heart to a man who didn't return her affection.

"I'm sure you'll be a great success," Adrian said. "You're easy to talk to, since you say what you mean. So many young ladies say one thing but mean another, and that can be awfully confusing."

"I can see how it would."

"And you don't intend to carry a fan, do you?"

"I hadn't thought about it," Felicity replied with a chuckle.

"Don't," Adrian advised succinctly. "Young ladies look very silly when they simper and wave their fans about. My friend Corky—Francis McCorquodale, you know—was stabbed by a fan at a ball last year. He almost lost an eye."

"Someone attacked him with a fan?" Felicity asked incredulously.

"Oh, I don't think it was deliberate," Adrian assured her. "But a young lady was waving her fan quite vigorously, you know, and if Corky hadn't ducked, she would have taken his eye out. As it was, she only scratched his forehead."

"That's horrible."

"Well, Corky was quite startled, but it all worked out in the end. The girl apologized, of course, and Corky could see she felt quite bad about it, so he asked her to dance. He ended up marrying her."

"How unexpected."

"It was," Adrian agreed. "Of course, Corky made her promise never to carry a fan again, and I think they've been quite happy together. Until they got the cat, that is."

"The cat?" Felicity asked.

Adrian nodded. "Corky's great-uncle died a few weeks ago and left him his cat. By all accounts, it's an ill-tempered beast, and doesn't like females. Corky's wife slinks around in fear of the animal, and Corky even suggested she carry her fan again, in case she needs it for self-defence."

"That seems only reasonable."

"Well, Corky's at his wits' end, and he really doesn't know what else to do. He feels obligated to give the cat a home, out of respect for his great-uncle, but he also has a duty to his wife."

"I suppose he does," Felicity agreed. "It sounds as though he has competing obligations."

Adrian nodded. "That's the problem in a nutshell. I would take the creature—the cat, I mean, not Corky's wife—but my landlady has a strict rule against pets."

A smile tugged at Felicity's lips. "It sounds like a difficult problem."

"I don't suppose you know anyone who would like a

cat?" Adrian asked hopefully. "I owe Corky a favour, and I told him I'd look for a home for Cleopatra."

"I don't think I do, but I'll keep it in mind," Felicity replied.

"I say, Miss Taylor," Adrian said as they rounded a corner. "Did you know Kincaid was behind us?"

Felicity turned and saw that Kincaid was indeed behind them, riding his grey stallion. Despite the distance, she could tell his eyes were hard and his mouth was set in a grim line.

"Oh, Mr. Kincaid rides often," she said blithely. "He's probably headed to the park to exercise his horse."

Adrian looked back and almost lost his grip on the reins. "Perhaps," he said dubiously. "But he looks as though he's following us."

"Nonsense," Felicity said dismissively.

"It's a little disconcerting, you know," Adrian confessed. "It's almost as bad as being followed by my brother."

"Does Lord Langley often follow you when you drive?"

"Well, not often," Adrian told her. "But I offered to take his wife driving last month, and he threatened to follow us if I did. Robert seems to think he's the only man who can drive a curricle."

"That must be very frustrating," Felicity remarked, as Adrian swerved to avoid a pedestrian.

"It is!" Adrian exclaimed, pleased to have found a sympathetic listener. "Robert's a good driver, but he's far too cautious. Just because I like to drive with a bit of dash, he thinks I'm dangerous."

"He sounds most unreasonable."

"Well, I don't think he means to be," Adrian said generously. "And I suppose he can't help worrying about his wife. But Mr. Kincaid reminds me of my brother, and I expect he's a cautious driver too."

"Mr. Kincaid is an excellent driver," Felicity said loyally, as Adrian sailed through an intersection and narrowly avoided a collision with a phaeton. The driver of the phaeton, who had held the right of way, let out a blistering stream of curses that Adrian didn't seem to notice.

Adrian finally slowed his pace at the entrance to Hyde Park, and Kincaid took the opportunity to draw his horse alongside them.

"Good afternoon, Mr. Kincaid," Adrian said politely.

"Afternoon, Adrian," Kincaid replied. "I'm sure she's too shy to ask, but I know Felicity would love to drive your curricle. She was talking about it after we saw you the other day."

"Oh, I would," Felicity agreed, giving Adrian a limpid smile. "Do you think you could teach me to drive, Mr. Stone?"

Adrian looked at Felicity skeptically before turning back to Kincaid. "I'm not sure this is the best time for it, you know. The park's crowded, and if the horses bolted—"

"Do you think they might?" Felicity asked, looking at him with concern. "Your horses do look strong . . ." She let her sentence trail off and chewed her lip.

Kincaid gave her a look that promised severe consequences if she did not behave, and Felicity gave him an almost imperceptible nod. "Your horses look strong, but

I'm confident I can handle them," she told Adrian. "I've driven a pair before, you know."

"Well, perhaps for a short distance," Adrian agreed dubiously. He handed Felicity the reins, and she set off down the path at a smart trot. She expected Kincaid to continue to follow them, but unlike Adrian, she didn't fear his scrutiny of her driving. She kept the reins for the rest of the drive, and as she drew the curricle to a stop in front of 23 Bentley St., Adrian remarked that she drove very well.

Felicity stood at the window and watched Adrian drive away. After he had turned the first corner, she walked down the street to 29 Bentley, where the butler reluctantly admitted that Kincaid had just returned. She was shown to the drawing room, where Kincaid joined her moments later.

"You shouldn't be visiting here without Miss Flint," he admonished.

Felicity rolled her eyes. "I won't be here long." She cast a critical eye around the drawing room before taking a seat on a hideous burnt-orange sofa. "You have better taste in furniture than the Smith-Lyons do."

"Thank you."

"Did you enjoy your ride this afternoon?"

"Not particularly," Kincaid replied. "I had other plans for the afternoon, and I was forced to reschedule a meeting with my banker."

"So you admit that you followed Adrian and me?"

"Of course I admit it, Felicity," Kincaid said with a look of exasperation. "You know I did, so there's no point in denying it. And since we're on the subject, I don't want you to drive with Adrian again."

"So you forbid it?"

"Yes, Felicity, I do forbid it. You have to understand, your parents entrusted you to my guardianship until you turn twenty-one. Can you imagine how I would feel if you were harmed in a road accident a month before you came of age?"

"Worse than if I was harmed in a road accident at another time?"

"Of course not." Guardian or not, Kincaid would be devastated if Felicity came to harm. "But at least I wouldn't have to live with the knowledge that I could have prevented it."

"I don't think Adrian's so very dangerous," Felicity argued. "I don't think he's ever come to serious harm himself, and with the traffic in town, no one can drive very fast."

"Perhaps I'm irrational," Kincaid said. "But you won't change my mind." His expression softened. "If you want to go driving, I'll take you."

"All right."

Kincaid could hardly believe she had agreed, and he decided to change the subject before she thought of another argument. "Have you thought about who you would like to be your chaperone?"

"Yes," Felicity said. "But I haven't reached a decision. I would prefer Miss Flint, but I'm afraid she would find it stressful. I think she's rather shy, you know."

"Do you think so?" Kincaid had attributed Miss Flint's taciturn nature to eccentricity, but he realized Felicity could be right.

Felicity nodded. "And Lady Delphinia would probably enjoy it, so I suppose it makes sense for her to do it."

Kincaid fought to keep his expression neutral. "Why don't you take a little more time to think about it? If you still feel this way next week, you can speak to Lady Delphinia."

Felicity looked at him strangely. "I've been thinking about it for close to a week."

"I know, but a decision like this shouldn't be rushed."

Felicity sighed. "All right, Mr. Kincaid."

Six

Wainwright opened the door to the drawing room and cleared his throat. "Mr. Kincaid," he announced.

Kincaid shot his butler a warning look as he strode past him into the room. Even though he lived down the street, 23 Bentley St. still belonged to him, and there was no need for him to be announced at the door of his own drawing room.

He found Felicity sitting by the window, with her sketchbook open on her lap.

"Good afternoon, Mr. Kincaid," she said, as she closed her sketchbook and stood to greet him. "I was beginning to think you had forgotten about us." She was pleased to see him, and it showed in her expression. Three days had passed since her drive with Adrian, and Felicity was bored. The house seemed very quiet since Kincaid had moved out, and if he hadn't come to see her, Felicity would have walked down the street to visit him.

Despite her welcoming smile, Kincaid looked

nervous. "There's something I want to talk to you about, Felicity."

"You look very serious, Mr. Kincaid," she said playfully. "I haven't been up to any mischief lately. You can ask Miss Flint."

"Miss Flint wouldn't tell me if you had," he replied with a chuckle. Miss Flint was known for both her economy of speech and her fierce loyalty to Felicity. "But I haven't come to reproach you. In fact, I hope you'll think I've brought good news."

"Oh?"

"I've been thinking about the question of your chaperone for the Season, and I don't think Lady Delphinia would be a good choice."

"I see," Felicity said slowly. "You think Miss Flint would be better?"

"I don't think Miss Flint is ideal either," Kincaid continued. "You see, Felicity, I've decided it's time I was married."

Felicity's eyes widened. "Yes!" she blurted impulsively.

Kincaid looked surprised by her enthusiasm. "You also think it's time I was married?"

"Oh, yes," Felicity said. "Lucas, I've dreamed about this for years."

He looked at her with amusement. "I had no idea you were so concerned about my bachelor state."

"Well, I understood why you had to wait, but sometimes I worried you would never come to the point," Felicity confessed. "How soon can the wedding be?"

"Aren't you going to ask the name of the lady?"

Felicity's expression of joy changed to one of dismay. "The name of the lady?" she repeated numbly.

"Yes, her name," Kincaid said, giving her a strange look. "Surely the name of the bride is more important than the date of the wedding?"

"Oh, of course," Felicity said, in a deceptively cheerful tone of voice. The name of the lady hardly mattered, since it wouldn't be Felicity Taylor. "Who is the fortunate young lady?"

"Miss Jane Harris."

Felicity frowned. "I don't recall you ever speaking of a Miss Harris. Don't you think this is rather sudden?"

A faint blush tinged Kincaid's cheeks. "I'm thirty-one, Felicity," he pointed out. "You agreed it was time I was married."

"I did say that," Felicity acknowledged. "And I think that thirty-one is a perfectly reasonable age at which to marry. I'm more concerned about the speed with which you offered marriage to Miss Harris, since I've never heard you mention her before."

"I've been acquainted with Miss Harris for several years," Kincaid explained. "She made her debut four years ago, and I've danced with her several times."

"How interesting." Felicity wondered why, after an acquaintance of four years, Kincaid had chosen to propose to Miss Harris now. "You've done an excellent job of keeping your affection for Miss Harris a secret."

"It's hardly a subject that I would discuss with you," Kincaid said dryly.

"I suppose not," Felicity agreed. "Tell me about Miss Harris. Will I like her, do you think?"

"Oh, I'm sure you will," Kincaid assured her. "Her father is a baronet, with an estate in Gloucestershire, and she is the eldest of five sisters."

Felicity nodded, reflecting that he had told her nothing about Miss Harris herself. "It sounds like quite a romantic story," she remarked. "You've been acquainted with Miss Harris for four years, but have only asked her to marry you now. Did something happen to make you see her in a different light, or have you been secretly in love for months? Perhaps there was a barrier to your marriage that no longer exists?"

"I didn't want to rush into anything," Kincaid said carefully.

"I can understand that," Felicity said. "But four years seems like a long time to wait. You were fortunate that no one swooped in and stole Miss Harris from under your nose."

"I suppose I was."

"How did you propose to her?" Felicity asked.

"What do you mean?"

"Did you sneak her away from a party and take her for a moonlit stroll? Or take her rowing on the Serpentine—"

"Felicity, it's the beginning of March," Kincaid protested. "Hardly the season for moonlit walks or boat rides."

"I suppose not," she conceded, but the look on her face made it clear that she was disappointed in him. "How did you propose?"

"I called upon the Harrises two days ago," he explained. "Miss Harris and I had a very pleasant conversation. So I returned this morning, and Lady Harris was kind enough to let me speak to Jane alone. Jane accepted my proposal, and her father has given his consent."

"I see," Felicity remarked slowly. "Now that I think

about it, Mr. Kincaid, there is something rather romantic about a proposal in the bright light of day, without the help of moonlight or wine. A gentleman who can successfully make an offer of marriage in an unromantic location—say, at the breakfast table—must have either a marvellous way with words, or a lady who loves him very much."

"I didn't propose to Miss Harris at the breakfast table," Kincaid protested.

"Oh, I know that," Felicity said, smiling kindly. "I was simply using it as an example of an uninspired setting."

Kincaid could tell she thought his method of proposing marriage had been similarly uninspired, and it irked him. "I'm not sure I have a marvellous way with words, Felicity, but Jane and I have a great deal of respect for each other."

"I'm pleased for you, Mr. Kincaid. When will the wedding be?"

"We plan to get married in three weeks' time."

"So quickly!" Felicity exclaimed.

"We don't want a big ceremony or a lot of fuss, so it seemed . . ." He trailed off when he realized that Felicity looked amused. "What?"

"Oh, I just think it's convenient that you've found a young lady whose views are so compatible with your own," Felicity said lightly. "Who doesn't want a big wedding, I mean." She privately thought that a lady who had secured a very eligible offer of marriage after four unsuccessful Seasons might want a little fuss.

"Yes, Miss Harris and I are quite well matched," Kincaid said with a smile. "I told her that my preference was for something understated, but that I would defer to her wishes."

"And her wishes matched yours?"

"Yes, they did."

"What a fortunate coincidence," Felicity murmured.

"Yes," Kincaid agreed. "So we will be married next month, and then we will both move into this house. There can be no question of impropriety after I'm married."

"Certainly not. Some people might even expect you to live in the same house as your wife."

Kincaid chuckled. "I mean there will be no question of impropriety between you and me."

"Oh, of course not," Felicity said, as though the very idea was absurd. "But there never was, was there?"

"Of course not," Kincaid said. "I told Jane about you, and explained that you're making your debut this Season. She said she would be delighted to act as your chaperone. Our wedding will be three days before your debut ball, so the timing will be perfect."

"That sounds wonderful," Felicity said brightly.

"Well, Miss Harris is a sensible woman, and with four younger sisters, she's well suited to the task of chaperoning you. And now you won't need to worry about whether to ask Lady Delphinia or Miss Flint."

"Very convenient," Felicity said with a nod.

Kincaid studied her face and frowned. "Felicity, are you feeling all right? You're looking rather pale."

"Oh, yes," she assured him. "I didn't sleep very well last night, that's all."

Kincaid's brow cleared. "All right. I will invite Jane

and her mother to tea sometime this week, so you can get to know each other."

Felicity forced a smile. "I am looking forward to it."

The following morning, Kincaid sat at the breakfast table after an entirely unsatisfactory meal. The Smith-Lyons' cook didn't seem able to prepare eggs that weren't over-cooked, and Kincaid had finally told the man that he preferred to eat only bread and butter at breakfast.

Kincaid not only missed the food at 23 Bentley St., he missed the company. Although he didn't reach his stride until after he finished his morning coffee, Felicity could carry a conversation with minimal assistance from anyone else. Miss Flint would comment on the excellence of the food, and all in all, it was a pleasant way to spend an hour. He had thought of returning to 23 Bentley St. for meals, but he feared that would defeat the purpose of moving out. If he wished to convince society there was nothing improper about his relationship with Felicity, visiting her home three times a day would hardly help his cause.

Since he had no other engagements that morning, he decided to call upon Jane. An hour later, he was shown to the Harrises' drawing room, where he found Jane, her mother, and her four sisters occupied with needlework. Jane rose to greet him with a bright smile.

"I hope you'll forgive me for calling at such an early hour," he began.

"Nonsense, Mr. Kincaid, there is nothing to forgive," Jane said with a little laugh. "We are betrothed, after all.

Please have a seat, and I'll ring for tea. Our cook made seed cakes yesterday, and I think they're very good."

Although the offer of seed cakes was tempting, the prospect of remaining in the drawing room was not. Jane's four sisters had put down their needlework and were staring at him with undisguised curiosity. Kincaid didn't think he could enjoy cake under such conditions, and he almost wished he hadn't come.

"Actually, Miss Harris, I hoped to persuade you to take a walk with me," he said. "Provided your mother has no objection, of course."

Lady Harris gave her permission and Jane went up to change, leaving Kincaid to the scrutiny of her mother and sisters. Three of the Misses Harris stared at him shyly, but Sophronia filled the silence by reciting the names of all the gentlemen she had danced with since the beginning of the Season. By the time Jane returned, clad in a practical grey pelisse, Kincaid was eager to make his escape.

"Mama thinks very highly of you," Jane remarked, as they descended the stairs to the street. "Otherwise she would never have allowed me to walk with you unchaperoned."

"I'm pleased to hear it," Kincaid said with a smile.

Jane shivered and drew closer to him. "It's a pity it's so cold today. I don't think I'll be able to walk farther than the first cross street."

"That will suit me very well," Kincaid replied. He was surprised to hear she was cold, since the weather was unusually warm for March, but he realized he had very little experience of walking with ladies. He rarely spent time outdoors with any girl but Felicity, who never seemed to feel the cold.

"You must think me very delicate," Jane said apologetically.

"Not at all," Kincaid said gallantly.

"It was kind of you to call."

"I wanted to see you," he said politely. "And I'd like to invite you and your mother for tea tomorrow."

"Oh, I would like that very much."

"It will give you the chance to meet my ward, Felicity Taylor," Kincaid continued.

"I've been looking forward to meeting Miss Taylor ever since you told me about her," Jane said, smiling up at him. "Is she a relative of yours?"

"No. Felicity's mother was my godmother."

"I see," Jane remarked. He could tell she wanted to ask why he had been appointed guardian to his godmother's daughter, but she was too well-bred to do so. "And how long have you been her guardian?"

"Seven years. Her parents died when she was fourteen, and I've been her guardian ever since."

"So she's twenty-one," Jane murmured. "Only a year younger than me."

"About to turn twenty-one, yes." Kincaid hesitated for a moment before deciding that Jane deserved to know a little more about the young lady she had agreed to chaperone. "Felicity's upbringing was rather unconventional. I hired governesses, of course, but we had some difficulty with them."

"Difficulty?" Jane asked curiously.

"Yes," Kincaid replied, with a rueful smile. "Felicity would tell you that I lack skill in selecting governesses. Most of the ladies I hired were unsuited to the position and left within a year."

"How strange."

"Yes, it was," Kincaid admitted. He had no doubt that Felicity had deliberately driven the governesses away, for reasons that were still unclear to him. "Felicity's manners may not be entirely conventional, and she has a tendency to be stubborn, but she has a good heart."

Jane was rapidly reaching the conclusion that Felicity was an unprincipled hoyden. "That sounds very difficult," she sympathized. "It was good of you to take on the responsibility of being her guardian."

"It wasn't difficult, exactly," he hedged.

"I understand completely, Mr. Kincaid," Jane said, determined to do her duty by Felicity. "And I will be pleased to share the burden. I think I'm still too young to take on a maternal role, but I hope Miss Taylor will see me in the guise of an older sister."

Kincaid nodded. "I expect she will."

"These kippers are delicious," Miss Flint remarked at breakfast the following day.

"Oh, yes," Felicity agreed, although she hadn't managed to eat more than a few bites of bread and butter. Her appetite seemed to have deserted her, and she had spent the meal pushing her food around her plate. Ever since she had received a note from Mr. Kincaid, informing her that Jane and her mother were expected for tea later that day, she hadn't been able to think about anything else.

"Excellent eggs, too," Miss Flint said.

"Yes."

"Are you ill, Felicity?" Miss Flint asked, looking at her with concern.

"Oh, no," Felicity said quickly. She forced herself to take another bite of toast, and then to chew and swallow it. "I'm merely a little distracted. The news of Mr. Kincaid's engagement came as quite a surprise."

"It's about time he was married," Miss Flint remarked.

Felicity pasted a smile on her face. "Yes, I suppose it is."

When she had eaten all she could stomach, Felicity slipped on an old cloak and made her way down to the stables. After nodding to the groom, she picked up a brush and currycomb and made her way to Sugarplum's stall. The mare nickered a greeting, and Felicity set to work brushing her neck.

Sugarplum had belonged to Felicity since the summer after she lost her parents. It had been Kincaid's idea to buy her a horse; he hadn't known what to do with a grieving fourteen-year-old girl, so he had decided to teach her to ride. Although Felicity's previous riding experience had been limited, she had a natural aptitude for it, and Kincaid was a good teacher. He had visited her often at Fairleigh Manor, where she was living with a governess, and they had spent hours riding around the countryside together.

There was something relaxing about the smell of the stables and the familiar task of grooming her horse. Sugarplum had been one of the few constants in Felicity's life since her parents' death, and a frequent source of comfort. And Felicity needed comfort as her thoughts turned to Mr. Kincaid, who had been the other constant presence in her life for the past seven years. In less than a month, she would turn twenty-one, and Kincaid would no longer be her guardian. He would keep control of her fortune until she married, but Felicity hoped to relieve him of this responsibility soon. Kincaid would be busy with his own family's affairs, and Felicity was determined to find her own husband as quickly as she could.

"Good morning, Felicity," Kincaid said from the door to the stall.

Felicity started and dropped the brush. "Mr. Kincaid!" she exclaimed.

"I didn't mean to scare you," he said apologetically, striding forward to pick up the brush.

"Oh, you didn't," Felicity said quickly. "It's just that I had been thinking about you, so when you appeared, it seemed as though I had conjured you up."

Kincaid stared at her curiously. "What were you thinking about?"

"Nothing of any significance," Felicity said. "Just that it will be a relief for you when I marry, and you're no longer responsible for me or my money."

His expression changed. "You've never been a burden, Felicity," he said quietly.

She looked at him skeptically. "Never?"

"I suppose interviewing governesses did grow tedious," he said with a chuckle. "Especially when I was trying to fill the position for the ninth time."

"I know some of them quit because I was difficult," Felicity admitted thoughtfully. "But an equal number left because you disappointed them."

"I disappointed them? Felicity, I barely had anything to do with them!"

"That was the problem," Felicity said placidly. "They

were hoping you would take a romantic interest in them, and they were frustrated when you didn't."

"That's absurd," Kincaid protested, but a flush crept over his cheeks. "In any case, I came to make sure you received my note. About Jane and her mother coming to tea."

"I did," Felicity said with a nod.

"Perhaps we should return to the house," he suggested, with a glance at Felicity's well-worn cloak and muddy boots. "You'll need time to change before the Harrises arrive."

"All right," Felicity agreed, giving Sugarplum's neck a farewell pat. "What time are they coming?"

Kincaid pulled out his fob watch. "You have an hour."

"Don't worry, Mr. Kincaid," Felicity said, as they started back to the house. "It won't take me an hour to change my clothes. I am looking forward to meeting Miss Harris, and I promise I won't keep her waiting."

Seven

True to her word, Felicity descended the stairs half an hour later in a charming pink muslin gown. She found Kincaid in the drawing room with Miss Flint, who appeared to be engrossed in her knitting.

Felicity had barely sat down when Wainwright announced Lady Harris and her daughter, Miss Jane Harris. Kincaid bowed to Lady Harris before greeting his betrothed with a polite smile. Felicity watched with interest as he awkwardly pressed Jane's gloved hands.

"Lady Harris, Miss Harris, I'd like to introduce my ward, Miss Felicity Taylor," Kincaid said. "And this is her companion, Miss Theodora Flint."

Lady Harris was a middle-aged lady of comfortable proportions, dressed in an unremarkable navy-blue gown. Felicity made her a very proper curtsy before turning to face her daughter.

Jane Harris was several inches shorter than Felicity, with soft brown eyes and an upturned nose. "I'm pleased to make your acquaintance, Miss Taylor," she said with a condescending smile. "Mr. Kincaid said you were a pretty child, but I'm afraid he didn't do you justice."

For an instant, Felicity's eyes glittered with anger, but she composed herself quickly. "Mr. Kincaid has told me a great deal about you as well," she said brightly. "But I can't believe he described me as pretty; it doesn't sound like the sort of thing he would say. I hope you haven't mistaken your betrothed."

"I can assure you I have not mistaken him." Jane beamed with pride as she glanced at Kincaid. "Mr. Kincaid has told me all about your unfortunate situation, Miss Taylor, and I would be pleased to act as your chaperone. I hope you will think of me as a sister."

"Well, if we are to be like sisters, there is no need to stand on ceremony," Felicity declared. "You must call me Felicity, and I hope I may call you Jane?"

"Of course, Felicity," Jane said with a forced smile. She had planned to suggest they use first names, but she resented the fact that Felicity had done so first.

Lady Harris seated herself opposite Miss Flint, and Felicity led Jane to a sofa at the far end of the room. After a moment's hesitation, Kincaid crossed the room and took the chair next to Jane.

"It's very kind of you to agree to be my chaperone," Felicity said to Jane.

"Oh, I'm sure I will enjoy it," Jane said. "But we will be very busy for the next few weeks. I have so much to teach you before your debut."

"Indeed?" Felicity asked, arching an eyebrow. "What sorts of things will I need to be taught?"

"Oh, dancing, etiquette, how to converse with a

gentleman. And we'll have to visit the modiste, of course, to ensure you have a suitable wardrobe."

"Felicity's had lessons from dancing masters," Kincaid put in. "She's quite a good dancer."

Felicity waited for him to say that she didn't need to be taught etiquette or conversation either, and she was disappointed when he didn't. "But as for the rest of it—it does seem like a lot to achieve in a few weeks," she said thoughtfully.

"I've always liked a challenge," Jane said with a laugh. "I know some people might consider me young to be a chaperone, but I think—"

"Oh, I'm pleased to have a chaperone so close to my age," Felicity interrupted blithely. "You'll understand all the modern customs. My companion, Miss Flint, was going to be my chaperone, and she has the most outdated notions of propriety. I don't think I'll catch a husband by being *proper*." Her eyes flicked to Kincaid before turning back to Jane. "I imagine you must have used all your feminine wiles to snare Mr. Kincaid?"

Jane's brow furrowed, and Kincaid gave Felicity a reproachful look.

"That's all right," Felicity said with a giggle. "You can tell me about it later, when he's not in the room. I'm sure you'll have some excellent advice on how to catch a husband."

Jane took a deep breath. "I don't think I would describe it that way," she said carefully.

"How would you describe it?" Felicity asked curiously.

"Well . . ." Jane said slowly. She looked to Kincaid for help, but he appeared to be studying the carpet. "There is a great deal more to a Season than meeting gentlemen. This will be your opportunity to become acquainted with the leaders of society, and to meet young ladies who will become your lifelong friends."

"I hope my friends won't be interested in the same gentlemen as I am," Felicity remarked. "It would be awkward to be friends with one's rivals."

"It isn't a competition," Jane said primly.

"Is it not?" Felicity asked skeptically. "My knowledge of gentlemen is limited, of course, but it seems to me that some gentlemen are more desirable than others."

"Felicity!" Kincaid exclaimed.

"And if that's the case," Felicity continued, "it stands to reason that young ladies would compete for the most eligible men. Wouldn't you agree?"

"Well, I . . ." Jane said weakly.

"You may not have heard, but I'm an heiress," Felicity informed her. "So I'm hoping to catch myself a man with a title. And as soon as I set eyes on you, Jane, I knew you would be the one to help me do it. I'm sure you can find a way for me to enjoy a little flirtation without compromising my reputation?"

Kincaid stared at her in disbelief. Felicity had always been spirited, but he had never known her to be vulgar.

"If Mr. Kincaid is going to glower like that, we'll have to leave him at home when we go to balls," Felicity teased. "Otherwise, he'll scare all my prospects away." She leaned closer to Jane, as though preparing to share a confidence. "I think you're very open-minded to take him as he is. I can assure you that his fits of melancholia never last more than a week, and the doctor thinks marriage will improve the condition."

Although Felicity had lowered her voice, Kincaid heard every word. "Felicity has a keen sense of humour," he said weakly.

"And it's fortunate that I do," Felicity agreed. "Mr. Kincaid is so serious, you know, it takes a great deal of effort to make him laugh. I would offer to tell you all his secrets, but I'm afraid he doesn't have any! If he does, he's very discreet. I've never known him to receive love letters from other young ladies, or anything of that sort."

There was a moment of shocked silence. "I know Felicity has been anxious about meeting you, Miss Harris," Kincaid finally said. "Sometimes when she's nervous, her humour can be inappropriate."

"Oh, Mr. Kincaid, you paint a very false picture of me!" Felicity protested. "As though I would be nervous to meet your betrothed!"

Jane seemed to think Kincaid's explanation was perfectly reasonable. "Your anxiety is understandable," she told Felicity gently. "But I assure you it's entirely unnecessary."

"You're very kind," Felicity remarked with a giggle. "Now, let's talk about how I can win myself a lord."

"Felicity, I'm not sure—" Jane began.

"But I am," Felicity interrupted confidently. "I can tell we're going to be the best of friends. As you said, we'll practically be sisters."

"Yes," Jane said slowly.

"But I'm not in any rush to be married," Felicity continued. "My father's family was in trade, you know, and he used to say that when you have something valuable to sell, you should never take the first offer you receive. You never know when a better opportunity will come along."

"It isn't a game, Miss Taylor," Jane admonished.

"Well, I'm sure your case is different," Felicity said. "Mr. Kincaid is quite the matrimonial prize, so I don't think my father's advice would apply."

"Felicity," Kincaid said in a pleading tone.

But Felicity ignored him and turned back to Jane. "I know it's not entirely proper of me to say that Mr. Kincaid is a matrimonial prize," she said with a laugh. "Since he is my guardian, many people would think I can't be impartial, but since you're already betrothed to him, I don't see how it can do any harm."

"I suppose not," Jane acknowledged. "But I do think, Felicity . . ." She trailed off as a ginger cat emerged from under the sofa and streaked across the room towards her. The cat stopped about a foot away from Jane and hissed, and Jane recoiled in alarm.

Kincaid looked as shocked as Jane. "What is that?"

"*She* is Cleopatra," Felicity explained, as she moved to pick up the cat. "She's apt to take offence if you refer to her as a what."

Sensing Kincaid's interest, Cleopatra jumped down from Felicity's arms and began to lick his boots.

"I didn't know you had a cat," Jane said feebly.

"I don't," Kincaid said grimly, turning back to Felicity. "What is *she* doing in our drawing room?"

"She is my cat," Felicity replied simply.

"Where did she come from?" Kincaid asked sternly.

"Adrian Stone," Felicity explained. "She belonged to his friend Corky, but apparently Corky's wife was afraid of her."

"I can't imagine why," Kincaid remarked dryly.

"Yes, some ladies are afraid of the silliest things," Felicity remarked. "Cleo is purebred, you know, and a very rare breed. And because of the circumstances, I was able to get her for a very fair price."

"Is that right?" Kincaid asked. He thought the only way the transaction could have been fair was if Adrian had paid Felicity to take the cat.

Felicity smiled innocently. "Yes, although I've always thought it was distasteful to buy and sell pets. As though Cleo was a commodity, rather than a member of the family!" The truth was that Adrian had brought Cleopatra to meet Felicity the previous afternoon, and had managed to leave without her. Felicity hadn't paid a thing for Cleopatra, and she was beginning to think she had received excellent value.

"I see," Kincaid said skeptically, as Cleopatra rubbed her flank against his leg.

"She likes you!" Felicity said, in a delighted voice. "I thought she would."

But Cleopatra decided she had shown Kincaid enough affection, and approached Jane again. Jane bravely reached down to scratch the cat behind her ears, but Cleopatra rejected the overture of friendship and walked away with her tail in the air.

"She takes a while to warm up to people," Felicity said lightly. "I'm sure the two of you will be dear friends in no time."

"I'm afraid I don't like cats," Jane said stiffly.

"Felicity," Kincaid said, in a tone that she dared not disobey. "Please take Cleopatra upstairs."

Felicity carried Cleopatra up to her bedchamber and

left her in the care of her maid. When she returned to the drawing room, she saw that tea had arrived and Jane was pouring out. After helping to distribute the tea, Felicity turned her attention to the plate of lemon tarts.

"I think our cook makes the best lemon tarts in all of London," she remarked, as she offered the plate to Lady Harris. "Will you try one, Jane?"

"No, thank you, Felicity."

"Oh, but you must," Felicity insisted, offering the plate of tarts to Jane. "They really are delicious."

"I've never liked lemon tarts."

"You haven't tried these," Felicity pointed out.

"I think we've had lemon tarts too often recently," Kincaid interrupted. He rang the bell and instructed the housemaid to have cake and sandwiches sent up immediately. "I'm sorry, Jane," he said contritely. "The staff must have forgotten that we have company. Lemon tarts are Felicity's favourite, so when we're alone, the cook rarely sends anything else." He gave Jane a conspiratorial smile. "But I'm getting rather sick of lemon myself."

Felicity stared at him, aghast. Kincaid liked lemon tarts far more than she did.

"I suppose I should be glad the staff don't see me as company," Jane said. "And I would hate for you to alter your routine on my account."

"I am pleased to have a reason to alter my routine," he replied.

"You have a beautiful house," Jane remarked, glancing around the drawing room. "Mama and I talked about having an engagement party, but our drawing room is so small, we couldn't imagine where we would put everyone."

"You are welcome to host a party here," Kincaid told her.

"Oh, I wouldn't want to impose," Jane demurred. "Although if we held a small party, Felicity could attend, even if she hasn't made her debut." She gave Felicity a patronizing smile. "It would give you a chance to practise your conversation."

"That's an excellent idea," Kincaid agreed.

"Perhaps in two weeks' time?" Jane suggested. "It is short notice, but Mama and I can handle all the arrangements. All you'll need to do is give me a list of people you want to invite."

"I'll speak to my housekeeper," Kincaid said with a nod. "Make whatever arrangements you like, and have the bills sent to me."

"Perhaps you would like to help plan the party, Felicity?" Jane asked.

"Oh, perhaps," Felicity said easily. "But right now, I would rather hear about the first time you met Mr. Kincaid. Was it love at first sight, or did your affection grow more gradually?"

"We met at a ball," Jane began.

"Did you waltz?" Felicity asked. "Did he try to manoeuvre you into a quiet corner so he could behave dishonourably?"

Jane frowned. "Mr. Kincaid has always behaved like the gentleman he is," she said primly.

Felicity's face fell. "How disappointing. But I don't think he's completely hopeless; if you give him time, he may redeem himself."

Kincaid ran a hand through his hair and studied her

in amazement. "Felicity, you are not yourself. Perhaps you should go up and rest?"

Felicity winked at Jane. "He's taking my advice already! Now he just needs an excuse to send your mother and Miss Flint away, so he can get you alone."

"Felicity!" Kincaid exclaimed.

"I'm sorry, Mr. Kincaid," she said contritely. "I don't mean to tell you how to conduct your courtship. But if you want my advice—"

"I don't," he said curtly. "Right now, I want you to go upstairs."

Felicity could tell she had pushed him too far, and she crossed the room to curtsy to Lady Harris. When she said goodbye to Jane, she impulsively pulled her into an embrace.

"I think it's silly to stand on ceremony when we're going to be family," Felicity remarked. "It was a pleasure to meet you, Jane."

Jane nodded stiffly and Felicity went upstairs, leaving Kincaid and Jane staring awkwardly at each other.

"I apologize, Miss Harris," Kincaid said. "Such behaviour is quite out of character for Felicity. I know she was anxious to make a good impression, and I imagine she was so nervous that she didn't know what she was saying."

Although Kincaid knew his explanation was foolish, he couldn't think of a better one, and it seemed to mollify Jane. "When I accepted your offer of marriage, Mr. Kincaid, I made a commitment to be your partner in all things," she said solemnly.

"That is very generous of you, Miss Harris. Are still

willing to serve as Felicity's chaperone after we are married?"

Jane nodded. "Felicity is clearly in need of feminine guidance, and I flatter myself that I will be able to provide it. I am the eldest of five sisters, after all."

Kincaid let out a small sigh of relief. "Felicity and I frequently ride in the park," he said. "Would you care to ride with us next week?"

Jane's face fell, and spots of colour tinged her cheeks. "I like to ride, but I'm afraid we couldn't bring my horse to London this Season."

Kincaid realized he shouldn't have assumed that Jane had a horse to ride. Her father's fortune wasn't large, and stabling costs in London were expensive. "We keep a horse for Miss Flint's use," he told her. "You could ride her, if that would suit."

"I would enjoy that very much," Jane agreed. "Thank you, Mr. Kincaid."

Eight

Kincaid spent the evening in the study of 29 Bentley St., debating what to say to Felicity about her uncharacteristic behaviour. The following morning, he remembered Oliver had mentioned that he found it easier to express himself by letter, so he sat down at his desk and picked up a pen. After three failed attempts, he settled on the following communication:

Dear Felicity,

I found your behaviour yesterday confusing, but I can only assume you were nervous about meeting Miss Harris. I assure you there is no need for concern. Miss Harris is eager to become acquainted with you, and she is looking forward to chaperoning you for the season.

I realize that since Miss Harris is close to you in age, you may not have known how to behave towards her. I would ask that you show her the same respect that you would my mother, or Miss Flint.

Yours truly,
Lucas Kincaid

The letter was rather vague, but he was reluctant to put his specific complaints down on paper. Felicity's comments about catching a man with a title, and of Mr. Kincaid being a matrimonial prize, were really best forgotten. He sealed the letter and gave it to a footman to deliver.

The footman returned half an hour later with the following reply:

Dear Mr. Kincaid,

I am disappointed by your decision to reprimand me by letter. If you have concerns about my behaviour, it would be courteous of you to discuss them with me in person. We live only three houses apart, after all.

Yours truly,
Felicity

Kincaid stuffed the letter in his pocket and walked down the street to 23 Bentley St. to discuss the matter with Felicity in person.

Wainwright smiled with amusement when he opened the door to his employer. "Good morning, sir," he said politely. "Shall I see if Miss Taylor is at home?"

Kincaid was not in a joking humour, so he handed Wainwright his overcoat and gloves and brushed past him into the house. He found Felicity and Miss Flint in the breakfast parlour, lingering over cups of coffee.

"Good morning, Mr. Kincaid," Felicity said politely. "You're rather early for a morning call, but you're welcome to share our breakfast."

"No, thank you, Felicity. I've already eaten." Although the offer of breakfast was tempting, he feared it would distract him from his purpose. "I wanted to talk to you."

He started towards a chair on the opposite side of the table, but a high-pitched yelp caused him to stop abruptly. He looked down and saw Cleopatra hissing at him angrily.

"I'm afraid you stepped on her tail," Felicity said reproachfully.

"That's another thing I wanted to talk to you about," Kincaid said. "Why did you buy such a ridiculous cat?"

"I thought you liked cats, Mr. Kincaid." Felicity looked very disappointed in him.

Kincaid couldn't recall having ever expressed an opinion about cats. "I suppose they're all right," he said cautiously. He looked down at Cleopatra, who had stopped hissing and was now staring up at him with a hopeful look in her eyes. "Why is she looking at me like that?"

"We gave her some kippers, you see, and I expect she's hoping for more," Felicity explained. Kincaid looked down again, and he could see that Cleopatra was standing next to a little china plate. "She looked at us with such a pitiful expression, didn't she, Miss Flint?"

"She did," Miss Flint confirmed. "And it's no wonder. These are excellent kippers."

"Only the best for Cleopatra," Kincaid said sarcastically. He had no doubt that the kippers were excellent, since the chef he had left behind at 23 Bentley St. was a culinary genius. This reflection did nothing to soften his mood.

The cat was looking at him with a haughty expression, as though she had a perfect right to share the breakfast. "Cleopatra's a fitting name for her, at least," Kincaid said with a laugh. "Your idea?"

"Oh, no," Felicity said. "I believe Adrian's friend's uncle chose the name. Adrian suggested I change it to Cleopawtra, because of her paws, of course, but I didn't think it had the same dignity."

"And for that, the cat owes you a debt," Kincaid said dryly. "But you can't keep her, Felicity. Miss Harris doesn't like cats."

Felicity frowned. "I know she said so yesterday," she acknowledged. "But I think she'll grow to like Cleo when she gets to know her better."

Kincaid eyed Cleopatra skeptically, and the cat returned his gaze. "Miss Harris won't have the opportunity to further her acquaintance with Cleopatra," he said firmly.

"Oh, I'm sorry," Felicity said sympathetically. "Has Miss Harris decided to end your engagement?"

Kincaid looked at her strangely. "Of course she hasn't decided to end the engagement. But she won't have the chance to become acquainted with Cleopatra, since you will get rid of the cat."

Felicity looked so disappointed that Kincaid's expression softened. "I'm sorry, Felicity, but you must see it would be rude to keep a cat after Miss Harris has told us she doesn't like them. Especially when the cat has been so recently acquired."

"I had no way of knowing that Miss Harris doesn't like cats," Felicity pointed out.

"But the fact remains that she doesn't," Kincaid said. "Give Cleopatra back to Adrian."

"His landlady won't let him keep a cat," Felicity said dejectedly. "But I will look for another home for her. It may be difficult, though, since not many people are broad-minded enough to take in such a spirited animal."

Kincaid looked at her through narrowed eyes. "I thought you said she was purebred, and that such cats were in great demand?"

"Oh, certainly," Felicity said. "They are in great demand as kittens, but once they grow to adulthood— well, the demand is far less." She bent to scratch Cleopatra behind the ears and was rewarded with a hiss. "The world can be cruel to aging ladies, can't it, Cleo?"

Kincaid's lips twitched. "Be that as it may, Felicity, you must find Cleopatra another home."

"But surely she can stay here until after your marriage?" Felicity asked hopefully.

"I suppose," Kincaid conceded grudgingly. "But if the demand for cats like Cleopatra is as low as you say, you should start looking for another home for her immediately."

"All right, Mr. Kincaid."

"Very good," Kincaid said. He walked to the sideboard to fill a plate with kippers and eggs.

"Is that why you've honoured us with such an early visit?" Felicity asked. "To discuss Cleopatra?"

"Not exactly." Kincaid carried his plate to the table

and took a seat facing Felicity. He considered asking Miss Flint to leave, but since he couldn't think of a diplomatic way to do so, he pushed on. "I received your letter, and I came to discuss my concerns with you in person."

Felicity's eyebrows arched in surprise. "Oh," she said. "Do you have more to say? Your letter didn't contain a sufficiently comprehensive reproof?" She knew her behaviour had been appalling, and Kincaid's letter had been far kinder than she deserved, but she wasn't prepared to admit it.

Kincaid was caught off guard. "I thought you wanted to discuss the matter?"

"Well, I wish you had chosen to discuss it with me from the start. What motivated you to write a letter?"

"I was boxing at Jackson's with Robert and Oliver," Kincaid began, before pausing to consider his next words.

"Oh, of course," Felicity said with a little smile. "That makes the matter perfectly clear."

"Robert and Oliver both said they sometimes find it easier to express their thoughts in writing," Kincaid continued through gritted teeth. "Oliver said that he and Isabelle sometimes write each other letters, so that they can reread them."

Felicity gave him a skeptical look. "I don't quite see the parallel," she said apologetically. "Oliver and Isabelle are married, so I imagine they write each other love letters."

Kincaid raked a hand through his hair in frustration. "You're deliberately misinterpreting me. You know our situation is different."

"I should hope our situation is different," Felicity said

with a laugh. "If that was your idea of a love letter, I don't envy Miss Harris."

"Felicity," he admonished.

"I'm sorry, Mr. Kincaid."

"Felicity, have you met Miss Harris before?"

"No," she replied slowly. "Why do you ask? Do you think she dislikes me?"

"Of course not," Kincaid said quickly. "But I wondered if you disliked Miss Harris."

"Why would you wonder that?"

"Your behaviour last night, Felicity—it was so unlike you. You said you were determined to catch yourself a man with a title, and you referred to me as a matrimonial prize."

Felicity grinned. "I suppose it's a bit of a stretch to think of you as a matrimonial prize," she agreed. "But I thought it sounded complimentary, and I wanted Miss Harris to be happy about her engagement."

He frowned. "You don't think she's happy about the engagement?"

Felicity had no doubt that Jane was overjoyed. "I'm sure she's happy about her engagement to you," she said. "But I was afraid she might not be happy about having to act as my chaperone, and I wanted to remind her of all the benefits of her marriage. The truth, Mr. Kincaid, is that I was nervous. I was worried that Miss Harris wouldn't like me, and that she might feel as though she has no choice but to act as my chaperone."

Kincaid looked at her carefully. Felicity certainly had her faults, but despite what he had told Jane, he had never known her to be nervous. But she met his eyes openly, and since he couldn't think of any other reason for her behaviour, he took her explanation at face value.

"Miss Harris is very keen to act as your chaperone," he reassured her. "I'm sure you will become very good friends once you get to know each other better."

"I'm sure we will, Mr. Kincaid," Felicity agreed. "Now that you have explained that she is eager to become acquainted with me, I'm sure the two of us will become excellent friends."

Kincaid looked at her suspiciously. "Really?"

"Of course," Felicity assured him. "And if I have any doubts about how to behave, I will refer to your letter."

The following afternoon, Kincaid walked down the street to 23 Bentley to ask if Felicity wished to join him on a visit to the Langleys. Felicity did, and they departed half an hour later in Kincaid's curricle.

"I invited Jane to ride with us next week," he told her as they set off down Bentley Street.

"That's an excellent idea," Felicity said blandly. Kincaid studied her face carefully, but neither her tone nor her expression told him what she really thought about it.

"Jane doesn't have a horse in town, so I thought she could borrow Stella from Miss Flint," Kincaid continued. "I've already spoken to Miss Flint about it."

"All right," Felicity agreed, without taking her eyes from the road. "Watch out for that carriage," she warned him.

Kincaid, who had already adjusted his course to

accommodate the passing carriage, frowned. "It's a wonder I'm able to manage when I don't have you to tell me how to drive."

"Yes, I often think so."

"I can tell when you're trying to provoke me," he muttered. "If I recall, you recently told me you thought I drove well."

Felicity looked at him innocently. "I rarely try to provoke you, Mr. Kincaid," she said. "It seems to happen without any effort."

Kincaid didn't reply, but Felicity could tell he was trying not to smile.

"Take care, Mr. Kincaid," she advised. "That child is about to step into the street."

"Next time we'll walk," Kincaid grumbled, as he reined in his horses to allow the child to cross in front of him.

They arrived at the Langleys' townhouse and were following the butler to the drawing room when Amelia came hurrying down the stairs.

"I saw you arrive through the window," she said, greeting Felicity with the familiarity of an old friend. "Isabelle's visiting, and we've been up in the nursery with Julian." She turned to Kincaid with a smile. "I understand congratulations are in order," she said. "Robert told me about your betrothal. He's in his study, if you'd like to join him there."

"Thank you," Kincaid replied, turning to make his way to Langley's study.

Amelia led the way to the nursery, where her sister Isabelle was watching Lord Julian Stone demonstrate his ability to crawl.

"Oh, Amelia, he's grown so much!" Felicity exclaimed. "How old is he now?"

"Almost nine months," Amelia said proudly.

Julian looked straight at Felicity and grinned. "He's smiling at me," Felicity said with delight. "He's clearly a very intelligent child."

"I think so," Amelia said. "Of course, Robert says I shouldn't praise him too much, or he'll grow up to be insufferably conceited."

"That's ridiculous," Isabelle said.

Amelia's eyes danced. "Especially since I recently overheard Robert tell Julian he was the cleverest child in England. He didn't know I was listening, of course."

They observed the baby in silence for several minutes, and Amelia noticed that Felicity seemed preoccupied. "You're very quiet, Felicity," she remarked. "Is everything all right?"

"I suppose I'm worried about Mr. Kincaid," Felicity admitted.

"Why?" Amelia asked curiously.

"I'm not sure Miss Harris appreciates how fortunate she is to be betrothed to him," Felicity explained. "And he seems to have rushed into the engagement, which is quite out of character for him. I'm sure women have been trying to trap him into marriage for years, but he never succumbed until now."

"Why do you think women have been trying to trap him into marriage?" Amelia asked curiously.

"I've seen the way they look at him when we ride in Hyde Park," Felicity explained matter-of-factly. "They blush and simper and flutter their eyelashes. I would be ashamed to make such a spectacle of myself."

"You might feel differently when you meet the right man," Isabelle suggested.

"Maybe," Felicity conceded. "I suppose I should say that I would be ashamed to make such a spectacle of myself over Mr. Kincaid. At first I thought the ladies were staring because he rides so well, but I realized that most of them don't even notice that." She sighed. "I think it's the combination of his dark hair and blue eyes. Objectively speaking, Mr. Kincaid is quite an attractive man."

"But what makes you think Miss Harris trapped him?" Amelia asked.

"Well, he's quite vulnerable, you know," Felicity said thoughtfully.

"Really?" Isabelle had never thought of Mr. Kincaid as particularly vulnerable.

"Does Miss Harris have a fortune?" Amelia asked delicately.

"No!" Felicity exclaimed, frowning at Amelia. "At least, I don't think she does, but it doesn't matter. Mr. Kincaid would never marry for a fortune."

"I didn't think he would," Amelia agreed. "But I don't understand. Is there some secret, or a scandal—"

"Oh, nothing like that," Felicity interrupted. "Mr. Kincaid isn't the type to be involved in a scandal. He's too honourable for that. And although he's very intelligent, he isn't cunning, and may not recognize when someone else is. He could easily fall victim to an unscrupulous character."

"And you think Miss Harris is an unscrupulous character?" Isabelle asked dubiously.

"I suppose I'm being silly," Felicity admitted. "It's just

that the news of the engagement came as such a surprise."

"Perhaps when Mr. Kincaid realized he loved Miss Harris, he didn't want to waste time," Amelia suggested.

"Perhaps," Felicity said doubtfully.

"Do you not like Miss Harris?" Isabelle asked cautiously. "She was probably nervous when she met you, you know. She must know that your opinion is very important to Mr. Kincaid."

Felicity thought that if Mr. Kincaid believed her opinion was of such great importance, he would have asked for it before proposing to Jane. "Oh, I do like Miss Harris," she assured her friends. "She's very kind, and very worthy, and she's going to be my chaperone for the Season. But—"

"Yes?" Amelia encouraged.

Felicity considered telling her friends about Kincaid's lack of emotion when he greeted Jane, and her fear that Jane didn't share his sense of humour. She could have explained how Jane had made her feel like a disobedient schoolgirl, and that she dreaded the thought of being chaperoned by a lady who seemed to have such a low opinion of her. But Felicity had never been good at sharing her feelings.

"Well, when Miss Harris came to tea, she said she didn't like lemon tarts," she said instead.

"I see," said Isabelle, who was aware of Felicity's love for lemon tarts. "I can see why you might consider that a character flaw, but I don't think it's so terrible."

"Oh, it got worse," Felicity assured her. "Mr. Kincaid assured Miss Harris that he didn't like lemon tarts either!"

"So perhaps they can instruct the cook not to make them?" Isabelle suggested.

"But Mr. Kincaid loves lemon tarts!" Felicity blurted. "He lied about it, to make Miss Harris feel better about not liking them."

"That doesn't seem like a very bad lie," Amelia remarked.

"But Mr. Kincaid never lies," Felicity pointed out. "I'm sure his conscience is still itching from having done so. And it doesn't reflect well on their relationship, if he's unable to tell Miss Harris the truth about what he likes. I think he has a duty to be honest with her before they are married."

Amelia gave Felicity a strange look. "Honest about his love of lemon tarts?"

"I'm not sure you realize the implications of the deception," Felicity said. "Is Mr. Kincaid going to live the rest of his life without enjoying another lemon tart? Or will he confess to Miss Harris that he lied to her about it?"

"I suppose he could pretend that he changed his mind, and suddenly acquired a taste for lemon," Amelia said thoughtfully.

Felicity frowned. "That would require him to lie again, and since he's fundamentally an honest man, I think it would weigh heavily on his soul."

"I didn't realize the problem was so complicated," Isabelle said. "Perhaps he could eat lemon tarts at his club?"

Felicity looked skeptical. "Do they serve tarts at White's?"

"I don't know," Amelia admitted. "I could ask Robert about it."

"Oh, please don't ask Lord Langley," Felicity said. "I don't want him to know that I'm worried about Mr. Kincaid."

"But Mr. Kincaid must care for Miss Harris," Amelia said sensibly. "After all, he asked her to marry him."

"Do you think so?" Felicity asked.

Isabelle nodded. "When Oliver asked me to marry him, I wasn't sure he loved me. But Amelia told me that in her experience, the most common reason for a man to ask a lady to marry him is that he wants to marry her. Perhaps Mr. Kincaid and Jane will be very happy together."

"I suppose they might," Felicity conceded, but her reply lacked conviction.

"I imagine you will come to like Miss Harris once you are better acquainted with her," Isabelle said optimistically. She glanced over at Amelia's son, who was gnawing on the leg of a wooden chair. "I think Julian is hungry, Amelia."

"His teeth are coming in, Isabelle," Amelia said with a laugh. "His Aunt Diana bought him a silver teething rattle, but he seems to prefer that chair."

"Well, I am hungry, even if Julian is not," Isabelle hinted.

Amelia chuckled and rang the bell. "I think there is still some almond cake in the kitchen."

"That sounds delicious," Felicity said, with an overly bright smile. Although she didn't raise the subject of Mr. Kincaid's engagement again, she was uncharacteristically quiet for the rest of the visit.

Nine

A date for the riding expedition was fixed for the following week. Kincaid suggested that he and Felicity could bring Miss Flint's horse to Jane, but Jane preferred to meet them at 23 Bentley St. She was hard at work planning the engagement party, and there were several matters she wished to discuss with Kincaid's housekeeper. Since Kincaid still hadn't told his betrothed that he had moved down the street, he made his way to 23 Bentley well before Jane was expected.

He found Felicity in the drawing room, reading a novel. She closed her book and stood to greet him. "Good morning, Mr. Kincaid," she said cheerfully.

Kincaid was silent for a moment as he took in her appearance. Everything about Felicity was elegant; her cherry-red riding habit, the tone of her voice, even the line of her neck. He could hardly believe she was the same girl who had giggled and told Jane she hoped to catch herself a man with a title. He hoped that whatever madness had afflicted her during her first meeting with Jane had been of a temporary nature.

"Good morning, Felicity," he finally said. "That riding habit suits you very well."

Her eyebrows rose at the compliment. "Thank you."

Kincaid hadn't meant to comment on her appearance, and he searched for something to say that would break the tension between them. "I hope you will be polite to Jane this morning."

"I hope I am always polite, Mr. Kincaid," Felicity said serenely.

Jane arrived then, saving Kincaid from having to reply. She was earlier than expected, but she explained that she had a great many things to discuss with his housekeeper.

"If the betrothal party is to be next week, we must send the invitations out tomorrow," she told Kincaid. "Have you made a list of the people you wish to invite?"

"It's almost finished," Kincaid lied, since he had completely forgotten about the need to make a list. An engagement party seemed like a great deal of unnecessary fuss, and he was having a hard time mustering much enthusiasm for it. "I'll send Mrs. Sutherland to you while I get the list from my study."

Felicity picked up her novel and read in silence while Jane and Mrs. Sutherland talked about the menu and decorations for the party. She only raised her eyes from her book when the discussion moved to the question of how many crab puffs would be needed.

"How many guests are you expecting?" Felicity asked curiously.

"I am inviting seventy people," Jane explained. "We

won't know the final number until we see Mr. Kincaid's list, of course."

"Of course," Felicity replied. "Have you considered hiring an orchestra?"

"I thought about it," Jane admitted. "But I was afraid it would be rather extravagant."

"Oh, I wouldn't worry about that," Felicity assured her. "You wouldn't want your engagement party to be shabby."

Kincaid rejoined them and caught the end of Felicity's sentence. "I'm certain the party won't be shabby, Felicity," he said, as he handed Jane a list of names.

Jane glanced at the list and then looked at him in confusion. "There are only five names on here!"

Kincaid nodded. "Yes. The Earl and Countess of Langley, the Marquess and Marchioness of Ashingham, and my Great Aunt Henrietta."

"But the rest of your family—" Jane stammered.

"The rest of my family is at Brentwood, and won't want to travel to London for a small gathering."

"They might, if they knew about the orchestra," Felicity said mischievously.

"The orchestra?" Kincaid repeated.

"I have decided not to have an orchestra," Jane said regretfully. "Unless you think we should, Mr. Kincaid?"

"Oh, no," he said quickly. "Music would make it difficult to converse." He turned to Jane. "Er—how many people are you planning to invite?"

"Seventy," Jane told him. "But if you only intend to invite five, perhaps I should decrease the number."

"There's no need," Kincaid said manfully. "If you wish to invite seventy people, you should do so. If you've finished discussing the plans, shall I ask for the horses to be brought round?"

"Oh, yes," Jane said. "I'm quite looking forward to riding."

"Do you ride often, Jane?" Felicity asked politely.

"As often as I can, when we're in the country," Jane replied. "I don't like to boast, but some of the young men back home say I have the best seat in Gloucestershire."

"Is that right?" Felicity asked, with a gleam of amusement in her dark eyes.

"Felicity's quite a good rider herself," Kincaid remarked.

"Mr. Kincaid exaggerates my talents," Felicity said modestly. "I ride well enough, but I've certainly never been told I have the best seat in Gloucestershire." She wasn't even sure she had ever been to Gloucestershire.

"Perhaps I can give you some suggestions," Jane offered. "I helped all my younger sisters learn to ride."

"That would be kind of you," Felicity said sweetly. "Mr. Kincaid rides very well himself, you know, but he never seems to want to give me advice."

Kincaid smothered a laugh and looked away. Felicity was one of the best riders he had ever met, male or female, and it had been many years since he had tried to give her advice on the subject.

They descended the stairs to the street, where two grooms waited with the horses. Kincaid helped Jane mount Stella, the pretty chestnut mare that they kept for Miss Flint's use, before stooping to help Felicity mount Sugarplum.

"Place your right hand a little higher on your horse's shoulder, Felicity," Jane called out helpfully.

Felicity took Jane's advice and Kincaid threw her up, but she somehow failed to swing her leg over the pommel of her sidesaddle. Kincaid was so surprised by this development that he wasn't prepared to catch her, and she fell clumsily to the ground.

"Felicity!" Kincaid exclaimed, reaching to help her up.

"Are you all right, Felicity?" Jane asked in concern.

"Oh yes," Felicity said apologetically. "I'm sorry, Mr. Kincaid, I must have misjudged the distance. Can we try again?"

"You might find it easier if you bend your right knee a little more," Jane suggested.

"Thank you, I'll try that," Felicity murmured. Kincaid threw her up again, and the second attempt was successful. She settled herself in the saddle, adjusted her skirts, and smiled down at Kincaid. "Thank you, Mr. Kincaid."

Kincaid mounted his own horse, a handsome grey named Apollo, and they proceeded down the street in the direction of Hyde Park. Kincaid rode next to Jane, and Felicity allowed herself to fall behind them.

"Take care, Felicity," Jane said solicitously as they made their way into the park. "The ground looks uneven up ahead."

"Thank you, Jane," Felicity murmured.

Kincaid watched in amazement as Jane gave Felicity advice on how to hold the reins and position herself in the saddle. Perhaps the most surprising thing was that Felicity acted as though she appreciated Jane's suggestions. Kincaid recalled that he had asked Felicity to be polite, but she seemed to be taking politeness to the extreme.

As they were approaching the Serpentine, the lake

that separated Hyde Park from Kensington Gardens, Sugarplum suddenly took off at a gallop.

"Felicity's horse has bolted!" Jane cried.

Kincaid stared at Felicity through narrowed eyes before dropping his hands and urging his horse to follow her.

Felicity and Sugarplum raced towards the Serpentine, and at one point, it looked as though they were going to gallop straight into the water. At the last instant, she pulled up and brought Sugarplum to a stop at the edge of the lake. As Kincaid watched in amazement, Felicity swung herself down from the horse and jumped into the water. A great deal of splashing ensued, and although the water only came up to her waist, Kincaid couldn't see what she was doing. He leapt off Apollo and watched in amazement as she emerged from the lake with a boy in her arms.

The child couldn't have been more than five years old, but his sodden clothes made him a heavy burden, and Felicity was relieved when Kincaid took him from her.

"I saw him fall in," she explained anxiously, as the boy coughed and sputtered. "It isn't deep, and he didn't go under right away, so I don't think he was submerged for more than a moment."

Kincaid laid the boy on the ground, rolled him onto his side, and firmly patted his back. After a last great cough, the child's breathing settled and he started to cry.

"You're all right," Felicity said briskly, as she helped him sit up. "I'm sure you're very cold, but we'll get you warmed up quickly."

Kincaid stripped off his coat and handed it to Felicity, who wrapped it around the boy. As she was chafing his small hands to try to warm them up, she saw a girl approaching them nervously.

"Are you this child's nurse?" Felicity asked abruptly.

The girl gaped at her for a moment before answering. "Yes, miss."

"We must get him home immediately," Felicity said. "Where does he live?"

"G-g-grosvenor Square, ma'am," the nurse stammered. "He is the Marquess of Willingdon's son." With that pronouncement, she burst into tears and ran off across the park.

"I know where Willingdon lives," Kincaid said. He had a passing acquaintance with the marquess, although they didn't move in the same circles.

"Good gracious!" Jane exclaimed as she rode up to them. "Don't tell me the child fell into the lake!"

"Well, I don't think he planned to go swimming in March," Felicity retorted.

"You shouldn't have been playing so close to the lake," Jane told the child reproachfully, before turning to Felicity and Kincaid. "We must get him home before he catches his death of cold."

The boy's eyes widened at Jane's suggestion that he might catch his death. "Nonsense, Jane," Felicity said, giving the child a reassuring smile. "I think this is the warmest day we've had so far this year, and there hasn't been ice on the lake for over a month. But I suppose we should go home and change into dry clothes." She realized she had forgotten about the horses, and was relieved to see that both Sugarplum and Apollo were patiently waiting several feet away.

"The boy will have to ride with you, Mr. Kincaid,"

Felicity told him as they retrieved the horses. "I'm afraid I won't be able to hold him while sitting sidesaddle."

"Of course," Kincaid agreed. After boosting Felicity onto Sugarplum, he lifted the boy on to Apollo and swung himself up behind him.

"What's your name?" Felicity asked the boy as they set off across the park.

The boy didn't reply, so Felicity kept talking. "My name is Felicity," she said conversationally. "And I like to swim, but this is the first time I've been swimming in March."

The boy still didn't speak, but he turned his head to look at Felicity. His features still held the softness of infancy, and she was surprised that his nurse had brought him from Grosvenor Square to the Serpentine on foot.

"I fell into a river once when I was three," Felicity continued. "Fortunately, my mother was watching, and she pulled me out."

"My mama died," the boy said shyly.

"I'm sorry," Felicity said simply. "You're clever to hold on to Apollo's mane, but you don't need to worry about falling off. Mr. Kincaid is a very good rider, and you're quite safe with him."

They turned a corner and spotted a carriage that had stopped on the side of the path. The coachman was reclining on the box seat with a loose grip on the reins, and Felicity suspected he was half asleep.

"That's Willingdon's coach," Kincaid said, recognizing the crest. His statement roused the coachman, who was alarmed to see his master's heir on a horse with an unknown gentleman.

"Lord Ernest!" the coachman exclaimed, before

turning to Kincaid with an accusatory look. "Where's Lizzy?"

"If you are referring to the boy's nurse," Felicity replied, "she ran away after I pulled Lord Ernest out of the Serpentine."

The coachman stared at Ernest in dismay. "T-the Serpentine?" he repeated numbly.

Felicity reflected that Lord Willingdon's servants didn't react well to surprises. "Yes," she confirmed. "We need to get him home."

The coachman hollered for the groom, and a lanky young man emerged from inside the carriage, where he had been taking a nap. The groom took in the situation more quickly than the coachman had, and moved to lift Ernest down from Apollo. Ernest, however, had grown comfortable with Mr. Kincaid, and loudly declared that he did not want to get in the coach.

"I'll take him home," Kincaid told Willingdon's servants. "You can follow us there." Neither the coachman nor the groom looked happy with this plan, but they wisely decided not to argue with Kincaid, who was looking rather formidable.

"You should go straight home to change, Felicity," Kincaid told her, when they reached the edge of the park. "Jane can go with you, and I'll take the boy to Grosvenor Square."

"Oh, I'll be all right," Felicity said dismissively. "My skirts are already starting to dry, and I'd like to see Ernest home."

"But you must be cold," Kincaid insisted. Although it was warm for March, there was still a nip to the air. "Go home and get dry, and I'll look after Ernest. If you like, I'll take you to Willingdon's later today so you can check on him."

"Thank you, Mr. Kincaid, but I'll be fine," Felicity replied.

When they reached Willingdon's townhouse, the groom jumped out of the coach to lift Ernest down, then watched in surprise as Felicity dismounted without assistance. She handed Sugarplum's reins to the startled groom before turning to the coachman. "You had best go look for the child's nurse. I daresay she should be able to find her way home, but she seemed like the type of girl who would get lost."

The coachman opened his mouth to question Felicity's authority, but realized he had no wish to be nearby when Willingdon learned that his son had fallen into the lake. The coach drove away, and Felicity took Ernest up to the house.

When Willingdon's butler answered the door in response to Felicity's impatient knock, he was astonished by the scene that met his eyes. Young Ernest was still swaddled in Kincaid's riding coat, which was comically large on his small frame, and Felicity was holding the tails of the coat to keep them from dragging on the ground. For his part, Ernest was clinging to Felicity's own skirts, which were dripping on the doorstep.

Felicity offered no explanation for their bedraggled appearance, but boldly declared that she wished to see the marquess. Since Ernest showed no desire to let go of her skirts, the butler wisely decided to take them to his master. Jane and Kincaid caught up to them in the entrance hall, and the entire party was shown to a large library.

Lord Willingdon rose from behind an imposing mahogany desk to stare at his young son and unexpected guests. The marquess was tall and dark, with pale skin and slightly stooped shoulders that testified to the fact that he spent most of his time indoors. His wife had died in a carriage accident the year before, and he had rarely been seen in society since.

"Willingdon," Kincaid said awkwardly. "Allow me to introduce Miss Jane Harris and Miss Felicity Taylor. While we were riding in the park, Miss Taylor saw your son fall into the Serpentine and jumped in to rescue him."

Willingdon's eyes widened. "Dear me."

Kincaid nodded. "I think your boy's all right, although I expect he's taken a chill. He needs a hot bath and some dry clothes."

To Felicity's surprise, the marquess didn't go to his son, but simply ordered a footman to fetch the house-keeper. A moment later, an efficient-looking woman bustled in and swept Ernest from the room.

The marquess turned to Felicity and bowed. "I am in your debt, Miss Taylor."

"In that case, perhaps you'll let me give you some advice," Felicity said boldly. "You should hire a different nurse for your son, since the current girl can't be trusted to keep him safe. Ernest was struggling in the water and she stood staring."

Willingdon frowned, and Kincaid groaned inwardly. "Felicity," he tried, but Felicity would not be deterred.

"I imagine it's difficult to find a competent nurse," she continued. "But if he were my child, I wouldn't let a nurse take him out of the house until I knew she could be trusted to look after him."

"You're right, Miss Taylor," Willingdon said stiffly. "The situation is regrettable, and I'm grateful it didn't end in tragedy. As I said, I owe you a debt. May I ask my housekeeper to find you some dry clothes?"

"No thank you, my lord," Felicity replied. "But there is one other matter. On our way home, we found your coach stopped at the side of the path. Your coachman was half asleep, your groom was napping in the coach, and the horses were standing in the cold!"

"Felicity," Kincaid said again, but Felicity persevered.

"You have fine horses, and if they were mine, I wouldn't entrust them to a man who fell asleep while they were in harness."

Willingdon acknowledged this with a stiff nod. "I will attend to the matter, Miss Taylor."

"Excellent," Felicity replied. "Good day, my lord. Tell Ernest we wish him well."

"You were rather hard on Willingdon, Felicity," Kincaid remarked as they rode home. "I'm sure he feels guilty enough."

"Maybe he should feel guilty," Felicity retorted. "Leaving his son in the care of such a nurse! The girl was positively bird-witted!"

"Now, Felicity," Jane began primly. "There's no need to be unkind—"

"You're right," Felicity interrupted. "Such a comparison is insulting to birds."

A low chuckle escaped from Kincaid, and Jane frowned. "Even if the nurse lost her head, there was no reason to lecture Lord Willingdon," she told Felicity. "He had no way of knowing how the girl would react in a crisis."

Felicity opened her mouth to argue the point, but Kincaid spoke before she could. "It's barely a year since the marquess lost his wife," he pointed out. "From all accounts, he loved her dearly, and he's had a difficult time."

"If he loved her dearly, he should take better care of their son," Felicity replied. "Perhaps he could take Ernest to the park himself. It might distract him from his grief."

In her outrage over Willingdon's parenting choices, Felicity hadn't noticed that the wind had strengthened, but as her indignation faded, she realized she was uncomfortably cold. Her damp skirts clung to her legs, and she wished she had accepted Willingdon's offer to have his housekeeper provide her with dry clothes. As they approached Bentley Street, she started to lose feeling in her fingers, and it was all she could do to keep hold of the reins.

They drew up in front of 23 Bentley St., and Kincaid dismounted first. "P-perhaps you would help me down?" Felicity asked.

Kincaid looked over and was surprised to see that she was shivering violently. He lifted her down from the horse, but she stumbled when he let go of her waist.

"Felicity!" he exclaimed, taking her arm.

"I'm fine, just a little c-cold," she stammered. She started towards the house but couldn't keep her balance, and would have collapsed if Kincaid hadn't caught her. Since it was clear that Felicity was in no condition to walk, he gathered her in his arms and carried her to the door.

"Fetch Mrs. Sutherland," he barked to Wainwright as he carried Felicity towards the staircase. The house-keeper arrived as he reached Felicity's bedchamber and opened the door so he could carry her through.

"She went into the lake to rescue a child," Kincaid explained, as he set Felicity gently on the bed. "I'm afraid she's fallen ill from the cold. You'll need to remove her wet clothes as quickly as you can, then she'll need a hot bath."

"Yes, sir," Mrs. Sutherland said calmly. Felicity's maid appeared, and the two women worked at the laces of Felicity's boots.

"Do you need help with the laces?" Kincaid asked, hovering over his housekeeper's shoulder.

Mrs. Sutherland turned to give her employer a speaking look. "We'll look after her, sir," she said gently. "Perhaps you could ask Wainwright to send a housemaid to build up the fire. We'll also need something hot to drink, and water for the bath."

Kincaid reluctantly left the room and hurried down the stairs to find the butler. After relaying Mrs. Suther-land's instructions, he told Wainwright to send someone for the doctor.

"Yes, sir," Wainwright replied. "Which doctor, sir?"

Kincaid was silent for a minute as he tried to think of a doctor's name. He had very little experience with illness, and he hadn't seen a doctor since he was a child.

"I don't know, Wainwright," he admitted in frustra-tion. "Do you have any suggestions?"

Wainwright's brow furrowed. "My previous employers thought highly of Dr. Mackenzie."

"Excellent," Kincaid replied. "Send a man for Mackenzie and tell him to be quick about it."

Wainwright bustled away to find a footman, and Kincaid was left with nothing to do. He wanted to go upstairs to check on Felicity, but his housekeeper's message had been clear; despite Felicity's indisposition, Kincaid didn't belong in her bedchamber. He was cursing the rules of propriety when the front door opened to admit Jane.

"Miss Harris," he said sheepishly. In his concern for Felicity, he had forgotten about her. "I'm sorry, I was worried about Felicity, and—"

"I understand perfectly," she assured him. "One of the grooms helped me dismount. How is Felicity? Can I do anything to help?"

Kincaid gave her a distracted smile. "Thank you, Jane. But our housekeeper is with her, along with her maid, and I've sent a footman for the doctor."

"I didn't realize Felicity was sick enough to need the doctor," Jane remarked. "It was reckless of her to try to save the boy herself."

Kincaid looked at her in surprise. "I suppose it was, but it was also very brave. She saved his life."

"I suppose she did," Jane said grudgingly. "But since we were riding with you, it would have been more sensible for Felicity to have told you when she saw him fall in."

The corner of Kincaid's mouth quirked up. "So I could have played the hero?"

"It has nothing to do with being a hero," Jane said primly. "Felicity could have been thrown from her horse, galloping off the way she did. Although I suppose she's a better rider than she let on?"

Kincaid didn't try to deny it. "She is."

"Aside from that," Jane continued, "she might have got into trouble in the lake, and then you would have had to rescue her as well as the boy."

"But Felicity didn't have trouble in the lake," Kincaid pointed out. "She pulled the child out all by herself."

Jane smiled stiffly. "She was fortunate."

"Yes." Kincaid thought Willingdon's son was the one who had been fortunate, but he didn't want to debate the point. He was impatient for the doctor to arrive, and he hoped the footman had conveyed the urgency of the situation.

Jane seemed to sense his distraction. "I should go home," she said.

"I'll order the carriage," Kincaid said with a nod. "I'm afraid I won't be able to escort you, since I want to be here when the doctor arrives."

"I don't need to be escorted home," Jane insisted. "My maid accompanied me here, and I expect she's waiting in the kitchen."

Dr. Mackenzie arrived shortly after Jane left, and Kincaid met him in the entrance hall. "Thank you for coming, Dr. Mackenzie," Kincaid began.

"Yes, well, that's my job," Dr. Mackenzie said briskly. He was a spare man in his mid-fifties, with ruddy cheeks and a brusque manner. "I understand a young lady fell into the Serpentine?"

"Miss Taylor didn't fall," Kincaid corrected. "She jumped into the lake to save a child."

Dr. Mackenzie nodded. "Did she succeed?"

"Yes, she did. We took the boy home before we returned here, so she was in her wet clothes for over an hour."

Dr. Mackenzie nodded again. "It's not surprising that she took a chill."

"This was more than a chill!" Kincaid exclaimed. "Felicity was shivering so badly that she almost fell off her horse. I had to carry her up to her bedchamber."

Dr. Mackenzie eyed him speculatively. "I see. And Miss Taylor is your . . ."

"She's my ward," Kincaid said quickly. "I'll take you to her now."

Mackenzie gave him a knowing look. "I'll find my way," he assured him. "Relax and have a drink. I don't expect this will take long."

But Kincaid found he was unable to sit, and he paced the hallway while he waited for the doctor to come down. True to his word, Dr. Mackenzie returned ten minutes later.

"As I suspected, she's taken a chill," the doctor said matter-of-factly. "But she's young and healthy, and she seems to be recovering well."

"Isn't there any medicine we could give her?" Kincaid asked anxiously.

"She doesn't need medicine," Dr. Mackenzie replied. "Miss Taylor is simply cold, and she needs to be warmed up. Your housekeeper seems like a sensible woman; she has the situation well in hand."

Under different circumstances, Kincaid might have thought that Dr. Mackenzie's advice was very practical, but since Felicity was the patient, the prescription seemed inadequate. "Surely you can recommend a tonic, or something to build up her strength?"

"I can leave you some medicine, if you like," Dr. Mackenzie said, in the tone of a man who was prepared to humour a fool.

Kincaid sighed. "If you don't think it will help, I suppose there's no point. Is there anything else we should do for her?"

"I advised her to avoid the Serpentine in the winter," Dr. Mackenzie said dryly.

Ten

Kincaid didn't even consider returning to 29 Bentley St. to sleep. He spent the night in his old bedchamber, down the hall from Felicity's, listening anxiously for a sign that something was wrong. Felicity's maid, Louise, was sleeping on a truckle bed in Felicity's room, but Kincaid wasn't sure he could trust her to call for help if Felicity needed it. Louise might dismiss a worrisome symptom as insignificant, or sleep so deeply that Felicity would have difficulty waking her up.

So Kincaid tossed and turned, but he couldn't fall asleep. Whenever he started to drift off, he remembered how blue Felicity's lips had looked, or the way she had shivered in his arms. He wished he had thought to ask Dr. Mackenzie about hiring a professional nurse, although he suspected the man would have laughed at the idea. He wrestled with the temptation to walk down the hall and check on Felicity himself, but held back for fear that he would wake her up.

Since Kincaid had ordered the staff to keep fires

burning in every room of the house, his night was not only sleepless, it was also uncomfortably warm. Shortly after dawn, he abandoned his efforts to sleep and rang for his valet, who had been fetched home from 29 Bentley St. His spirits improved a little after he had shaved and dressed, and he was able to convince himself that Dr. Mackenzie was right. Felicity simply needed a few days of rest, and there was no reason to doubt that she would make a full recovery.

But Felicity seemed to think she had rested enough, and Kincaid found her at the breakfast table, eating a slice of toast. Her cheerful yellow morning gown set off her glowing complexion, and she looked to be the picture of health.

"What are you doing out of bed?" Kincaid asked in alarm.

"I know it's early for breakfast, but I was hungry," Felicity explained. "All I had for dinner yesterday was broth, and I was ravenous when I woke up this morning."

"Your maid could have brought up a tray. Really, Felicity, after what happened yesterday—"

"I wasn't sick, Mr. Kincaid. I simply caught a chill, but now I'm warm," she told him dismissively. "Hot, in fact. When I awoke this morning, I was convinced I had a fever. Is there a fire burning in every room of the house?"

"Yes," Kincaid admitted. "I wanted to make sure you were warm enough. Are you sure you should be out of bed?"

"Very sure," Felicity said confidently. "Surely Dr. Mackenzie told you there was nothing to worry about?"

"Yes, he explained that you were simply cold and

needed to be warmed up," he said dryly. "I expect to receive a large bill for this valuable advice."

Felicity laughed. "Unless you've gambled my fortune away, it shouldn't be hard to meet the expense."

"Felicity, you know that's not what I meant. I'm not worried about the doctor's bill."

"But I'm sure that when my parents appointed you as my guardian, they never intended for you to pay for my expenses out of your own purse."

"It's a trivial expense, Felicity," Kincaid replied.

"You just said you expected it to be a large bill," Felicity pointed out.

Kincaid sighed. "I'll pay it with your money, if that will make you happy."

"It will, thank you." Felicity studied him carefully and thought he looked exhausted. "Did you spend the night here?"

"Yes."

"You don't look as though you got much sleep. Was the house too hot for you?"

"Something like that," he grumbled, noting that Felicity looked perfectly rested. He almost told her the truth, that worry for her had kept him awake, but he held his tongue.

"I was thinking about Ernest," Felicity told him. "I thought we might send a note to Lord Willingdon to ask how he's doing."

"Apparently, he's well. One of Willingdon's footmen came round yesterday evening to return my coat, and he brought a note from the housekeeper. They sent for their doctor as a precaution, but he saw no cause for concern."

"That's a relief," Felicity said, gesturing to the chair beside hers. "You should join me for breakfast."

A cup of coffee and a well-cooked breakfast were too tempting to resist, and they went a long way to restoring Kincaid's good humour. As he was finishing his second cup of coffee, Felicity met his eye.

"Thank you, Mr. Kincaid," she said quietly.

Kincaid looked at her in confusion. "For what?"

"For not pointing out how foolish I was yesterday. You wanted me to go directly home from the park, but I insisted on staying with Ernest. I think I was so afraid for Ernest that I didn't realize I was cold."

"You were very brave yesterday, Felicity. That boy would have died if you hadn't been there."

"I suppose," she agreed. "But I should have accepted Willingdon's offer to have his housekeeper find me dry clothes. There was no need for me to get into a state where I had to be carried into the house. And then all the fuss with the doctor, and the worry I caused you—I'm sorry."

Kincaid knew how much the apology cost her. During his time as her guardian, Felicity had gone to great lengths to convince him that she didn't need anyone's help.

"I was worried, Felicity," he admitted. "But you have nothing to apologize for."

Felicity still looked troubled, so he continued. "Not many people could have done what you did yesterday, Felicity," he said quietly. "But when you saw Ernest fall in, you didn't stop to think about the risks, you just galloped across the park and ran into the water. I've never seen anything like it."

"Really?" Felicity asked.

"Really. It was incredibly reckless, but I can't criticize you for it." Indeed, the look in his eyes was something close to admiration. "And you shouldn't be too hard on yourself for waiting to change your clothes. If you were the sort of girl who always acted sensibly, you probably wouldn't have jumped in the lake."

"Oh." Felicity was so surprised by his praise that she didn't know how to reply.

"And I hope you never put me through something like that ever again," he continued. "My heart almost stopped when you collapsed."

"I suppose it was a challenge for you to carry me up the stairs," Felicity teased.

"Oh, yes," Kincaid agreed lightly. "It's a pity you're so tall. I almost asked Dr. Mackenzie to examine me when he was through with you."

Kincaid left the breakfast parlour and sought out his butler, who assured him that everything was running smoothly at 23 Bentley St. He received a similar report from his housekeeper, which was hardly a surprise, since Felicity had been giving Mrs. Sutherland her orders for over a year.

Having run out of reasons to linger, Kincaid looked for Felicity, and found her in the drawing room, bent over a sketchbook. She was so absorbed in her work that she didn't hear him approach.

"Felicity," he began.

Felicity looked up with a startled expression, then quickly closed her sketchbook and set it on the table beside her.

Although Kincaid had barely noticed the sketchbook

before, the haste with which she closed it made him curious. "Are you plotting something?" he asked warily.

"Plotting something?" Felicity asked, in a tone that implied she thought the idea was ridiculous. "What do you think I could be plotting, Mr. Kincaid?"

"I don't know. That's the problem."

Felicity pretended to consider the matter. "I don't think that's a problem," she replied. "This way, if I'm plotting something you wouldn't approve of, you won't have to worry about it before it happens."

"You're very kind to me, Felicity," Kincaid said dryly.

"Well, you're very good to me, so I think it's only fair," she replied, taking his words at face value. "As it happens, I wasn't plotting anything, merely amusing myself with some sketching." She had been sketching a design for a gown, and although she knew it was irrational, she didn't want Kincaid to see it. He had drawn the conclusion that she only visited Madame Sylvie to order dresses, and she had no wish to change his mind.

To her relief, he didn't ask to see her sketchbook. "I came to tell you I'm returning to Number 29," he told her. "But please send someone for me immediately if you're feeling unwell. And I think . . ."

He trailed off when Wainwright entered to announce Lady Delphinia and Mr. Nethercott.

"Felicity, I am so relieved to see that you're well," Nethercott said, striding briskly into the room. "We heard you rescued Willingdon's boy from the Serpentine. It sounds like you were quite the heroine."

Lady Delphinia followed her son at a more leisurely pace and lowered herself gracefully into a wing chair. Cleopatra emerged from under the sofa and prowled towards her, and Felicity moved to intercept her cat. Lady Delphinia, however, proved more than a match for Cleopatra, and fixed the cat with a look of disdain that sent her scampering behind the curtains.

"It does sound like a heroic feat, Felicity," Lady Delphinia murmured. "But I don't understand why you had to be the one to do it."

"The boy's nurse was in shock," Felicity explained. "So she was in no condition to help him. But she shouldn't be put in charge of a child if she's unable to keep her wits, and I told Lord Willingdon so."

"Very few nursemaids are to be trusted," Lady Delphinia remarked. "What I don't understand is why you were riding in the park by yourself. It isn't proper, Felicity."

Felicity frowned. "But I wasn't by myself, ma'am. I was with Mr. Kincaid and his betrothed, Miss Jane Harris. I can assure you it was perfectly proper."

Lady Delphinia turned to stare at Mr. Kincaid. "I see." Her tone conveyed her opinion of a man who would stand by and watch a lady rescue a child from a lake.

"Felicity saw the child fall in and was the first to reach him," Kincaid explained through gritted teeth.

"Of course," Nethercott said with a smirk.

"I came to invite you to stay with me while you recover," Lady Delphinia told Felicity.

"Thank you, Lady Delphinia," Felicity replied, "but as you can see, I've already recovered."

"I'm not sure if Mr. Kincaid told you of my invitation, but I would be happy to have you live with me for the Season," Lady Delphinia persisted. "I could chaperone you to parties, and Martin could escort you when you ride in the park."

"I can assure you, Miss Taylor, that I am an excellent swimmer," Nethercott said gallantly. "If we encounter any children in the Serpentine, I would be pleased to rescue them on your behalf."

"You must not have heard the good news," Felicity said brightly. "Mr. Kincaid is betrothed to Miss Jane Harris. They are to be married in two weeks' time, and Jane will act as my chaperone for the Season."

Lady Delphinia's face fell, but she recovered her composure almost immediately. "How fortunate," she said. "But Miss Harris is not family, and I wonder—"

"But she will not be Miss Harris, she will be Mrs. Kincaid," Felicity pointed out. "And since Mr. Kincaid is practically family, she will be too."

Lady Delphinia knew when to accept defeat. "Of course," she said with a little smile. "How very fortunate."

Jane arrived shortly after Lady Delphinia and Mr. Nethercott departed.

"Dear Felicity, I didn't expect to see you out of bed," Jane said, with a hint of censure in her tone.

"You and Mr. Kincaid agree on that point," Felicity said mildly. "But I was bored, so I got up."

"Are you sure that was wise?" Jane asked doubtfully. "If you're not careful, the chill may settle in your lungs."

"Do you think it's more likely to do so in the drawing room than in my bedchamber?" Felicity asked.

Jane appeared to consider this question. "I suppose

not," she conceded. "But you should take care to keep warm and avoid exertion."

"Oh, Mr. Kincaid has done his best to keep me warm," Felicity said innocently. "He ordered the staff to keep fires blazing in every fireplace in the house. When I woke this morning I was uncomfortably hot, but I feel perfectly well now."

"I'm pleased to hear it," Jane replied solicitously. "But I hope you won't overexert yourself. I'm sure you wouldn't want to cause further worry for Mr. Kincaid."

"Well, I can't control whether Mr. Kincaid worries," Felicity remarked. "But I certainly don't intend to overexert myself. I had planned to go to the modiste today, but after yesterday's adventure I've decided to wait until tomorrow."

"Oh, I will join you," Jane declared. "Mr. Kincaid thought I could advise you on a dress for your debut."

"Did he really?" Felicity asked, with a quizzical glance at Kincaid. "He is an optimist."

"What do you mean?" Jane asked suspiciously.

"Merely that I am very stubborn, and rarely take advice in matters of dress," Felicity said, smiling blandly at Jane. "But if you would like to accompany me to the modiste, you are welcome to do so."

"I would like to."

"In that case, Miss Flint and I will call for you tomorrow morning."

"I am looking forward to it," Jane replied.

Eleven

The following morning, Felicity directed the coachman to pick up Jane on the way to Madame Sylvie's. Jane had evidently been waiting by the window, and she strode quickly down the stairs as soon as the carriage drew to a stop. The groom jumped down to help her into the carriage, but Jane walked past him to speak to the coachman.

"I would like to go to Miss Latham's on Oxford Street," she told him.

"Yes, Miss," the coachman replied impassively.

Jane was assisted into the carriage, where Felicity greeted her warmly and Miss Flint gave her a nod.

"I wanted to speak with you about the importance of being cautious in your speech," Jane told Felicity. "I understand you don't mean any harm, but when you're out in society, you will meet many high sticklers. Even the most innocent comment might be misinterpreted, and the consequences could be disastrous."

"Dear me," Felicity remarked. "It's a wonder that young ladies dare to speak at all."

Jane nodded. "You may be intimidated at first," she said kindly. "But it's important to make an effort. You might make an observation about the weather, for example."

"The weather," Felicity repeated with a nod, as though she were trying to commit it to memory.

"Yes. Or you could mention a book you enjoyed, or an artist you admire."

"I'm afraid I don't know much about art," Felicity said apologetically. "It has never interested me."

Jane reflected that Felicity's education had been sadly limited, and it was a shame that she had driven so many governesses away. "We will have to visit the Exhibition at the Royal Academy this summer," she suggested.

"You can tell me what to say about the paintings," Felicity said agreeably.

Jane forced out a laugh. "You can just say what you think of them. But the most important thing is to know which subjects should never be discussed in company."

"Which subjects are those?"

"First of all, you should never mention your fortune," Jane said primly.

"But how will the gentlemen know I have one?" Felicity asked innocently.

Jane looked perplexed by the question. "They will probably have already heard of it."

"So a gentleman may discuss a lady's fortune with other people, but not with the lady directly?"

"He will have discussed it discreetly," Jane explained.

Felicity furrowed her brow. "So if I want to know

about a gentleman's fortune, I should take care to be discreet?"

Jane frowned. "If you want to know if a gentleman is eligible, you can ask me. If I don't know, I will ask Mr. Kincaid."

Felicity resented the suggestion that she would need to use Jane as an intermediary to ask Kincaid a question. "But what if I want to know the amount of a gentleman's fortune?"

"All you need to know is whether he has enough money to support you in comfort," Jane replied. "The amount is not important."

Felicity raised an eyebrow and looked at her skeptically. "Surely you don't believe that?"

As Jane was considering her answer, the carriage slowed to a stop, and she resolved to continue the discussion after they were through at the modiste's. The ladies descended, and Jane was surprised to find that they were in front of Madame Sylvie's establishment instead of Miss Latham's. She stared at the shop in confusion for a moment before turning back towards the carriage, intending to tell the coachman he had erred. To her chagrin, the coachman had decided to walk the horses, and the carriage was already some distance away.

Jane turned to Felicity instead. "The coachman has made a mistake," she complained. "I told him quite clearly that I wished to go to Miss Latham's."

"Yes, I heard you say so," Felicity said.

Jane's brow furrowed. "Is he new to the post? It seems like a foolish mistake for a coachman to make."

"Oh, there was no mistake," Felicity said. "I had

already told him to bring us to Madame Sylvie's. He knows I would never buy a gown from anyone else."

Jane's eyes narrowed. "But I told him I wanted to go to Miss Latham's! And he said—"

"He said, 'Yes, Miss,'" Felicity agreed. "But to be fair, you didn't ask him to take you to Miss Latham's, you simply told him you wished to go there."

"Quite right," Miss Flint put in. "I heard that too."

Jane's cheeks flushed with anger, and Felicity adopted a conciliatory tone. "But I'm sure he understood what you meant, and he'll take us to Miss Latham's next. My business here shouldn't take long."

Jane grudgingly followed them into the shop, and Sylvie emerged from the back room to greet them.

"Ah, Madame Sylvie," Felicity said brightly. "Allow me to introduce Miss Jane Harris. She is engaged to Mr. Kincaid."

Madame Sylvie smiled at Jane. "*Enchantée,* Miss Harris."

"Madame Sylvie," Jane acknowledged coolly.

"Jane is here to help me choose a gown for my coming-out ball," Felicity explained. She gave Sylvie a speaking look, and the modiste correctly deduced that Jane didn't know about the red satin gown that Felicity was sewing.

"I will show you my book of designs," Sylvie said. She moved to an elegant rosewood desk and pulled a book from a drawer.

"Felicity," Jane said in a loud whisper. "I imagine this shop is very expensive."

"Oh, yes," Felicity confirmed. "Madame Sylvie makes the finest gowns in London."

"They must cost a fortune."

Felicity frowned. "Not more than I can afford."

"I must say, Felicity, I'm surprised that Mr. Kincaid permits such extravagance," Jane said. "I couldn't justify spending such a large sum on a gown for myself." She glanced at Madame Sylvie and coloured when she realized the modiste had overheard. "What I mean to say is that . . ."

Madame Sylvie's smile never wavered. "I understood what you meant, and I quite agree," she said, in a deceptively gentle tone of voice. "It would be a waste."

Felicity shot Madame Sylvie a look of warning before turning to Jane with a cheerful expression. "Jane, you must let me buy you a gown."

"Oh, no," Jane protested. "I couldn't allow you to do that. Why, Mr. Kincaid thinks you spend far too much money on clothes already, and—"

Felicity's expression changed. "Did he say so?"

"Well, yes, he did," Jane told her, undeterred by the look in Felicity's eyes. "And he also said you spend far too much time thinking about clothes."

"Ees zat right?" Sylvie asked Jane. Her French accent had a tendency to become more pronounced when she was speaking to customers she didn't like. "Would Mr. Kincaid criticize a poet for spending too much time thinking about poetry?"

"He might, you know," Felicity said with a laugh. "Mr. Kincaid is a very practical man."

"I wouldn't want to do anything that would displease him," Jane said. "I'm afraid, Madame Sylvie, that your gowns are too expensive for me."

"Nonsense," Felicity said brightly. "We will both have

new gowns for the ball, and I will pay for them. Madame Sylvie, what would you suggest for Jane?"

Madame Sylvie cast a professional eye down Jane's figure and turned the pages of her book. "This one," she said, pointing at a drawing of an elegant gown with a high waist and puffed sleeves.

"Oh, I like that," Felicity said enthusiastically. "Jane, what do you think?"

"It's very nice," Jane remarked. "But I don't think—"

"And Sylvie, you must have some beautiful fabrics?" Felicity interrupted.

Sylvie nodded and led them to another room, where bolts of exquisite silks and satins were displayed on specially built shelves. "Ze blue satin would look lovely on Mademoiselle Jane," she suggested.

But Jane was determined to choose her own fabric, and her eye had been caught by a mint green silk.

"Ze green silk would be an excellent choice," Madame Sylvie agreed. Felicity stared at the modiste in disbelief, for she didn't think green was a good choice for Jane at all. Jane suffered from a sallow complexion, and the mint green would make her look jaundiced. Felicity had no doubt that Sylvie saw it too, and it was unlike her to lie to a customer to make a sale.

"I much prefer the blue," Felicity said quickly. "It will bring out the colour of your eyes, Jane."

"I have decided on the green," Jane said stubbornly.

Felicity frowned, as though struck by an idea. "The Countess of Langley told me she has just bought a green gown for the ball," she said. "If I recall, Madame Sylvie, she ordered it from you. It might even be the same fabric."

Madame Sylvie opened her mouth to contradict Felicity, since the most recent gown she had made for the Countess of Langley had been blue. But she couldn't ignore Felicity's pointed look, so she nodded. "Yes," she said slowly. "I had forgotten."

Felicity turned to Jane. "I'm sure you wouldn't want to go to a ball wearing the same colour gown as your hostess."

"I suppose not," Jane said with a frown.

"So perhaps the blue satin?" Felicity suggested gently. "You would hate to outshine the Countess of Langley."

Sylvie clucked her tongue. In her opinion, there wasn't a dress in the world that would allow Jane Harris to outshine the Countess of Langley, and the very idea was laughable. Since Sylvie had long suspected that Felicity was infatuated with Mr. Kincaid, she found her behaviour curious. If Felicity had suggested a colour that wouldn't flatter Jane, Sylvie wouldn't have approved, but she would have understood. But when Jane could be made to look dowdy by simply giving her what she wanted—well, Felicity was far more generous than Sylvie would be in her place.

"You're sure, Felicity?" Sylvie asked dubiously.

"Oh, yes," Felicity assured her. "Jane must have the blue."

"All right," Jane agreed reluctantly. "Now we'll have to choose fabric for you, Felicity. It must be white, of course, for your debut ball." She surveyed the bolts of fabric before pointing to one of ivory crepe. "I think this would be suitable."

"Yes, that looks lovely," Felicity answered easily.

"Then it's decided," Sylvie said. "If you'll step this way, Miss Harris, my assistant will take your measurements."

"You have a kind heart, Felicity," Madame Sylvie said quietly, after Jane had been led away by an assistant. "In your place, I would have let her wear the green."

"I'm hoping to be rewarded for my kindness eventually," Felicity said vaguely. Allowing Jane to go to her ball in an unflattering gown, looking like a pitiful creature, would not serve her purpose at all.

"Miss Harris may notice that Lady Langley isn't wearing mint green silk."

"I was hoping you could make a mint green gown for Lady Langley," Felicity said. "I'll pay for it, of course, as well as the blue satin for Jane. It will be a way to thank Lady Langley for hosting the ball, and Jane for acting as my chaperone."

"All right," Sylvie said with a sigh. "Lady Langley will look magnificent in the green. I don't expect you actually want a gown of ivory crepe?"

"No," Felicity said with a smile. "I've made great progress on the red satin. Miss Flint's been helping with the fitting, but I'd like your opinion before I finish the bodice. I would have brought it today, but Jane decided to come, so I'll have to come back another day."

"Do you still wish to visit Miss Latham's?" Felicity asked Jane as they left Madame Sylvie's.

"I don't think there's any need," Jane replied irritably.

"No, you're quite right," Felicity agreed. "We will drive Miss Harris home first," she instructed the coachman.

"Oh, no," Jane protested. "I would hate to put you to the trouble. I thought I might return with you to Bentley Street, to call upon Mr. Kincaid."

"Certainly." Felicity directed the coachman to take them to 29 Bentley.

"I thought you lived at 23 Bentley St.," Jane remarked. "I suppose I should learn the address, since it will soon be my home."

"Oh, I do," Felicity replied. "But Mr. Kincaid lives at 29 Bentley."

Jane's eyebrows drew together in confusion. "But I thought you were living in his house?"

"Yes, I am."

"But why is he at Number 29?"

"He was worried about gossip," Felicity explained. "He thought people might think we were engaged in an improper relationship if we were living under the same roof."

"An improper relationship?" Jane repeated, looking at Felicity through narrowed eyes.

"Yes, isn't it nonsensical?"

"Very," Jane said curtly. Her expression did not invite further conversation, and the remainder of the drive passed in silence.

Kincaid hadn't expected visitors at Number 29, but he greeted them warmly and rang for tea.

"How are you feeling, Felicity?" Kincaid asked, as he took a seat on the sofa beside her. He studied her face for signs of illness and was relieved to see that she looked healthier than ever.

"Perfectly well, thank you," Felicity replied. "No ill effects from having jumped into the lake."

Jane seated herself next to Miss Flint and attempted to engage her in conversation. Several minutes later, Miss Flint announced she had a headache and was going to return to 23 Bentley.

"I'll come with you, Theodora," Felicity offered.

"No need," Miss Flint said gruffly. "It's only a step down the street. I'm sure Mr. Kincaid will walk you home later."

Kincaid agreed that he would, and Miss Flint departed. After she had left, Jane turned to Kincaid. "Miss Flint was very quiet this afternoon," she began.

Kincaid smiled. "Miss Flint is always quiet."

"That's a relief," Jane said with a little sigh. "I was beginning to think she didn't like me."

Kincaid frowned. "I'm sure that's not true. By her standards, she just had an unusually long conversation with you."

"I was reassuring her that I would help her find a new position," Jane explained.

"I'm afraid you've lost me," Felicity said in a deceptively sweet voice. "Why would Miss Flint need a new position?"

"Well, after Mr. Kincaid and I are married, you will no longer need a companion," Jane said matter-of-factly. "I thought Miss Flint might be worried about where she would go, so I told her she can stay with us until she finds a new place."

"How kind of you," Felicity said, but there was a dangerous look in her eyes that belied her words. Jane didn't recognize her expression, but Kincaid did.

"Felicity—" he began, but Felicity interrupted him.

"Have you decided to dismiss any other members of

137

the staff, Jane?" she asked. "The housekeeper, perhaps, or Mr. Kincaid's valet?"

Jane looked at Felicity in confusion. "Of course not. I am hardly going to replace Mr. Kincaid's valet."

"How generous of you to let him stay."

"Felicity—" Kincaid tried again.

"If you'll excuse me, I'm going to speak to Miss Flint," Felicity declared. She stood and swept out of the room, leaving Jane and Kincaid staring after her.

"Well!" Jane exclaimed. "I was only trying to be helpful. I don't see why she flew into a miff."

Kincaid studied her carefully. "Don't you?"

"No, I don't!" Jane insisted. "And I don't understand the talk about your housekeeper, or your valet. It's not as though I intend to dismiss all your staff."

"You relieve my mind."

Jane could see that she didn't have his sympathy, and she grew defensive. "Felicity must see that she won't need a companion after you and I are married. Unless she doesn't think my companionship will be enough for her?"

Kincaid was caught between loyalty to his betrothed and his belief that Felicity was in the right. "I imagine Felicity thinks that since Miss Flint is her companion, she should be involved in any discussions about her future in the household."

Jane frowned. "Well, Felicity should have said that, instead of making irrational references to your valet."

"Perhaps." Kincaid wondered if Jane really couldn't see Felicity's point. "But you wouldn't dismiss my valet, would you?"

"Of course not. It wouldn't be my place."

Kincaid nodded. "Miss Flint has been Felicity's

companion for two years," he said quietly. "They've developed a friendship. Miss Flint was referred by a connection of my mother's, so I don't know the details of her background, but it may not be easy for her to find a new situation."

"But I assured her that she could remain with us until she finds a new position," Jane said peevishly.

"And it may not be pleasant for her to feel as though she's here on sufferance."

"But Miss Flint must not expect to stay with Felicity forever? Surely she doesn't think Felicity will keep her on after she marries?"

"I don't imagine she does," Kincaid said. "But since she's Felicity's companion, she might have thought it was Felicity's place to have that conversation."

"I see," Jane said curtly. "Thank you for explaining the situation so clearly."

"Jane, I know that things with Felicity can be complicated," he said, in an effort to be conciliatory. "I'm fortunate that you're so understanding."

"In the future, I'll be sure to speak to you before making any decisions about the staff."

"It might be best," Kincaid agreed. "I've run a bachelor household for a long time, and will take me some time to adjust to my new circumstances."

Twelve

When Kincaid called at 23 Bentley St. three days later, he was informed that Felicity was in the drawing room.

"But I believe she's occupied, sir," Wainwright said mysteriously.

"Occupied?" Kincaid asked. "With what?"

"She's interviewing a man for the position of butler."

"You're not leaving, Wainwright?" Kincaid asked curiously.

"No, sir. I understand Miss Taylor is looking to hire staff for her new household."

"Her new household?" Kincaid repeated.

Wainwright nodded. "Yes, sir."

Kincaid jumped to the conclusion that Felicity had contracted a betrothal, and her new household would be her husband's. Although she would lose her fortune if she married without his consent before she came of age, there was nothing to stop her from entering into an engagement. Of course, after her birthday she could marry whomever she chose, and she would turn twenty-one in two weeks' time.

If Kincaid had been in a cooler frame of mind, he might have stopped to question why Felicity was rushing to replace her future husband's servants, but fury made him irrational. He stormed past Wainwright into the drawing room, where he found Felicity sitting across from a soberly dressed young man. Across the room, Miss Flint was nominally playing the role of chaperone, but she appeared to be absorbed in her knitting.

"What is the meaning of this?" Kincaid thundered. The look on his face terrified the prospective butler, but Felicity met his eye calmly.

"Good afternoon," she said with a look of feigned confusion. "Are you here to apply for a position?"

"I beg your pardon?" Kincaid exclaimed.

"I wasn't aware that there was another appointment today," Felicity replied, "but if you would care to wait in the hallway—"

"I'm not going to wait in the hallway!"

"You'll have to learn to mind your manners if you hope to work in my household," Felicity said reproachfully. "And if you were hoping to work as the butler, I'm afraid you're too late, for I intend to offer the position to Mr. Jones here."

"I'll survive the disappointment," Kincaid said sarcastically.

"I'm relieved to hear it," Felicity murmured, casting a critical eye down his figure. "You could apply to be a footman, but I was hoping to find someone a little more muscular. But if you're willing to train . . ." She paused and looked at Mr. Jones. "Do you think you could train this man to be a footman?"

"A f-footman?" Jones stammered nervously. He was perceptive enough to see that Kincaid's accent and attire weren't those of a servant, and he wondered if this was some sort of test.

"You're right, Jones," Felicity said. "He appears to have a temper, and I'm afraid he would disturb the harmony of the household."

"I'm done playing games, Felicity," Kincaid bit out.

Felicity turned to Jones. "Perhaps you could demonstrate how you would get rid of an unwanted caller?"

"Felicity," Kincaid said, with ice in his tone.

Felicity sighed and turned apologetically to Mr. Jones. "It seems this man is insisting on an immediate interview. I think I have all the information I need from you, and I'll be in touch with more details about the position."

As soon as Jones had departed, Felicity faced her guardian. "I hope you haven't frightened poor Mr. Jones," she remarked. "I think he would make an excellent butler."

"Who is he, Felicity?" Kincaid asked abruptly.

Felicity's brow furrowed. "Mr. Jones? He's the man I mean to hire as my butler."

"Not Jones," Kincaid said impatiently. "The man you mean to marry."

"Well, I don't know yet," Felicity said with a laugh. "I thought that was the point of having a Season."

Now Kincaid looked confused. "So you haven't entered into an engagement?"

Felicity shook her head. "Of course not. I haven't had the opportunity to meet anyone."

Kincaid couldn't hide his sigh of relief. "Then why are you hiring a butler?"

"Miss Flint and I intend to set up our own household," Felicity explained. "I went to see Mr. Battersby two days ago, and he agreed to help me find a house to let."

Kincaid took a moment to process this, and the room was silent apart from the clicking of Miss Flint's knitting needles.

"You can't set up your own household, Felicity," he finally said.

"Why not?" Felicity asked reasonably. "I will be of age in two weeks, and you promised to let me have the income from my fortune. It will be more than enough to cover the rent and expenses."

"It's not a matter of money."

Felicity raised an eyebrow. "If you're worried about the proprieties, you needn't. Miss Flint will come with me, so it will be perfectly respectable."

"It won't be respectable, because you're not going to do it," Kincaid retorted. He took a deep breath and continued in a gentler tone. "I know Jane spoke of helping Miss Flint find another position, but I've explained that she's welcome in my home for as long as she wishes to stay. So there is no reason for you to establish your own household."

"No reason, except that I wish to do so."

"But you can't!" Kincaid exclaimed.

"Explain to me why not," Felicity said calmly.

"Because I don't want you to!"

"No doubt that seems like an excellent reason to you," Felicity replied with unimpaired calm. "But I'm not convinced you've thought it through. What about Jane?"

"What about Jane?" Kincaid asked.

"She doesn't like Cleopatra," Felicity said. "And I've grown attached to dear Cleo, you see, and I don't want to give her up. So Miss Flint, Cleopatra and I will set up our own establishment, where we won't have to worry about Jane's fear of cats."

"Of all the ridiculous reasons to set up your own household, that has to be the worst," Kincaid muttered.

"You and Jane will be newlyweds, and I'm sure you'll want the house to yourselves."

"I can assure you, we will not."

"I suppose you and Jane will be so delirious with passion that you won't even notice the other occupants of the house," Felicity agreed. "Miss Flint and I, however, might find it awkward."

"Jane and I will not be delirious with passion," Kincaid said crisply. "Really, Felicity, I don't know what novels you've read, but I doubt they gave you an accurate idea of what marriage is like."

"But I think that's how it's supposed to feel," Felicity told him. "As though you're the first couple in the world to have discovered love."

"That's nonsense, Felicity," Kincaid said dismissively. "I can assure you that neither Jane nor I will lose our wits. And there is no need for you to move out. Jane understands that your home is with me, until you marry or choose to leave it."

"And when may I choose to leave it?" Felicity inquired.

"Well, clearly not now!" Kincaid insisted. "It would be completely inappropriate."

"How so?"

"Because beautiful young ladies don't set up their own households!"

"Do you think I'm beautiful, Mr. Kincaid?" Felicity asked curiously.

"I'm sure many men do," Kincaid hedged.

Felicity was gratified by the flush of embarrassment that was creeping over his cheeks. "That doesn't answer my question."

"My opinion on the subject is irrelevant."

"Well, I'm glad you realize that," she agreed. "Now, if I could only convince you that your opinion of my place of residence is equally irrelevant, we might reach an understanding."

"Never!" he exclaimed. "I won't be your guardian for much longer, Felicity, but I will still have control of your fortune, and if I have to, I'll stop your allowance."

"Mr. Battersby didn't seem concerned about the idea," Felicity murmured.

"I doubt Mr. Battersby could remember what he had for breakfast this morning!" Kincaid retorted. "He's losing his wits, Felicity."

"Do you think so?" Felicity asked thoughtfully. "I seem to recall that when Mr. Nethercott raised that concern last year, you said that Battersby was as sharp as ever."

Kincaid's expression darkened at the mention of Martin Nethercott. "Don't bring your cousin into this," he said in frustration. "It's not Nethercott's business."

"Perhaps not," Felicity said. "Although if Battersby is truly losing his wits, Mr. Nethercott might have a reason to be concerned."

"You don't trust me to manage your affairs on my own?"

"Well, if Battersby's incapable, it leaves you with a great deal of power," Felicity mused. "You might be tempted to take advantage of it."

Kincaid knew she was being deliberately provocative, but her words still stung.

"Is that really what you think, Felicity?" he asked, fighting to keep his tone even. "I've been scrupulously careful with your money, but if you're concerned I'll take advantage—"

"Oh, I'm not concerned about my fortune," Felicity said quickly. "I don't think anyone could have managed it better."

"Oh," Kincaid said, taken aback. "Then I don't understand what you mean."

"You might abuse your position in other ways," Felicity explained. "By issuing autocratic decrees. You promised to give me the income from my investments, but now that I wish to do something you don't like, you intend to go back on your word."

"No one could expect me to let you establish your own household at the age of twenty-one," he retorted. "You must have known I wouldn't agree to it, so you went to Battersby because you thought you could manipulate him."

"No," Felicity said thoughtfully. "I don't think I tried to manipulate Mr. Battersby. I made a straightforward request, and he said yes."

"I'll talk to Battersby," Kincaid said grimly. "Have you thought of what this will do to your reputation? Living by yourself—"

"I won't be by myself," Felicity pointed out. "I'll be with Miss Flint."

"And you think Miss Flint could protect you if a man tried to take liberties?"

Felicity shrugged. "Since you moved out, I have been living with only Miss Flint and the servants for protection. If I set up my own household, my situation would hardly be different than it is now."

Kincaid could see the logic of this, but he didn't want to admit it. "Yes, but I trust my servants, and you don't know anything about the people you mean to hire. Take that Mr. Jones, whom you hope to hire as your butler. What do you really know about him? Far from coming to your defence, he might try to take advantage of you himself."

Felicity's dark eyes sparkled with amusement. "Do you think I'm that irresistible, Mr. Kincaid?"

Kincaid didn't meet her gaze. "I think there are a great many men who don't treat women with the respect they deserve."

Felicity smiled. "You have a poor opinion of your sex, Mr. Kincaid," she said lightly. "And of me, if you think I wouldn't be able to defend myself."

"How would you defend yourself, Felicity?"

"It would depend on the circumstances," she replied. "But I can assure you that I would put up a fight." She arched an eyebrow. "Would you like a demonstration?"

The temptation was great, and Kincaid fought the urge to take Felicity in his arms and show her how a man might behave if he wished to take advantage of her. He could teach her how difficult it was to resist a man in the grip of a passionate emotion, and it might convince her to take better care of herself in the future.

If Felicity noticed the dangerous look in his eyes, she didn't let on, and they faced each other silently for a moment. Kincaid gritted his teeth and reminded himself that what he felt for Felicity wasn't desire, but frustration. She was playing a game with him, and she had him at a disadvantage since he didn't know the rules. All he knew was that he couldn't win, since his opponent was willing to risk both her reputation and her safety to win her point.

It was Cleopatra who finally broke the tension by emerging from under the sofa with a hiss.

"Of course, the cat," Kincaid muttered, as Cleopatra stalked towards him.

"Of course," Felicity said. "I think Cleopatra likes the idea of a new home. And as you see, I won't be unprotected. I think any man would think twice about trying to ravish me while I have Cleopatra."

As though to disprove Felicity's point, Cleopatra remembered that she liked Kincaid. He watched warily as the cat sniffed the toe of his boot before rubbing her flank against his lower leg.

"I'm relieved to know she's standing guard," he said dryly.

Felicity laughed. "She might distract an attacker, at least. I could run away while Cleopatra licks his boots."

Kincaid pressed his lips together to suppress a laugh. "It isn't a joke, Felicity," he said when he had collected himself. "You will remain in my house until you marry."

"But—" Felicity began.

"Don't you see, Felicity," he said gently. "If you leave, I'll feel as though I've driven you out."

Felicity opened her mouth to deliver a flippant reply, but the look in his eye made her pause.

"You can keep Cleopatra," Kincaid coaxed. "I'll tell Jane the cat isn't negotiable."

"All right," Felicity agreed quietly.

Kincaid smiled with relief. "I'll tell Battersby he can stop looking for a house, and if you give me Mr. Jones's direction, I'll inform him that you will no longer need a butler."

"Thank you."

Felicity and Kincaid were so absorbed in their conversation that they didn't hear Wainwright enter the room.

"Miss Harris," Wainwright announced.

Kincaid stood and bowed to Jane. "This is a pleasant surprise," he said with a teasing smile. "Dare I hope that you've come to visit me and not my housekeeper?"

Jane looked bewildered by the question, so Kincaid continued. "My staff have told me how hard you've been working to prepare for tomorrow's party," he explained. According to his valet, Jane had visited Mrs. Sutherland every day for the past week, and she always had 'one more detail' to discuss. The entire household was feeling the strain, and Kincaid realized Jane was in danger of alienating his servants before she formally became their mistress.

"I'm sure Jane and Mrs. Sutherland would have been pleased to involve you in the preparations," Felicity put in. "And there is likely still work to be done, you know."

"On the contrary, I have just spoken to Mrs. Sutherland, and I think everything is in order for tomorrow,"

Jane said. "But I was hoping to talk to you, Felicity. I understand this will be your first *ton* party, and I realized we haven't discussed what you will wear to it."

"That's very thoughtful of you, Jane," Felicity said. "But I think I'll be able to dress myself."

"Perhaps you could show me the gown," Jane suggested.

"If you like," Felicity agreed, with a small shrug of her shoulders. She led Jane to her bedchamber and rang for her maid. Jane cast a critical eye around the room, which was tastefully decorated in pink and cream, and found little to reproach. Felicity was glad that the red satin dress for her debut ball was safely out of sight in her dressing room.

"I am concerned about Mr. Kincaid," Jane remarked, as they waited for Felicity's maid to appear. "This engagement party will be very important for him."

"Do you think so?" Felicity asked curiously.

"Of course," Jane replied. "It will be his opportunity to meet my family and friends."

"And your opportunity to meet his family and friends," Felicity pointed out.

"Yes," Jane said slowly, recalling that Mr. Kincaid had only invited five people to the party. "I would hate for him to be distracted."

"Distracted?" Felicity repeated.

"Yes," Jane said carefully. "Mr. Kincaid worries about you, you know."

"Does he?" Felicity asked. "Has he discussed it with you?"

"No," Jane admitted. "But I've seen the way he looks when he talks about you. You're a big responsibility, Felicity. When I arrived this afternoon, it was clear you were discussing something important."

"Yes, it was important," Felicity agreed. To Jane's disappointment, she didn't elaborate on what they had been discussing.

Felicity's maid entered and dropped a curtsy, and Felicity smiled.

"Ah, Louise," Felicity said. "This is Miss Harris. She is engaged to Mr. Kincaid, and she would like to see my peach silk gown."

"Your peach silk, Miss Taylor?" Louise repeated.

Felicity nodded. "I intend to wear it to the party tomorrow, and Miss Harris wants to be sure it's suitable."

Louise didn't think Felicity's gown was any concern of Jane's, and she fixed Jane with a look of acute dislike before leaving to fetch the gown.

Jane barely looked at the peach silk, confirming Felicity's suspicion that her real aim had been to speak to Felicity privately.

"Would you like to see it on, Jane?" she offered politely.

"No, thank you."

Felicity dismissed her maid with a nod. "Thank you Louise, that will be all."

When Louise had disappeared with the dress, Felicity turned back to Jane. "So you are worried about Mr. Kincaid," she said thoughtfully.

"Yes, I am," Jane agreed. "As I said, Mr. Kincaid does not need any distractions at tomorrow's party. I wanted to remind you to be on your best behaviour. I know you don't have much experience with society parties, so I hope I you won't take offence."

"Not at all," Felicity lied. "I appreciate your candour. Shall we return downstairs? I have just remembered that I promised to call upon Isabelle this afternoon, so I must take my leave of you."

"Isabelle?" Jane inquired curiously.

"The Marchioness of Ashingham," Felicity explained. "Are you acquainted with her?"

Jane shook her head.

"Mr. Kincaid invited her and her husband to your party," Felicity said with a smile. "I'll introduce you tomorrow."

Thirteen

Letter from The Hon. Lucas Kincaid to his brother Archie, the Earl of Brentwood.

Dear Archie,

I hope this letter finds you and your family well.

I am writing to inform you that I am engaged to Miss Jane Harris, the eldest daughter of Sir Barnaby Harris of Gloucestershire. We are to be married next week. Please don't feel obliged to come to London for the wedding; it is to be a small affair, and we don't want a lot of fuss.

Miss Harris is a very dignified young lady, and she is going to act as Felicity's chaperone for the Season. I hope she will be a good influence on Felicity, who is as spirited as ever. Felicity recently decided to establish her own household when she comes of age, and she even persuaded old Battersby to help her do it! Naturally, I put a stop to that scheme, and I had some choice words for Battersby on the subject. But I suppose I can hardly blame him; I'm sure Felicity bewitched him.

I expect Felicity will bewitch the gentlemen of the ton in a similar fashion, and although she claims she's in no rush to be married, I think she will receive numerous offers. I'm sure she'll lead her husband a merry dance, and if he's not careful, she'll run through her fortune within a year. If you can believe it, last week she ordered two evening gowns for Miss Flint from the most expensive modiste in London. It was recklessly extravagant, though I suppose it was thoughtful. Miss Flint certainly seemed pleased.

Give my love to Mama and the rest of the family.

Yours,
Lucas

Kincaid knew that by the time his letter reached Brentwood, it would be too late for his family to travel to London for the wedding. He felt a twinge of guilt over not having written earlier, which he tried to dismiss with the rationale that weddings were dull affairs, and he was really doing his family a favour. But women could be funny about things like weddings, and his mother might have wanted to attend his. He appeased his conscience by writing his mother a separate letter, so she wouldn't have to learn the news from his brother.

That duty done, Kincaid made his way to 23 Bentley to check on the preparations for his engagement party, which was to take place that evening. He found the house bustling with activity: the maids were dusting every visible surface, the footmen were polishing the chandeliers, and his housekeeper was supervising the delivery of a vast quantity of hothouse flowers.

Wainwright emerged from the chaos with a letter in his hand.

"Mr. Kincaid," the butler said. "Miss Taylor left a letter for you. I was just on my way to deliver it."

Kincaid plucked the letter from his hand, broke the seal, and spread open the sheet.

Dear Mr. Kincaid,

I'm afraid my presence at your party may prove a distraction, so I have decided to go away with Adrian Stone. Don't worry; we are not headed to Gretna Green, and we will return soon.

Sincerely,
Felicity

Kincaid looked up from the note and glared at his butler. "When did she give you this?" he thundered.

"Perhaps an hour ago, as she was leaving. She said it wasn't urgent, and I've been supervising the cleaning of the chandeliers—"

"She left an hour ago?" Kincaid interrupted.

"A travelling coach came to call for her—a very fine vehicle, with a crest on the panel," Wainwright explained. "I assumed you knew that she planned to take a trip."

"I was not," Kincaid said curtly. "I don't suppose Miss Flint went with her?" As soon as he spoke the words, he realized the absurdity of the question. Felicity's letter implied that she had eloped with Adrian, and she wasn't likely to take a chaperone on an elopement.

"Miss Flint is upstairs, sir," Wainwright said nervously.

"I see. And when you saw Miss Taylor leave in a travelling coach, without a chaperone, you didn't think to inform me immediately?"

Wainwright gathered his courage. "I didn't think it was my place, sir."

Kincaid decided he would deal with his butler later. "Please ask Miss Flint to join me in my study, and have the coachman prepare the curricle," he said grimly.

Miss Flint presented herself at his study five minutes later.

"Did Felicity tell you where she was going?" he asked abruptly.

Miss Flint blinked at him. "No, sir. She simply said she was going away, and asked me to look after her cat."

Kincaid looked down and saw that Cleopatra had followed Miss Flint into the study.

"Is something wrong, sir?" Miss Flint asked.

Kincaid took a deep breath in an attempt to keep hold of his temper. "Felicity left me a note," he explained. "It is rather cryptic, but I believe she has eloped with Adrian Stone. I understand they left only an hour ago, so we should be able to catch them. I will need you to come with me to act as Felicity's chaperone. We will leave as soon as the curricle is ready."

Miss Flint blinked at him again. "Certainly, Mr. Kincaid, if you wish it," she said, in her usual deliberate way. "But your engagement party is tonight."

"It's of no consequence," said Kincaid, who had completely forgotten about his engagement party.

"And what about Cleopatra?"

"What about Cleopatra?" Kincaid retorted.

"Felicity has entrusted her cat to my care," Miss Flint explained. "It's quite a cold day, and I'm not sure she would want me to bring Cleopatra on the journey."

Kincaid stared at her in disbelief. "Leave the cat with Wainwright," he said crisply. His butler deserved some sort of punishment for failing to inform him that Felicity had left; perhaps the cat would terrorize him.

Miss Flint had no further objections, and Kincaid helped her into the curricle ten minutes later. He tried to think of where Adrian would have taken Felicity, but no answer presented itself. Since Felicity wasn't of age, they wouldn't be able to marry unless they went to Scotland, but Felicity had explicitly written that they hadn't gone to Gretna Green.

But Wainwright had said the travelling coach had a crest on the panel, and since Kincaid was fairly certain Adrian didn't own a coach, he guessed they had borrowed Lord Langley's vehicle. He doubted Adrian had told his brother the true reason he wanted the coach, but since he didn't have any other ideas, he decided to visit Langley.

Fifteen minutes later, Kincaid marched up the steps of Langley's townhouse with Miss Flint trailing behind him. They swept past the astonished butler and into the drawing room, where they found Langley and Amelia playing chess.

Kincaid didn't waste time with pleasantries. "Robert!" he demanded. "Did you lend Adrian your travelling coach?"

Langley glanced up from the chessboard and frowned. "Certainly not."

"Then he must have taken it without your permission," Kincaid declared. "I'll need to question the stablehands."

"Even Adrian wouldn't take my coach without permission," Langley said. "And besides, Lucas—"

"Then you don't know Adrian as well as you think," Kincaid retorted. "Because he's taken your coach and eloped with Felicity."

"No, he hasn't," Langley replied calmly. "He's gone to Ashingham, with Oliver and Isabelle. Oliver got word yesterday that there was a fire in the tenant cottages. No one was injured, but three of the cottages were badly damaged, and he wanted to inspect things himself. They left this morning, and Adrian went with them."

Kincaid's brow furrowed. "Adrian can't have gone to Ashingham! Felicity left a letter stating she'd gone off with him, and my butler saw her get into a travelling coach with a crest on the panel."

"It must have been Oliver's carriage," Langley deduced. "Felicity has probably gone to Ashingham with them."

"How do you know?"

"Adrian had dinner with us last night," Amelia explained. "He was visiting Oliver when the news came about the tenant cottages, and I think he invited himself along."

"Why would he do that?" Kincaid asked suspiciously.

"I no longer try to understand why Adrian does anything," Langley said with a sigh. "But I expect he was bored."

"I don't believe it," Kincaid said.

Langley shrugged. "Oliver was going to write you a

letter to explain why he and Isabelle won't be able to attend your engagement party tonight. It should have arrived by the morning's post."

This reminded Kincaid of Felicity's letter, which he waved under Langley's nose. "What do you make of this?" he asked hotly.

Langley cast his eye down the page. "The letter seems quite clear, Lucas. It says they haven't gone to Gretna Green."

"But that's even worse!" Kincaid exclaimed. "Felicity doesn't turn twenty-one for two more weeks, so she can't get married in England without my consent. If Adrian doesn't have the sense to take her to Scotland, they'll be living together unmarried, and Felicity will be ruined."

"I'm telling you, Lucas, they've gone to Ashingham with Oliver and Isabelle," Langley said. "Adrian would be the first person to tell you that he doesn't have the means to elope with anyone. I make him a lamentably poor allowance, you know."

"It isn't a joke, Robert!" Kincaid exclaimed. "I recall hearing you weren't nearly as calm when Adrian ran off with the woman you loved!" Shortly before she had become betrothed to Langley, Amelia had asked Adrian to drive her to London, and Langley had mistakenly believed they had eloped.

Langley and Amelia exchanged a speaking look.

"You're right, Lucas," Langley replied. "I was mad as fire when I thought Adrian had run off with Amelia. But that was a misunderstanding, and I'm sure you'll find that this is too."

"But why would Felicity go to Ashingham?" Kincaid asked. "It doesn't make sense."

"Your engagement party is tonight," Langley said, studying his friend closely. "If Felicity heard that Isabelle was leaving town, she might have persuaded her to take her along."

"Felicity went to see Isabelle yesterday afternoon," Kincaid said, brightening at the idea. "But what does the engagement party have to do with anything?"

"Your marriage will mean a significant change for Felicity," Langley said carefully.

Kincaid frowned. "I suppose, but she's not sentimental like that."

"She may worry that you will have less time for her after you marry."

"But she has no desire to spend time with me now," Kincaid protested. "She's always after me to let her manage her own affairs."

"I find women don't always mean what they say."

"I don't understand this affair at all," Kincaid said. "But I'm going after them and bringing Miss Flint. That way, if Isabelle isn't with them, I can pretend that Miss Flint was chaperoning Felicity all along."

"You'll miss your engagement party," Langley pointed out.

"The engagement party can go hang," Kincaid retorted. "You can't expect me to smile and make polite conversation while Felicity's on the verge of marrying your brother?"

"I suppose not," Langley admitted. "Have you—er—informed Miss Harris that you won't be able to attend the party?"

Kincaid huffed out a sigh of frustration. "I don't know

why everyone's so fixated on this engagement party. It's hardly an event of great significance."

"Miss Harris might disagree."

"I'm allowing her to hold the party in my house," Kincaid pointed out. "Surely that's enough of a contribution to the affair."

Langley didn't reply, but his expression conveyed his belief that Jane might have a different opinion.

"You're planning to go to the party," Kincaid told Langley thoughtfully. "You could explain the situation to Jane."

Langley raised an eyebrow. "I'm sorry, Lucas, but I'm not sure I could."

"I'll write her a letter," Kincaid declared. "Can I borrow some paper, Robert?"

A pen and paper were supplied, and Kincaid considered what to write. He was reluctant to tell Jane the truth about what Felicity had done, especially since he didn't know the whole of it himself. After a moment's reflection, he dashed off the following missive:

Dear Miss Harris,

I regret that I will be unable to attend our engagement party this evening. An emergency has called me out of town.

Yours sincerely,
Lucas Kincaid

Kincaid sanded his letter, folded it, and handed it to Langley. "Can you see that this is delivered?"

Langley looked at him with a concern. "If you wish, Lucas, but are you sure?"

"Of course I'm sure!" Kincaid said impatiently. "I've wasted far too much time already."

The journey to Ashingham Court took a little over four hours, but it felt like an eternity to Kincaid. The roads were good and Miss Flint was a silent travelling companion, so there was nothing to distract him from the problem of Felicity's whereabouts. Much as he wished to believe that Langley was right and Felicity had gone to Ashingham, he wouldn't be able to relax until he found her.

When he finally reached the estate, Kincaid jumped from his carriage, thrust the reins at a groom and impatiently helped Miss Flint to alight. The butler escorted them to a drawing room, where they found Felicity drinking tea with Isabelle, Oliver and Adrian.

"Good afternoon Miss Flint," Felicity said politely. "And Mr. Kincaid. I didn't know you were coming to Ashingham."

Kincaid's face was a study in emotions, and Felicity watched as the tension in his eyes turned to relief and then to anger. "Good afternoon, Felicity," he said tersely. "The next time you decide to leave town, I would appreciate being informed in advance."

Felicity's brow furrowed. "I left you a letter," she said innocently.

"A letter that implied you were eloping with Adrian!" Kincaid exclaimed.

Isabelle and Oliver stared at him in dismay. "I'm sure there was some misunderstanding—" Isabelle began.

"You didn't tell me you wanted to elope, Miss Taylor,"

Adrian interrupted. "Had I known, I would have applied for a special licence. It's a bad time of year for a journey to Scotland, you know."

Kincaid looked at Adrian in disbelief. "You will not marry Felicity," he said grimly.

"Well, no, I hadn't planned to," Adrian agreed. "But now that you've suggested it, I think it's a splendid notion. We're of a similar age, and she seems to know how to look after herself. And after all, she is an heiress."

"If Felicity marries without my consent before she comes of age, she won't see any of her fortune," Kincaid pointed out. "It will go to her cousin, Martin Nethercott."

"But my twenty-first birthday is in less than two weeks," Felicity said impishly.

"Since I hadn't thought of it until today, I think I could wait two weeks," Adrian said pensively. "I don't have the funds for a big wedding, but perhaps you could advance me some of Felicity's money to finance it."

"There will be nothing to finance, since Felicity is not going to marry you," Kincaid said through gritted teeth.

"But I won't need your consent after I'm twenty-one," Felicity replied. "You will no longer have a say in the matter. And I'm sure Miss Harris will be relieved to learn that she will no longer be required to chaperone me."

"Don't forget that your money remains under my control for another two weeks," Kincaid said hotly. "I'd throw it in the Thames rather than see it go to Adrian."

"Mr. Battersby might have something to say about that," Felicity said thoughtfully. "He might think you were overstepping your role as my trustee."

"No man of sense would blame me if he knew the circumstances," Kincaid retorted.

Adrian bristled. "Now Lucas, you're not being fair. I may not have a title or a fortune, but I would make Miss Taylor a good husband. And she doesn't need to marry a man with a fortune, because she has her own."

Kincaid gave him a scathing look. "Your arguments for marriage are that you're of a similar age, she seems to know how to look after herself, and she's an heiress!"

"What of it?" asked Adrian, who thought those seemed like excellent reasons for marriage.

"Felicity deserves to marry a man who loves her," Kincaid exclaimed.

"Mr. Kincaid believes everyone deserves to be as happy as he and Miss Harris are," Felicity explained.

"Yes," Kincaid said curtly. "I do."

Adrian looked mollified. "I suppose I can't blame you for that." He turned to Felicity. "While I respect you a great deal, Miss Taylor, I'm afraid I don't love you."

"I understand, Adrian," Felicity said solemnly. "I'm afraid I don't love you either."

"Although," Adrian said thoughtfully. "There is always a chance that love would develop in time. I understand that often happens when a gentleman and lady are given the chance to spend time together. Perhaps after a courtship—"

"No!" Kincaid barked. "I'm sorry, Adrian, but I'm convinced that you and Felicity would not suit."

"Mr. Kincaid was fortunate to fall in love quickly, you see," Felicity remarked. "Almost unbelievably so. I don't think he believes that two people may fall in love gradually."

"I apologize, Lucas," Oliver said, in an attempt to play the diplomat. "Isabelle and I thought you knew Felicity was coming to Ashingham with us. This is an unfortunate misunderstanding, but there's been no harm done, and there's no need to make too much of it."

"Most unfortunate," Kincaid agreed, looking at Felicity through narrowed eyes. "But now that the misunderstanding has been cleared up, we shall go home."

Felicity raised an eyebrow. "Do you mean to turn around without letting your horses rest?"

"I'm sure Oliver will lend us horses to return to London." Kincaid was itching for the chance to speak to Felicity without an audience.

"I'll certainly lend you horses if you're determined to leave today," Oliver agreed. "But won't you consider staying the night? Isabelle and I would enjoy showing you the estate."

"I haven't brought any clothes with me," Kincaid admitted sheepishly. In his haste to catch Felicity, he hadn't thought to pack a bag.

Oliver smiled. "We won't dress formally for dinner, and I can lend you what you need. I'm sure Isabelle can find spare clothes for Miss Flint."

"All right." Although he wasn't keen to stay at Ashingham, Kincaid was tired of driving, and even if they left immediately, they wouldn't reach London until after dark. With his luck, he would arrive home to find his betrothal party in full swing.

"I'll have the housekeeper prepare rooms for you and Miss Flint," Isabelle said.

"We'll leave first thing in the morning, Felicity," Kincaid told her.

"If you wish," Felicity said easily. "Did you come in the curricle?"

"Of course."

Felicity smiled at him before glancing at Miss Flint. "We will be a cozy party on the journey home."

Kincaid's face fell as he realized his curricle couldn't accommodate three passengers.

"Miss Taylor is welcome to stay at Ashingham and return with us," Oliver suggested. "We were only planning to stay two nights, but we could return tomorrow if it's more convenient."

"But I'm afraid our travelling coach only seats four," Isabelle said apologetically.

"I could ride," Oliver suggested.

"That won't be necessary," Kincaid said. "Miss Flint can return with me in the curricle."

"But it's so cold outside," Felicity pointed out, with a hint of criticism in her tone. "It's a long time for Miss Flint to be exposed to the elements, and she's already endured the journey here today."

"I brought Miss Flint to save what I could of your reputation!" Kincaid exclaimed. "You don't seem to appreciate how easily a young lady's reputation can be lost."

"But my reputation was never at risk," Felicity pointed out, with a little laugh. "I have been in Isabelle's company all day."

"You may ride in the curricle with me tomorrow, Felicity," Kincaid declared. "If you find the cold uncomfortable, it will be no more than you deserve."

Oliver and Isabelle exchanged a look. "I'm not sure that's a good idea, Lucas," Oliver said carefully.

"Surely you're not worried about the proprieties!" Kincaid retorted.

"It's not a question of propriety," Oliver said. "But if you quarrel with Miss Taylor, you might be distracted from the road. It might be safer for you to travel with Adrian."

"Safer for whom?" Kincaid asked, giving Adrian a look of acute dislike.

"Oliver and I will return to London tomorrow, and Miss Flint and Felicity can travel with us," Isabelle said quickly. "Now that we've settled that, why don't we give you a tour of the house?"

There were many beautiful things to see at Ashingham, but Kincaid wasn't in the mood to appreciate any of them. He was angry with Felicity for having orchestrated the deception, and with Adrian for having unwittingly participated in it. He knew it wasn't rational to blame Adrian, who had been a pawn in Felicity's scheme, but for some reason this annoyed him further. Mostly, he was angry at himself for leaping to the worst possible conclusion when he read Felicity's letter.

When it was time to dress for dinner, Oliver provided Kincaid with a set of evening clothes and the services of his valet. Since Oliver's valet was highly efficient, Kincaid was the first to come downstairs, but Felicity joined him several minutes later.

"Good evening, Mr. Kincaid," she said nonchalantly.

Although his temper had cooled, her carefree greeting made it flare again. "You know, Felicity, I'm tempted to lock you in your bedchamber until you come of age. After this little trick, I don't think anyone could fault me for it."

"There was no trick, Mr. Kincaid. Isabelle invited me to come to Ashingham with her, and I did."

Kincaid sighed. "You have your faults, Felicity, but stupidity isn't one of them. You knew exactly what I would think when I read your letter."

"You're right, Mr. Kincaid," she said quietly. "It was the result of a foolish impulse, but I know I made you anxious, and I'm very sorry."

She looked truly contrite, and Kincaid's anger faded. "I should still lock you in your room, you know."

"Are you considering doing so?" Felicity asked curiously.

Kincaid frowned. "I didn't expect you to look so happy about the idea."

"Well, it would give me a reason to complain about your behaviour as my guardian. I could argue that you should be dismissed as my trustee, and that I should be given access to my fortune."

"To whom would you complain?"

"Mr. Battersby."

Kincaid raised an eyebrow. "And you think Battersby could stay awake long enough to reply?"

"Probably not," Felicity admitted. "I suppose I would have to think of a way to escape from the bedchamber. I imagine you would send a footman to deliver food, since I might overpower a maid. Unless you plan to bring the food yourself?"

"Of course not."

Felicity smiled. "A footman, then. I would bribe him."

Kincaid shook his head. "I'm afraid you would be out of luck. I trust my servants."

"Really, Mr. Kincaid?" Felicity's dark eyes sparkled. "You're convinced your servants are incorruptible?"

"They know they will be dismissed if they don't follow my orders."

"You don't think I could charm one of your footmen?"

"My footmen will do what they're told," he said unconvincingly.

"Even if I explain the size of my fortune? And promise a large payment if they help me escape from you?"

Kincaid shook his head. "Even then."

Felicity tried a different tack. "I wonder what Miss Harris would think about your plan to keep me locked in a bedroom? Or your friends, if they learned of it? It sounds like something from a Gothic novel!"

"It has nothing to do with Miss Harris," Kincaid said dismissively.

"She might disagree. And if you were worried about gossip before, imagine what people would say if they learned you were holding me prisoner?"

"This argument is ridiculous," Kincaid declared, conveniently forgetting that he had started it. "Not to mention improper. If you spoke like this in company, Felicity, people would get the wrong idea."

"As I've explained, Mr. Kincaid, I don't speak like this in company. But since you're like a brother to me, I feel I can speak my mind with you."

For some reason, Kincaid found that remark the most irritating of all. "I'm not your brother, and you would do well to remember that."

"Yes, Mr. Kincaid," Felicity said meekly.

~

In the end, Kincaid made the journey back to London with Adrian as his passenger.

"Would you like me to drive?" Adrian offered, shortly after they had departed.

"No," Kincaid replied curtly.

"I understand you're about to get leg-shackled," Adrian said casually.

"Yes."

"What's her name?"

"Miss Jane Harris."

"I've never heard of her," Adrian remarked. "Is she beautiful?"

Kincaid was silent as he considered his reply, which gave Adrian his answer.

"Beauty isn't everything," Adrian said philosophically. "I mean, I do think it's important, but perhaps it's less important as you get older."

"I'm thirty-one!" Kincaid exclaimed. "I don't know why everyone speaks of me as though I'm ancient!"

"Well, you're not exactly ancient," Adrian said kindly. "But then, I never said you were. I only said you were older, and you can't deny that you're older than many people. You're older than I am, and older than Isabelle and Felicity—"

"And older than Miss Harris, and older than your nephew Julian," Kincaid added. "This will be a very tedious journey if you plan to share a list of everyone you know who is younger than me."

"I don't think the list is *that* long," Adrian said thoughtfully. "And the fact that you're older than Miss Harris may not be such a bad thing. I've noticed that many young ladies seem to enjoy being married to older men."

Kincaid fought to hide a grin. "You've noticed that, have you?"

Adrian nodded. "I expect it makes them feel secure. And a lot of ladies are upset by the thought of getting old, but since Miss Harris is younger than you, she'll always be young in a relative sense."

"I suppose she will."

"What does Felicity think of Miss Harris?"

"What do you mean?" Kincaid asked sharply.

Adrian looked surprised by his tone. "Oh, I don't know. It's just that you'd be in an awkward spot if they didn't get along."

"Felicity and Miss Harris are already good friends."

Adrian nodded. "That must be a relief for you."

Fourteen

The following day, Kincaid mustered his courage and went to call upon Jane. The Harrises' butler greeted him with a frown, leaving him in no doubt that the servants had heard about Kincaid's absence from his own betrothal party. He was shown to the drawing room, where he found Jane sitting with her mother and her sister Mary.

After bowing to Lady Harris, Kincaid addressed Jane. "Good morning, Miss Harris."

"Good morning, Mr. Kincaid," Jane replied crisply, before returning her attention to her needlework.

"I want to apologize for missing the betrothal party," Kincaid began. "I was called away to deal with an emergency—"

"Yes, you said as much in your note," Jane interrupted. "Did you catch them in time?"

"What?" Kincaid asked. He had hoped to avoid telling her of Felicity's prank, but it seemed she already knew of it. "What do you mean?"

"Miss Taylor and Mr. Stone," Jane continued coolly. "Were you able to catch them before she was compromised?"

Kincaid glanced uncomfortably around the room and noticed that Jane's mother and sister were listening to the conversation with great interest. "Lady Harris, I wonder if you would allow me a few minutes alone with your daughter?"

At first he thought Lady Harris was going to refuse, but after a moment's consideration she nodded and stood.

"I will be just outside the door, Mr. Kincaid," she told him. She motioned to Mary, who reluctantly followed her out of the room.

"Now, Miss Harris," Kincaid said. "I must ask you to explain what you meant."

"I understand that Felicity eloped with Mr. Adrian Stone," Jane said primly.

"Where did you hear that?"

"When I received your letter, I was worried that someone in your family had suffered an accident," Jane explained. "So I went to your house, and your butler told me you had rushed off to Lord Langley's."

"Go on," Kincaid said grimly.

"I went to the Langleys' house next, and asked to see Lady Langley."

"And what did you learn from her?"

"Lady Langley didn't want to tell me anything about it," Jane said. "She claimed she didn't know where you had gone, but I knew that was a lie."

Kincaid raised an eyebrow. "I see. How did you know that?"

"While I was waiting for Lady Langley in the drawing room, I came across Felicity's letter."

"You came across Felicity's letter?" Kincaid repeated. He realized that in his haste to chase after Felicity and Adrian, he had left the damning letter on a table in the Langleys' drawing room. "I suppose you make a habit of reading other people's correspondence?"

Jane had the grace to blush. "I didn't realize what it was until after I had read it. I knew Felicity's behaviour was unconventional, but such an elopement is unforgivable. I've never been more shocked in my life!"

"I can see why the letter would have been shocking, if you didn't understand it." Although Kincaid's tone was calm, there was a hardness to his eyes and a tightness about his mouth. "But contrary to what you assumed, Felicity did not elope with Adrian Stone. She travelled to the Marquess of Ashingham's estate, in the company of the marquess and marchioness."

Jane's expression of outraged dignity changed to a look of disbelief. "But why would Felicity leave you such a letter?" she asked. "The letter certainly implies that she ran off with Mr. Stone."

"Mr. Stone accompanied them to Ashingham," Kincaid explained. "But Felicity was in the company of the marchioness the entire time."

"Then Felicity deliberately misled you," Jane retorted. "She wrote that letter to trick you into thinking she was eloping."

Kincaid was tempted to tell Jane that he had known of Felicity's plans all along, but he realized that if he did, he wouldn't have an explanation for rushing to Ashingham. "The letter was carelessly written, and I know Felicity regrets having caused such a misunderstanding."

"I don't believe it," Jane said mulishly. "I think she wanted you to miss your betrothal party. What I can't understand is why, but I doubt I'll ever understand how Felicity thinks."

"That is unfair, Miss Harris," Kincaid said. "If Felicity's letter was confusing, it was merely because it was written in a rush."

"You're determined to make allowances for her!" Jane exclaimed. "Her behaviour has caused me a great deal of embarrassment. I had to sit through a betrothal party without my betrothed, and it was clear that everyone pitied me. I have never endured such an ordeal in my life!"

"How horrifying," Kincaid remarked dryly.

His sarcasm only served to inflame Jane further. "People asked where you were, of course. I told them you were unwell, but I'm afraid many of them didn't believe it."

Kincaid was relieved to learn that she hadn't spread gossip about Felicity. "That was wise, Jane," he said gratefully. "If anyone asks, I'll tell them I was suffering from influenza. Now that we've cleared that up, should we ask your mother and sister to return?"

Jane stared at him. "But what about Felicity?"

"I will ensure that Felicity apologizes to you," Kincaid said. "She should never have written such a careless letter."

"I don't believe it was careless," Jane insisted. "I'm sorry, Mr. Kincaid, but I can't possibly chaperone Felicity.

Her behaviour is unmanageable, and I've never heard such vulgar speech as I did when I was introduced to her! I hoped I could influence her, but this episode has convinced me that she is beyond redemption."

"Felicity lost her parents when she was young," Kincaid began.

"I thought you became her guardian when she was fourteen," Jane said with a frown. "That doesn't seem so very young."

Kincaid was silent for a moment, remembering how fragile Felicity had looked at the reading of her parents' will. "It does to me," he finally said quietly.

"I understand it must have been difficult for Felicity to lose her parents," Jane conceded. "But people will still expect her to behave a certain way. When she enters society, she will make herself an object of ridicule, and all of her connections will be tainted by association!"

Kincaid pressed his lips together tightly. "I see," he said curtly. "Since I am one of her tainted connections, may I ask if you still want to marry me?"

Jane's eyes widened. "Of course I still want to marry you, Mr. Kincaid," she said quickly. "I hold you in very high regard. But I won't be able to chaperone Felicity. I'm afraid she dislikes me, and I wonder if she would be more comfortable living with one of her relatives? I understand she has a cousin, Lady Delphinia Nethercott, and perhaps—"

"No," Kincaid said. "I am Felicity's guardian, and her home is with me."

"But you must admit that it's unusual for Felicity to live in your house while you live down the street. You don't think she would be happier living with family?"

"No," Kincaid repeated, and the look in his eyes told Jane not to push the matter.

"I see," Jane said stiffly. "Then I think we would be wise to delay our marriage by several months. Since I will no longer be chaperoning Felicity, there is no need to rush."

"Certainly," Kincaid agreed, a little too quickly. "When would you like to be married?"

"Would June be convenient?" Jane hoped that by then, Felicity would have married and left his house.

"Perfectly convenient," Kincaid said agreeably. "Let me know if you need me to help with the planning." He rose to leave and was almost at the door when he remembered something. "Do you know the current whereabouts of the letter you found at the Langleys'?"

Jane's cheeks heated, and Kincaid could tell she was wrestling with her conscience. "It's in my bedchamber," she finally admitted.

"I have no doubt that you took it so you could restore it to me," Kincaid said smoothly. "I'll take it from you now."

Jane left the room without meeting his eye, and returned a few moments later with the letter. She handed it to Kincaid with a look that told him she was disappointed in him, and although he was more successful in hiding his feelings, he was equally disappointed in her.

After Kincaid left Jane, he walked to 23 Bentley, where he found Felicity and Miss Flint drinking tea in the drawing room.

"Good afternoon, Miss Flint," he said politely. "I wonder if you would give me a moment alone with Felicity?"

"Certainly," Miss Flint replied, rising to leave.

Kincaid took the seat opposite Felicity and considered how to begin. "I went to see Jane this morning," he finally said.

Felicity tried to hide her curiosity. "I hope she wasn't upset that you missed your betrothal party," she said lightly.

"She was disappointed," Kincaid admitted. "The party was important to her, Felicity. She put a lot of effort into planning it."

Felicity chewed her lip. "What did you tell her?"

"I didn't have to tell her anything," Kincaid said. "She found the letter that you were kind enough to leave for me. I forgot it at the Langleys'. And yes, I know it was careless to leave it lying about."

"Jane is a resourceful young lady."

"She is," he agreed with a nod. "We've decided to delay our wedding until June."

"Until June," Felicity said thoughtfully. "Does Jane mean to punish you for missing the party?"

"Of course not," Kincaid replied. "She simply wants more time to plan the wedding."

"June is a lovely month for a wedding," Felicity remarked. "And you can have a larger ceremony, since you will have so much time to plan."

"Perhaps," Kincaid agreed. "I am leaving those details to Jane." He studied her carefully. "I'm afraid this means Jane won't be able to act as your chaperone this Season.

She doesn't think it would be appropriate for her to do so before we're married."

"That may be for the best," Felicity said quickly.

Kincaid nodded. "So we will need to find you a different chaperone. I could talk to Langley, see if he could ask his mother—"

"I think I would rather ask Miss Flint," Felicity said with a smile. "Her new evening gowns have arrived, and she told me she was looking forward to my debut ball. I think she might actually enjoy it."

"All right." Kincaid still had reservations about Miss Flint's suitability as a chaperone, but he realized that Jane's attempts to influence Felicity had provoked a rebellion. Felicity seemed to care about Miss Flint, and she might try to control her behaviour to avoid embarrassing her.

"I intend to behave, Mr. Kincaid," Felicity said, as though she had read his thoughts.

Kincaid chuckled. "I'm pleased to hear it. Are you excited for your debut ball?"

"Of course," Felicity said with a grin. "And I'm looking forward to coming of age. Don't forget, you agreed to increase my allowance when I turn twenty-one."

"I haven't forgotten."

"I suppose I'll need to find something to do with the money," Felicity mused.

"I'm sure you'll find a way to spend it."

"Oh, I'm sure I could," Felicity agreed. "But I thought the responsible thing to do would be to try to increase it."

Kincaid eyed her warily. "How would you do that?"

"Well, I have a good eye for horses, so I'm thinking of trying my luck at Newmarket." She paused and furrowed her brow. "But I don't know if women are allowed to place bets, or if I would have to employ a man to do so on my behalf."

Kincaid looked truly alarmed. "Felicity, I don't think that's a good idea," he told her. "Although I agree that you're a good judge of horses, the races are notoriously unpredictable . . ."

He trailed off when he saw the gleam of mischief in her eyes.

"Relax, Mr. Kincaid," Felicity said. "I'm not actually planning to bet on horse racing."

"I don't know why you insist on turning everything into a jest," he grumbled.

"I think it's because you're so quick to believe I'm irresponsible," she replied. "It's almost too easy."

Kincaid sighed. "What do you seriously mean to do with the money?"

"I thought I would leave it where it is."

"What do you mean?"

"I went to see Mr. Battersby the other day," Felicity explained. "And I persuaded him to tell me the amount of my fortune. It seems the money has more than doubled in value since you took over the management seven years ago."

"It has," Kincaid confirmed.

"It took me a while to figure out the arithmetic," she told him. "None of my governesses thought to teach me how to calculate compound interest, but I suppose I shouldn't blame them, since I never showed an interest in mathematics. But at a rough estimate, it seems you've achieved an average return of close to ten percent per year."

"Ten and a half," Kincaid admitted.

It had taken Felicity over an hour with a mathematics textbook to reach this conclusion, and she was gratified to hear that her calculation was close. "And that's assuming you haven't withdrawn any money for expenses, such as my horses or my allowance," she said, watching him carefully. "So either the actual rate of return was higher than that, or you haven't been using my money to pay my expenses."

Kincaid didn't comment, and Felicity knew better than to press the question.

"So I thought you must have some talent for investing, and I would do well to leave the money where it is," she continued. "I've done some reading about how the Stock Exchange works, and—"

"You've what?" he interrupted, looking at her skeptically.

"I've been reading, Mr. Kincaid," she said, a little defensively. "About the Stock Exchange. Mr. Battersby explained that a lot of my money is invested in stocks, and I wanted to understand how it works."

"What have you been reading?"

"I found some books in your library," she explained. "There's no need to look alarmed, I took very good care of them."

"I'm not alarmed, just surprised," Kincaid admitted. "I had no idea you were interested in your investments. If I had known, I would have tried to explain things to you sooner."

"I suppose I should have asked you," Felicity acknowledged. "My father used to talk to me about the investments he was making, and I always found it interesting. And now that you've agreed to increase my allowance, I expect to have money left over at the end of each quarter, and I thought I should invest it. I'll need you or Mr. Battersby to help with the logistics, and I was hoping I could ask for your advice occasionally."

Kincaid stared at her in disbelief. "You want my advice?"

Felicity shrugged. "If you have time, I would appreciate it. You seem to have achieved a good rate of return." She grinned mischievously. "Of course, I think I could have done better, especially if I had the benefit of a competent governess. Unfortunately, my guardian was a singularly poor judge of governesses—"

"Oh, no," Kincaid interrupted with a chuckle. "I doubt there's a governess in England who teaches her pupils about the stock market, or about compound interest. You can't blame your lack of knowledge on my inability to choose a governess."

"Maybe not," Felicity agreed thoughtfully.

"But I see I should have taught you myself," Kincaid said, looking at Felicity with new respect. "I still can, you know. We could start tomorrow afternoon."

Felicity was about to agree when she remembered that she shouldn't come to depend on Mr. Kincaid. After all, he was engaged to another lady, and she doubted he would have time to spend discussing Felicity's investments after he married Jane. She needed to learn to rely on herself, and surely she could learn what she needed from the books in his library.

"I'm afraid I'm busy tomorrow," she told him. "The gown for my debut ball is almost finished, and I need to visit Madame Sylvie for the final fitting."

"Of course," Kincaid said. "Another time, then." Felicity waited for a sarcastic remark about the critical importance of her visit to the modiste, but none came.

"I was hoping to wear my mother's pearls to the ball."

Kincaid nodded. "I'll visit the bank tomorrow. Would you like any of the other pieces?" The jewellery collection that Felicity had inherited from her mother was kept in a safety deposit box at the bank.

"No, thank you. Just the pearls." As a little girl, Felicity had frequently watched her mother dress for parties, and she knew the pearl necklace had been her mother's favourite. "I can hardly believe it's finally happening," she confessed. "I feel like I've waited years for this."

Kincaid chuckled. "Because you have, Felicity." She had been seventeen when she had first declared her intention to wait until she was twenty-one to make her debut. Every year he had expected her to change her mind and request to have a Season, but Felicity had been resolute. He still didn't understand why she had chosen to wait, since he had assured her that he wouldn't withhold his consent to a reasonable match, but he was grateful she had.

"Do you think I was foolish to wait?" Felicity asked, and Kincaid was surprised by the uncertainty in her eyes. He suspected it was the closest she would come to admitting she was nervous about her debut.

"Of course not," he said gently. "I think you were wise. Now that you're older, you're more likely to know what you want in a husband."

"I suppose."

Since she didn't look convinced, Kincaid tried a

different approach. "But I'm biased, of course," he said in a teasing tone.

"What do you mean?"

"Well, now that you no longer need my consent to marry, I won't feel responsible if you end up tied to a wastrel."

It was the truth, but as he had hoped, it made her laugh.

Fifteen

Kincaid only suspected that Felicity was nervous about her debut ball, but he knew that he was. He wasn't afraid that she would lack for dancing partners; Langley and Oliver had promised to dance with her, and after all, she was an heiress. But he hoped she wouldn't cause a scandal by sharing her frank opinions too freely, or lose her heart to a gentleman who was unworthy of it.

In the spirit of reconciliation, Jane had offered to help Felicity dress for the ball, but Felicity had politely declined her assistance. Despite this, Jane had declared that she wished to lend Felicity her support by travelling with her to the ball. If Kincaid found this surprising, in view of Jane's previous fear of being tainted by association, he didn't remark upon it.

On the evening of the ball, Kincaid had the added concern that they would be late. When it was time to leave to pick up Jane, Felicity still hadn't appeared, and he paced the hall impatiently. "Perhaps you should go up and try to hurry her along," he grumbled to Miss Flint.

"If you wish, Mr. Kincaid."

But as Kincaid watched Miss Flint move towards the stairs, he realized she was unlikely to succeed in hurrying Felicity. "On second thought, Miss Flint, I'll go pick up Jane and bring her back here. We are closer to the Langleys' than she is, so it should save us some time."

"All right," Miss Flint said agreeably.

When Kincaid returned with Jane, Miss Flint was still waiting patiently in the entrance hall, but there was no sign of Felicity.

"Would you like me to go up to see if I can help?" Jane offered.

Kincaid nodded. "Thank you, Jane."

But before Jane could reach the bottom of the staircase, Felicity appeared at the top of it, wearing her red satin dress. The bodice fit like a glove, showcasing her slender figure, and the elegant skirt swished pleasingly around her dancing slippers as she descended the stairs. Her dark hair had been arranged in an elegant knot, with a few curls left to brush against her shoulders, and her only jewellery was the pearl necklace she had inherited from her mother.

Both Kincaid and Jane stared at her in disbelief, and it was Miss Flint who finally broke the silence. "That's a very nice dress," she remarked.

"Thank you, Miss Flint," Felicity said cheerfully. "I was thinking the same about yours." Miss Flint's gown of navy-blue crepe flattered her complexion and fit her to perfection.

Kincaid finally found his voice. "Felicity, you can't wear that!" he exclaimed.

"You don't like it?"

"Like it?" he exclaimed. "Felicity, it's indecent!"

Felicity frowned. "What's indecent about it?"

Kincaid studied the dress carefully and tried to formulate an objection. Had the neckline been cut an inch lower he might have complained, but as it was, he could hardly argue it was improper. And he supposed it wasn't unusual for a lady's upper arms to be bare, as Felicity's were between her cap sleeves and white kidskin gloves. If he had seen the dress on a dashing young matron, he might not have thought much about it, but on Felicity it was different.

The real problem was that it was a dress for a lady, not a young girl, and Kincaid stared at Felicity as though seeing her for the first time.

"It's very red," he finally stammered.

Felicity smiled. "Yes, poppy red. Don't you like the colour?"

"But when we were at Madame Sylvie's, we discussed the ivory crepe!" Jane blurted. "I've never seen that colour."

"No?" Felicity asked innocently. "Madame Sylvie says poppy red is all the rage in Paris this season."

"I have seen the colour," Jane said tartly. "But never on a debutante. And I thought you agreed with me when I suggested the ivory crepe."

"Well, I agreed to think about it," Felicity said. "But I decided ivory wouldn't suit my complexion."

"Take it off," Kincaid said curtly.

"Well, I am wearing a chemise and petticoat underneath it," Felicity said thoughtfully. "But if you think the dress is indecent, I think the undergarments alone would be much worse."

Kincaid's face had turned almost as red as Felicity's dress. "I meant go upstairs and change into a different dress," he bit out.

"What about the dress is inappropriate?" Felicity asked.

Kincaid cast his eyes down the dress, then quickly averted his gaze. The truth was that Felicity looked entirely too desirable, but he could hardly tell her that. He had spent months training his mind to ignore her physical charms, but the sight of Felicity in that dress still stole his breath. He could only imagine what it would do to other gentlemen.

"You don't look like a debutante," he finally told her. "Young ladies are supposed to wear soft colours, and a red dress will attract a great deal of attention."

"But I'm not trying to avoid attention," Felicity countered. "Lady Langley is giving the ball in my honour."

"I'm not suggesting you try to avoid attention," Kincaid replied. "But it's traditional for young ladies to wear white, and society can be cruel to ladies who don't follow tradition."

"There are rules to these sorts of events, my dear," Jane put in. "A dress like yours suggests that either you don't know the convention, or you are trying to flout it. Gentlemen will be turned off by such behaviour."

"But I like the red," Felicity said. "And I don't see why the colour would offend anyone. Really, a gentleman who is offended by the sight of a red dress is not a man I would like to marry. I could understand why a man would protest if I wore a red dress with pink ribbons, but to object simply to the red—it doesn't seem rational."

"It's not conventional," Jane repeated.

"Perhaps not," Felicity acknowledged. "But I'm not always conventional myself. I suppose I could wear a white dress and pretend to be a demure young miss, and I might fool a gentleman into making me an offer of marriage. But can you imagine what would happen after the wedding?"

Jane's brow furrowed. "What do you mean?"

"I wouldn't be able to hide my true character for long, and my poor husband might feel as though he had been deceived," Felicity said with a shrug. "He would be right."

"But surely, if you made an effort, you could . . ." Jane paused to consider how to best phrase her words.

"Continue the deception?" Felicity asked. "I suppose I could, but I think it would make me miserable. So I won't try to sell a man a fantasy."

Jane pursed her lips. "Felicity, you shouldn't speak of selling yourself at all."

"You're right," Felicity agreed seriously. "I hope to find a man who appreciates me for who I am. And the truth is that I'm not entirely conventional, and I like the colour red."

"So you are determined to wear that dress?" Kincaid asked.

Felicity nodded. "I am."

Kincaid gave a nod of resignation. "All right. The carriage is waiting for us."

Before they made it out the door, Kincaid stopped and took a small velvet box from his pocket. "I almost forgot," he said, handing it to Felicity. "Your birthday gift."

Felicity opened the box and found a delicate gold brooch in the shape of a horseshoe. "It's beautiful," she breathed.

"It made me think of you," Kincaid explained. "You don't have to wear it tonight," he said quickly, since Felicity was already working to pin the brooch over her left shoulder. "You might not want to put holes in your dress."

"I can't think of a better reason to put holes in the dress," Felicity said with a laugh. She finished securing the brooch, then impulsively rose on her toes and kissed Kincaid's cheek. "It will bring me luck tonight. Thank you, Mr. Kincaid."

Jane stepped closer to Felicity to examine the brooch. "It's very pretty," she remarked.

Kincaid realized he should have brought jewellery for Jane as well as for Felicity, and vowed to buy something for Jane before he saw her next.

When their carriage drew up in front of the Langleys' townhouse, Kincaid assisted Miss Flint and Jane to descend before giving Felicity his arm.

"Jane's gown suits her very well, don't you think?" Felicity remarked as they made their way to the door.

Mr. Kincaid glanced at his betrothed, who was walking a short distance ahead of them with Miss Flint. The torches lining the path didn't give nearly enough light to see Jane well, but there was only one possible answer to Felicity's question. "Yes, it does."

"I imagine she will have many admirers tonight."

Kincaid gave her a strange look. "Have you forgotten that Jane is betrothed to me?"

"I could never forget that, Mr. Kincaid," Felicity replied blandly.

At first, Felicity was intimidated by the crush of elegantly dressed people who filled the Langleys' townhouse. The Langleys' warm greeting helped set her at ease, and she relaxed further when Lord Langley led her out for the first dance. Felicity had always liked to dance, and there was something comfortable about dancing with a man who had absolutely no interest in marrying her. She never lacked a partner in the dances that followed, and she was forced to disappoint several gentlemen who hadn't spoken quickly enough to secure places on her dance card.

Partway through the evening, Kincaid watched Felicity dance with Lord Illingham, a serious young man who had recently inherited a viscountcy.

"Miss Taylor is looking well tonight," Langley remarked.

Kincaid had been so absorbed in watching Felicity that he hadn't realized Langley had joined him. "Yes," he said thoughtfully. "Although I was concerned that her dress was a little too . . ." He let his sentence trail off, hoping Langley would understand his meaning. To his irritation, his friend just looked at him expectantly.

"Too what, Lucas?" Langley finally said.

"Too daring?" Kincaid tried. "And it's very *red*."

"I'm hardly an expert on ladies' fashions," Langley remarked. "But I think Miss Taylor looks very attractive."

Kincaid thought Langley had summarized the problem very well. "Yes, I suppose she does."

"And Amelia was very pleased with the gown Miss Taylor sent her," Langley continued.

"Felicity gave Amelia a gown?"

Langley nodded. "I'm surprised she didn't tell you. It was delivered yesterday, with a card to thank Amelia for hosting the ball. Amelia's wearing it tonight."

Kincaid scanned the room until he spotted Amelia, who was wearing an elegant green gown that complemented her red hair. "One of Madame Sylvie's creations, I suppose?"

Langley nodded. "Miss Taylor has excellent taste."

"She certainly spends enough time at the modiste," Kincaid said dryly.

Adrian Stone joined them, sipping a glass of wine. "It doesn't seem right," he remarked. "Miss Taylor's wearing a dress made for sin, but she's only dancing with prosy bores."

"Adrian!" Kincaid exclaimed.

Adrian looked at him in surprise. "I don't mean to insult her partners, but it's true. She's with Illingham now, and he'd be more at home in a library than a ballroom. And before that there was Alversleigh, and—"

"I think Lucas was objecting to your description of Felicity's dress, not of her dance partners," Langley explained to his brother.

Adrian looked at Kincaid, who was glowering at him. "Oh," he said. "I meant it as a compliment, you know. It's the most beautiful dress in the room."

"I don't disagree, but it's not the sort of compliment a young lady's guardian will appreciate," Langley said.

"But Lucas isn't Miss Taylor's guardian anymore," Adrian pointed out. "Not now that she's turned twenty-one."

"It's not the sort of compliment any gentleman should appreciate," Kincaid said through gritted teeth.

"Perhaps not," Adrian said with a laugh. "Although Illingham certainly looks as though he appreciates the dress."

Adrian was correct, and as he spoke, Lord Illingham was telling Felicity exactly how much he admired her gown.

"Thank you, Lord Illingham," Felicity murmured. "Miss Harris was kind enough to advise me on the colour."

"Miss Harris?" Illingham repeated, as though trying to place the name.

"The young lady in blue, dancing with the Earl of Salford."

Illingham glanced briefly at Jane before returning his gaze to Felicity. "Isn't she the one who's betrothed to Mr. Kincaid?"

"Yes," Felicity murmured. "But I'm afraid there may be some trouble there."

"Oh?" Illingham asked.

Felicity nodded sadly. "They were to be married last week, but Miss Harris requested to delay the wedding until June," she confided. "Between you and me, I think there's a chance she'll cry off."

Lord Illingham looked surprised. "Why would she do that?"

Felicity sighed and chewed her lower lip, as though debating how much to tell him. "Miss Harris is very intellectual," she confessed in a whisper. "I think she's concerned Mr. Kincaid doesn't share her love of books and languages."

Illingham frowned. "I always thought Kincaid was quite an intelligent man."

"Oh, he is," Felicity said quickly. "But as you know, Lord Illingham, there is a great deal of difference between being intelligent and being an intellectual."

"You are wise to see the distinction," Illingham said, nodding sagely.

Felicity laughed modestly. "Oh, I'm merely repeating something I heard Miss Harris say," she lied. "I'm afraid I'm neither intelligent nor an intellectual."

To her dismay, Illingham seemed to consider a lack of intelligence a strength rather than a flaw. "You have more important qualities, Miss Taylor," he told her. "You are looking lovely tonight."

"You're very kind, Lord Illingham," Felicity murmured.

"I wonder if you would consider dancing with me again this evening?" he asked hopefully.

"I'm afraid my dance card is full."

Sixteen

Felicity danced the next set with the Marquess of Willingdon, who was soberly dressed in a dark grey waistcoat and black pantaloons.

"I wanted to thank you again, Miss Taylor, for what you did for my son," the marquess said solemnly. "When I think of what might have happened if you hadn't been near the Serpentine—"

"It's probably best not to think of it," Felicity said quickly. "How is Ernest doing? Have you engaged a new nurse?"

"I have," Willingdon told her. "My housekeeper conducted the interviews, and she has engaged a very suitable young lady."

"And does Ernest like her?"

Willingdon looked surprised by the question. "I assume so. He won't need a nurse for much longer, of course. He's almost old enough for a tutor."

"Surely not," Felicity argued. "How old is Ernest?"

"He will be five next month, so he will soon be ready for a more serious course of study."

"I think Ernest will need a woman's influence for a few years yet," Felicity said. "It can't be good for young children to study all day."

"I believe education is of paramount importance for young minds," Willingdon said with a frown.

"Well, yes," Felicity agreed. "But perhaps not for minds as young as five."

Willingdon's frown deepened, and it was clear he hadn't expected her to debate the point. "I have a strong interest in education, Miss Taylor," he told her. "At present, I am working on a new method of Latin instruction that I hope will be adopted at Eton."

"That sounds fascinating," Felicity murmured politely.

"Do you read Latin, Miss Taylor?"

"Very little, I'm afraid," Felicity confessed. "But I believe Miss Harris does. Don't you think she looks lovely in blue?"

"Yes, indeed," Willingdon replied, although he barely spared a glance for Miss Harris, who was dancing past with Mr. Kincaid.

Felicity refused to be discouraged. "Miss Harris was telling me how much she enjoyed meeting Ernest," she said cheerfully. "Did you know she is the eldest of five sisters? I suppose that's why she has such a way with children."

Willingdon merely nodded, and since they were separated by the pattern of the dance, Felicity had little opportunity to expound upon the theme.

The next dance was a waltz, which Felicity had purposefully kept free to give herself a chance to rest. Willingdon led her back to Miss Flint, who was sitting to the side with the other chaperones, and she was soon joined by her friend Isabelle.

"It seems you've made a conquest of Lord Willingdon," Isabelle remarked. "Apparently, this is the first ball he's attended since he lost his wife."

"I wasn't trying to conquer him," Felicity grumbled.

"Well, he must think highly of you, since you rescued his son from the Serpentine."

Felicity shrugged. "It wasn't as dramatic as it sounds. I really think . . ." she trailed off as her attention was caught by a couple at the other end of the ballroom. "I don't know how you tolerate it, Isabelle," she finished.

Isabelle's brow furrowed. "What do you mean?"

Felicity gestured across the room, where Isabelle's husband Oliver was dancing with a pretty blonde. "Watching your husband waltz with another lady. I think I could tolerate a country dance, or a cotillion, but there's something very intimate about the waltz."

"Don't you recognize his partner?" Isabelle asked.

Felicity squinted across the room at Oliver and his partner. "No."

"That's Letitia Hunt," Isabelle told her. "She's a friend of mine. You met her last summer, when we were all at the Langleys' estate?"

"Oh, yes," Felicity said. She vaguely remembered Letitia, a shy girl who had been bullied by her overbearing mother.

"Letitia looks different, doesn't she?" Isabelle

remarked. "She's much happier now that she no longer lives with her mother."

Felicity didn't reply immediately, as she was distracted by the sight of Mr. Kincaid and Jane dancing past them. She had been making a conscious effort not to stare at them, but she realized they were unlikely to catch her looking; Kincaid and Jane seemed to be absorbed in each other.

Felicity turned resolutely back to Isabelle. "Where does Letitia live now?"

"With her grandmother, in Tunbridge Wells," Isabelle explained. "But her grandmother has been ill, so they came to London to consult her physician. Letitia's terribly shy, so I asked Oliver to dance with her."

"So you have no one to blame but yourself," Felicity teased. "When I'm married, I won't want my husband to waltz with anyone but me."

Felicity hadn't expected Martin Nethercott to ask her to dance, and when he did, she couldn't think of a reason to refuse. She had never liked Nethercott much, but she was fair enough to admit that she wasn't an impartial judge. After all, for the past seven years he had stood to inherit her fortune if she married without Kincaid's approval, and such a circumstance was hardly conducive to friendship.

As the dance progressed, Felicity was also forced to admit that Mr. Nethercott was an excellent dancer, and he was certainly exerting himself to be charming.

"That's a beautiful necklace, Miss Taylor," he remarked.

"Thank you. It was my mother's."

"I know. I remember her wearing it."

Felicity raised her eyebrows in surprise. "You do? I didn't think you knew my mother very well."

"I suspect I knew her better than you think," Nethercott replied with a smile. "I admired your mother greatly."

"I didn't know."

"I admire you too, Miss Taylor," he said smoothly. "You were dealt a difficult hand, and you handled it with grace."

"Do you think so?" Felicity asked thoughtfully. "I know I've been quite a trial to Mr. Kincaid."

"I'm afraid, Felicity, that I don't have much sympathy for Mr. Kincaid. If he found his role as your guardian difficult, I'm sure it was his fault rather than yours."

If Nethercott had expected Felicity to be gratified by his criticism of Kincaid, he was disappointed. "I doubt you know enough about it to comment," she said coolly.

"Perhaps not," he said easily. "I'm sure he did his best."

"You must be disappointed that I didn't marry in defiance of Mr. Kincaid's wishes."

"Of course not," Nethercott said quickly. "Your parents wanted your money to go to you. I have no claim on it."

Felicity raised an eyebrow. "You never hoped that I would fall in love with someone entirely ineligible?"

"No," Nethercott insisted with a laugh.

"Then you're a better man than most," Felicity said lightly.

"You have a low opinion of men, Miss Taylor."

"I learned it from Mr. Kincaid," she said with a chuckle.

Nethercott's expression darkened. "What do you mean? I must say, Miss Taylor, I never thought Kincaid was fit to be your guardian, and if he did anything—"

"Oh, no," Felicity insisted, realizing how her statement could be misinterpreted. "Mr. Kincaid has always behaved like a gentleman. He merely encouraged me to be suspicious of men."

"I see," Nethercott said thoughtfully. "I suppose that's good advice, especially with your fortune."

"It's the curse of being an heiress, you know," Felicity said playfully. "I will never know if a gentleman is interested in me or my fortune."

Nethercott looked at her earnestly. "Miss Taylor, I hope Kincaid's advice hasn't given you a mistrust of all men. I know of at least one man here tonight who is wishing you didn't have a fortune."

"That seems rather cruel," Felicity said with a laugh. "Why would he wish such a thing?"

"So he could court you without being accused of being a fortune hunter."

"Well, he sounds very foolish," Felicity said bluntly. "I think I could be happy without the fortune, but I'm certainly not going to wish it away. It will make life more comfortable, and I wouldn't want to give it up simply to save my husband's pride."

"I see." Nethercott wasn't quite sure what to make of that speech, but he decided to try his luck. "I wonder,

Miss Taylor, if you would dance with me again later this evening?"

"We may be cousins, Mr. Nethercott," Felicity said. "But our relationship isn't so close that I can dance with you twice at one ball without giving rise to gossip. People would say we had an attachment, or even an engagement."

Nethercott met her eye. "And would that be such a bad thing?" he asked steadily. "I've always admired you, you know."

Felicity was so astonished that she could barely follow the pattern of the dance. She had never thought of her cousin as a potential suitor, but when she cast her mind back over their conversation, she realized he was working up to a proposal. She racked her brain for the words to let him down gently, but her stricken expression was answer enough.

"It was presumptuous of me to suggest it," Nethercott said lightly.

"N-not presumptuous," Felicity stammered. "It's just that—I have always known you as my cousin, and I can't imagine thinking of you any other way."

"I see," Nethercott said thoughtfully. "And do you think there is any chance your feelings will change?"

Felicity shook her head apologetically. "I'm afraid not."

"Then let's forget I ever spoke of this," Nethercott said easily. "I value your friendship, Miss Taylor, and I would hate to think that I've caused awkwardness between us."

"Oh, you haven't," Felicity lied.

"Then perhaps you would accompany me to the

opera on Friday?" he asked. "Liliane Leroux is singing, and she has the most beautiful voice I've ever heard."

Despite her insistence that there would be no awkwardness, Felicity hesitated, and Nethercott hastened to reassure her. "My mother will come too, of course. I intend to rent a box, and perhaps you would like to bring Miss Flint?"

Under those circumstances, Felicity didn't see how she could refuse. "I would be delighted."

The dance ended, and Nethercott led her back to Miss Flint.

"Miss Flint," Felicity said brightly. "Mr. Nethercott has invited us to join him and Lady Delphinia at the opera on Friday. Liliane Leroux is performing, and he is planning to rent a box. You will come, won't you?"

"Yes," Miss Flint agreed.

Felicity hadn't noticed that Kincaid was behind her until he spoke. "I was thinking of going to the opera myself," he said thoughtfully. "Perhaps I'll invite Miss Harris, and we could all go together."

For a second, Nethercott's face took on an ugly look, but he quickly schooled his features into a more pleasant expression. "I'm afraid there won't be space for everyone in the box," he said apologetically.

Kincaid looked at him in surprise. "You must be planning to rent an unusually small box," he remarked. "But it's no matter. My brother lets me use his box while he's in the country, and it will easily accommodate our party."

Nethercott gave in with grace. "That's very generous, Kincaid. Thank you."

A gentleman approached to claim Felicity for the next

dance, and Kincaid and Nethercott were left standing together at the edge of the ballroom.

"One would almost think you were jealous," Nethercott said casually.

"Well, certainly," Kincaid agreed. He smiled pleasantly at Nethercott. "I would hate to think of you enjoying the opera without me."

Kincaid had asked Felicity to save him a dance, and he claimed her for a waltz late in the evening. She moved lightly in his arms, and he couldn't help thinking that dancing with Felicity was much easier than dancing with Jane. He often felt as though Jane was half a step behind him, and he had to exaggerate his cues to ensure she could follow his lead. But dancing with Felicity required hardly any effort, as she seemed to anticipate his movements.

"You look very serious, Mr. Kincaid," Felicity teased. "Is there something on your mind?"

He met her eye. "I was thinking you dance remarkably well."

Felicity's dark eyes twinkled. "I'm sorry, Mr. Kincaid, I must ask you to repeat yourself. I'm afraid I misheard."

"You dance well, Felicity," Kincaid repeated with a grin. "Anyone listening to you play the pianoforte would think you had no appreciation for rhythm, but your dancing suggests otherwise."

"I suppose that's more like you."

"You know you dance well, Felicity," Kincaid said. "You don't need me to point it out to you."

"Do you usually save your compliments for people who aren't aware of their strengths?"

"Not generally, no."

"I'm pleased to hear it," Felicity replied. "Just because a lady knows she does something well doesn't mean she won't appreciate a compliment."

"Do you really think I criticize you so much?" he asked, looking at her with concern. "If I do, it's only because I care about you."

"I see," Felicity said lightly. The conversation was straying into dangerous territory, and if she wasn't careful, she might fool herself into thinking he cared for her the way she had always hoped he would. She reminded herself that he was speaking as her former guardian, and that he was betrothed to another lady.

She glanced around the ballroom until she spotted Jane. "Look, Mr. Kincaid, Jane is dancing with Adrian Stone."

Kincaid followed her gaze and saw Jane and Adrian waltzing together. "Just so long as you don't dance with him," he told Felicity. "He seemed to like the idea of marriage to you a little too much."

Felicity laughed. "I'll never forget the look on your face when Adrian said that marrying me seemed like a splendid notion."

"I'm pleased you found it so entertaining," Kincaid said dryly. "Have you enjoyed yourself tonight?"

"Very much."

"And have any gentlemen caught your eye?"

"If they had, I'm not sure I would tell you about them," Felicity replied with a laugh. "That's the sort of thing a lady might discuss with her friends, but not with another man."

"Are we not friends, Felicity?" Kincaid asked with a frown.

Felicity laughed. "I suppose I should have said I might discuss it with other ladies."

"But you can ask me, you know, if you want my opinion on any of your suitors. I may know things about a man that ladies wouldn't."

"I'll keep that in mind, Mr. Kincaid," Felicity said lightly. "If I want your advice, I will be sure to ask for it."

Seventeen

When Kincaid arrived at 23 Bentley on the evening of the opera party, he was afraid he would find Felicity in another daring gown, and he was relieved when she appeared in a demure pink silk dress.

"You look very nice, Felicity," he said appreciatively. She looked so pleased by the tepid compliment that he was tempted to elaborate on it, so he turned to Miss Flint before he could say something foolish. "You look very nice too, Miss Flint."

Miss Flint looked almost as gratified as Felicity had. "You look very nice yourself, Mr. Kincaid," she returned.

"We are a nice-looking party," Felicity agreed, and Kincaid's lips twitched as he led the ladies out to the carriage.

They stopped to pick up Jane, who was keen to discuss Felicity's ball.

"Was it everything you expected, Felicity?" Jane asked.

"Oh, yes," Felicity assured her. "I met so many interesting people, and everyone was very kind."

"You dance very well," Jane said politely.

"Thank you. I enjoyed seeing Lord Willingdon again," Felicity said casually.

"Oh, I danced with Lord Willingdon too," Jane said earnestly. "He seems like such a sensible man."

"Yes, he does."

"He told me that was the first ball he attended since his wife died," Jane continued. "He clearly loved her very much."

"Oh, certainly," Felicity agreed. "But I think he's wise to re-enter society. Poor Ernest needs a mother, so it's time for Lord Willingdon to think about finding a wife."

"Are you interested in Lord Willingdon, Felicity?" Jane asked curiously.

"Oh, I wasn't thinking of myself," Felicity said modestly. "Lord Willingdon is clearly a very intelligent man, and he needs a wife who will be his intellectual equal."

"Surely not his equal," Jane said with a frown.

"Well, perhaps not," Felicity said. "But someone who can discuss the classics and assist him with his educational projects. I'm afraid I'm not a scholar."

"Few women are," Jane said kindly.

Felicity was irritated by Jane's disparagement of their sex, but she fought to hide her feelings. "I wasn't a very good pupil," she remarked instead. "It was a source of great frustration to my governesses. One even said I was unteachable." It was the truth, although the governess had been frustrated by Felicity's preference for the stables over her books, not by her lack of aptitude.

Jane looked at Felicity with something akin to pity. "I see."

"I suppose you never gave your governesses any trouble?"

"I suppose I didn't," Jane admitted, with barely concealed pride.

They found Lady Delphinia and Mr. Nethercott in the foyer of the theatre. Felicity hadn't seen her Nethercott since the ball, and she was relieved when he greeted her easily, with none of the resentment she might have expected from a rejected suitor.

Kincaid led the way to his brother's box and solicitously helped Jane remove her cloak. Felicity watched them as she worked at the buttons of her own pelisse, and she was startled when Nethercott spoke in her ear.

"May I, Miss Taylor?" he asked. She turned to find him standing close to her, with his arm outstretched to help her with her pelisse, and she nodded quickly. As he slipped the garment from her shoulders, he paused and cursed softly.

"I'm sorry, Miss Taylor," Nethercott said apologetically. "My cufflink seems to have caught on your necklace." Felicity felt his breath on her neck as he leaned closer to extricate himself, and she was beginning to feel uncomfortable when he finally liberated his cufflink.

Although his arm was free, Nethercott continued to peer at her necklace. "I'm afraid I've damaged it," he said regretfully. "May I take the necklace off?"

"Yes," Felicity agreed.

Nethercott removed her necklace and studied the clasp. "The hook of the clasp is bent," he said. "I wouldn't trust it until you've had a jeweller examine it. I'm afraid

I'm responsible for this, Miss Taylor, and if you'll allow me, I'll arrange to have it fixed."

"Please don't worry about it, Mr. Nethercott," Felicity reassured him. "I was planning to take it in for cleaning, and the jeweller can see to the clasp at the same time." She reached out to reclaim the necklace, and slipped it into her reticule.

"What do you think of it, Felicity?" Kincaid asked during the intermission. Nethercott had left to stretch his legs, but the rest of the party remained in the box.

"I don't think I've ever seen so many beautiful gowns." Felicity's position at the front of the box gave her an excellent view of the other guests. "And I don't understand why you made such a fuss about the dress I wore to my debut. My red satin looks quite modest compared to the gowns some of the ladies are wearing here."

"I think Mr. Kincaid was asking what you thought of the opera," Jane remarked.

"Oh, the music is beautiful too," Felicity replied. It was her first experience of the opera, and she was enjoying it a great deal. "Madame Leroux has a lovely voice."

"Do you speak Italian, Felicity?" Jane asked.

"No, I never learned it."

"I'm surprised Mr. Kincaid didn't hire you an Italian master," Lady Delphinia said.

"I expect he knew it didn't interest me," Felicity replied with a smile. "French was enough, and I certainly had a great deal of that. But you know, Lady Delphinia, I don't think one needs to speak Italian to enjoy the opera."

"I suppose the music is enough," Jane remarked.

"The music is lovely," Felicity agreed. "But even

without knowing the language, the story seems perfectly clear."

Jane's brow furrowed. "What do you mean?"

"Well, the lady loves the gentleman, but he doesn't have the wit to see it, and he thinks he's in love with someone else."

Jane gave her a condescending smile. "I think it's a little more complicated than that."

"Oh, I don't doubt it," Felicity said. "Gentlemen have a way of making everything complicated." She gestured to the stage. "The first question is whether the gentleman will realize that the lady loves him. Many gentlemen are quite blind to that sort of thing."

"I don't think it's fair to blame the gentleman," Jane remarked. "He has no way of knowing how the lady feels if she doesn't tell him."

"She's too proud," Felicity explained. "Imagine her embarrassment if she told him of her feelings and he didn't return them."

Jane didn't look convinced. "Then perhaps she doesn't deserve him."

"Perhaps not," Felicity agreed lightly. "In any case, it makes for good entertainment."

Miss Flint sneezed loudly, and Lady Delphinia shifted in her chair to move farther away from her. Felicity studied her companion with concern. "Are you feeling well, Theodora?" she asked. "You're looking flushed tonight."

"Oh, I'm fit as a fiddle," Miss Flint assured her. "Just a tickle in my throat."

In Felicity's opinion, the second half of the opera degenerated into a farce, and she wasn't sorry when it ended. Nethercott escorted her and Lady Delphinia out of the theatre, while Kincaid walked behind them with Jane and Miss Flint.

"Step carefully, Miss Taylor," Nethercott said solicitously, as they emerged into a noisy throng of people and carriages. Felicity was searching the line of vehicles for Kincaid's coach when someone jostled her from behind.

"Are you all right, Miss Taylor?" Nethercott asked, reaching out his arm to steady her.

Felicity was focused on regaining her footing and didn't answer immediately, but when she had collected herself, she realized her reticule had been snatched. She glanced around to look for the thief, but quickly concluded it was futile. She had barely glimpsed the person who had bumped into her, and even if she had, she would never find him in the crush of opera-goers.

"Someone stole my reticule," she said numbly.

Nethercott's eyes widened, and he began to scan the crowd. "Did you see him? What did he look like?"

"I didn't see," she said disconsolately. "And we'll never find him in this crowd."

"I'm sorry, Miss Taylor," Nethercott said sympathetically. "Did you have much money in it?"

Felicity took a deep breath. "Only a few shillings," she told him. "But he took my mother's pearls."

"At least you weren't injured, Felicity," Jane remarked as they drove home.

"Yes," Felicity said listlessly.

"And the necklace can be replaced."

"Yes." Felicity was too distraught to argue with Jane, but she certainly didn't agree with her. She could buy herself another necklace, but nothing could replace the pearls she had inherited from her mother.

"Maybe your pearls can be recovered," Miss Flint said optimistically. "Mr. Nethercott said he would visit the Bow Street Runners tomorrow."

"Perhaps," Felicity said, forcing a smile for Miss Flint. She had little hope that the Runners would find her necklace, and she doubted Nethercott did either. She imagined her cousin simply felt guilty that she had been robbed while he was escorting her to the carriage.

Felicity, however, thought there was no one to blame but herself. If she had only allowed Nethercott to take charge of the necklace when the clasp broke, she wouldn't have lost her pearls. She had been a fool to wear such a precious possession to the opera in the first place, and she vowed that if she got the necklace back, she would never wear it out of the house again.

She looked up to see Kincaid studying her closely.

"There's a good chance we'll get your necklace back, Felicity," he said quietly. "I'll start making inquiries tomorrow."

"Thank you, Mr. Kincaid," Felicity said. "I suppose you could work with my cousin."

A strange expression crossed Kincaid's face, and he didn't reply for a moment.

"I know you're not overly fond of Mr. Nethercott, but it seems like it would be more efficient for you to work together," Felicity explained.

"You're right," Kincaid agreed. "I'll call upon Nethercott tomorrow."

The servants at 29 Bentley St. were no longer surprised to see Felicity at unusual hours, so when she knocked on the door the following morning, the butler didn't hesitate to show her to the breakfast parlour.

"I would like to help you search for my necklace," she announced.

Kincaid set down his coffee cup and sighed. "Have you eaten? Would you like to join me for breakfast?"

"I'm not hungry," Felicity said impatiently. "I thought we might call upon Mr. Nethercott and visit the Runners together—"

"Felicity," Kincaid interrupted. "You can't come with me."

Felicity's face fell. "Why not? You can hardly expect me to sit at home while you and Mr. Nethercott search for my necklace."

"You can't come with us, Felicity," Kincaid repeated simply. "It could be dangerous."

"Visiting the Runners?" she asked skeptically.

"I intend to make my own inquiries as well. There are a number of pawn shops in the East End that deal in stolen goods, and the thief may have already sold your necklace."

"But surely I could accompany you," Felicity insisted.

Kincaid shook his head. "It's not a nice neighbourhood, Felicity, and I won't take you there."

"I'm twenty-one years old, Mr. Kincaid," Felicity countered. "I wish you wouldn't treat me like a child."

"I assure you, Felicity, I don't see you as a child," Kincaid said with a sigh.

"I suppose that's worse," Felicity replied. "Although I'm a grown woman, you still see me as a helpless creature, incapable of looking after myself. But my mother's necklace is very dear to me, and—"

"I don't see you as helpless, Felicity," Kincaid said quietly. "But you are very dear to me."

Felicity was shocked speechless, and Kincaid appeared almost as surprised by his words as she did.

"If I'm worried about your safety, I won't be able to focus on the search for your necklace," he finally continued.

"Oh." Felicity found she couldn't argue with that.

"Perhaps you could go out with Miss Flint this morning," Kincaid suggested. "Walk in the park, or visit the modiste. I'll come by this afternoon to let you know what came of my inquiries."

"All right," she agreed.

Kincaid stood and offered her his arm. "I'll walk you home."

Eighteen

After Kincaid escorted her back to 23 Bentley, Felicity went in search of Miss Flint, hoping she would join her for a walk in the park. Unfortunately, the tickle in her companion's throat had progressed to a full-blown head cold, and although Miss Flint still claimed to be fit as a fiddle, Felicity insisted she rest in her bedchamber.

After taking Miss Flint some tea and toast, Felicity moved to the drawing room, where she stared out the window and wondered how long she would have to wait for Mr. Kincaid to return. To distract herself, she picked up her sketchbook and began to draw a whimsical series of bonnets.

She was finishing a sketch of a hat adorned with a bunch of grapes when she heard a timid knock at the drawing room door.

"A gentleman and a lady have called to see you, Miss Taylor," James announced nervously. James was the first footman, and although he didn't aspire to the butler's responsibilities, he was often forced to assume them on

Saturday mornings. Wainwright was in the habit of spending Friday nights at a pub with some friends, and rarely made an appearance before midday on Saturday.

"You may send them in, James," Felicity said with a kind smile.

Moments later, Lady Delphinia and Martin Nethercott strode into the room. As Felicity stood to greet them, she noticed Nethercott hadn't bothered to remove his greatcoat, and Lady Delphinia still wore a grey woolen cape over her travelling dress.

"I'm pleased we've found you at home, Miss Taylor," Nethercott said quickly. Although Lady Delphinia had taken a seat opposite Felicity, Nethercott was pacing the room as though he had too much energy to sit still. "I think I've found a lead on your stolen necklace."

"You have?" Felicity asked in surprise.

Nethercott nodded. "I visited the Runners early this morning. They've been investigating the pickpockets around Covent Garden, and they suspect that most are working for a gang. The stolen goods are being sent to Italy, by way of France."

"I see," Felicity said quietly, trying to hide her disappointment.

"So we'll have to move fast," Nethercott continued. "The Runners said this group works quickly. Your necklace is likely already on its way to Dover, with a collection of other goods that were stolen yesterday."

"You think there's still a chance to recover it?" Felicity asked, hardly daring to hope. She had resigned herself to the idea that her mother's necklace was lost to her forever.

"Oh, yes," Nethercott said confidently. "The thieves

are unlikely to sail before nightfall, since they won't want to attract the attention of the Customs men."

"Did you hire the Runners?"

Nethercott shook his head. "There was no one available to leave immediately, so I decided to go myself."

"Go yourself!" Felicity exclaimed. "But the thieves may be armed, and it could be dangerous—"

"Yes, that's what I said," Lady Delphinia agreed, with a delicate nod of her head. "The necklace isn't worth the risk."

"I'll be careful, Mama." Nethercott gave his mother a reassuring smile before turning back to Felicity. "I wondered if you would like to come with me."

He saw her look of surprise and rushed to reassure her. "My mother can come as your chaperone, so we won't have to inconvenience Miss Flint. We can travel to Dover together, then you and Mama can wait in an inn while I look for the necklace. You should be perfectly safe, but I understand if you would rather not come."

"I'd like to come," Felicity said hastily. "But what about Mr. Kincaid?"

Nethercott looked perplexed. "What about Mr. Kincaid?"

"He's searching for the necklace too. He was going to call on you this morning so you could work together."

"I must have missed him," Nethercott said with a frown.

"He was planning to go to the Runners too, and to visit pawn shops in the East End. We should tell him what you've learned. He may want to come to Dover with us."

"There's no time, Miss Taylor," Nethercott insisted. "If

we don't leave now, we won't reach Dover before dark, and once the necklace leaves England, we'll never recover it."

"You're right," Felicity agreed reluctantly. "Just let me pack a bag and write a note for Mr. Kincaid."

"I can write Kincaid a note," Nethercott offered.

Felicity gave him a nod of thanks before rushing upstairs to put on a cloak and hat. She found a valise in her closet and hastily packed a walking dress, two petticoats, and a pair of stockings. Her maid would be horrified by such careless packing, but she didn't have time to wait for Louise.

As she hurried out of her bedchamber, Felicity's eyes fell upon her jewellery box and she paused. On an impulse, she opened the box and found the little horseshoe brooch that Kincaid had given her for her birthday. Next to her stolen necklace, it was her favourite piece of jewellery, and as she pinned it to her shoulder, she hoped it would bring her luck.

When Nethercott had first suggested they go to Dover, Felicity had been so eager to take action that she hadn't stopped to think about the difficulties they faced. However, once she was in the Nethercotts' carriage she had little to do but think, and she realized the odds were stacked against them.

"How will you know where to look for the necklace?" she asked Nethercott. "If the thieves are trying to avoid attention, they may not leave from the principal port."

"I told him it would be impossible," Lady Delphinia

agreed, with an elegant shrug of her shoulders. "But Martin was determined to try."

"The Runners gave me an address," Nethercott explained. "They think they've found the house where the goods are being stored."

Felicity frowned. "If the Runners know where the goods are being stored, why don't they shut down the operation?"

"I'm afraid they didn't share all of their secrets with me," Nethercott replied. "The Runners may not have jurisdiction in Dover. Or they might be waiting them out, hoping the small fry will lead them to the head of the gang."

Felicity's brow furrowed. "In that case, why would they give you the address?"

"Because I'm so charming, my dear cousin, that they couldn't say no."

Felicity laughed in spite of herself. "Please be serious, Mr. Nethercott," she admonished when she had collected herself.

"I'm very serious, Miss Taylor," he replied, but the teasing look in his eye suggested otherwise.

But Felicity had concluded they would need a great deal of luck to find her necklace, and she couldn't understand why Nethercott seemed so confident. She was opening her mouth to question him further when she sensed the coach slowing down.

"Are we stopping already?" she asked.

Nethercott nodded. "We'll make better time if we change horses now, and the Lamb and Lion keeps a good stable."

They drew to a stop in front of the posting inn, where

the ostlers made quick work of changing the horses. As they prepared to return to the road, Lady Delphinia announced that she had a cramp in her leg.

"Help me down, Martin," she commanded. "I need to stretch my legs for a minute."

Nethercott leapt obligingly out of the coach to hand his mother down, and Lady Delphinia walked towards the inn at her usual leisurely pace. She certainly didn't move as though her leg was troubling her, and Felicity fought to hide her impatience.

"Do you really think we can reach Dover in time?" she asked Nethercott, who had climbed back into the carriage and taken the seat opposite her. "Where are we now?"

Nethercott's thin lips curved upwards. "We are in Barnet, Miss Taylor."

"Barnet," Felicity repeated slowly. "But I thought Barnet was to the north of London, and Dover to the east."

Her cousin's smile broadened. "You're right on both counts, Felicity. You might say we're taking an unconventional route." He tapped the roof of the carriage with his cane, and seconds later, the carriage began to move.

"We've left Lady Delphinia behind," Felicity protested. "Tell the coachman to turn back."

"I'm afraid my mother dislikes long journeys and has decided to return to London," Nethercott said apologetically. "She can hire a post-chaise at the inn."

"But we'll be spending the night in Dover," Felicity said. "I'll need a chaperone, or my reputation—"

"We're not going to Dover, Felicity," Nethercott interrupted smoothly. "And you certainly won't need a chaperone."

～

An hour after Felicity left with the Nethercotts, Kincaid knocked on the door of 23 Bentley St.

Wainwright greeted him with a nervous expression. "Mr. Kincaid!" he blurted anxiously. "I was just coming to look for you."

"I'm flattered, Wainwright," Kincaid said dryly, striding into the house. "But I've actually come to see Miss Taylor. Where is she?"

Wainwright seemed to shrink into himself. "That's actually what I wanted to talk to you about."

"Yes?"

"It's rather delicate."

"Just tell me, Wainwright."

Wainwright swallowed and gathered his courage. "The thing is, sir, Miss Taylor had callers this morning. A gentleman and a lady. James answered the door, since I was—er—indisposed."

"Yes," Kincaid said impatiently. He knew exactly why Wainwright was indisposed every Saturday morning and had spoken to him about it several times. He supposed he should replace him with a more reliable butler, but for all his foibles, Wainwright was familiar, and there was something to be said for that.

"James didn't ask for the callers' names," Wainwright said in a disapproving tone. "But he overheard part of their conversation with Miss Taylor. They spoke of travelling to Dover to search for Felicity's pearls. Felicity left with them about an hour ago."

"If they hope to find the pearls in Dover, they'll be disappointed," Kincaid remarked sardonically. Felicity's pearls were currently reposing in his pocket, having been redeemed from an East End pawn shop an hour earlier. He had been looking forward to giving her back the necklace, even though he still hadn't decided what to tell her about how he had found it.

"Yes," Wainwright said slowly. "But the thing is, sir, I'm not sure they've gone to Dover. Albert—the new groom, you know—went out to look at their horses, and got talking to the coachman. And the coachman told him they're headed for Gretna Green!"

If Wainwright had hoped for a reaction to the news that Miss Taylor had departed in a carriage with an unknown gentleman and lady, bound either for Dover or Gretna Green, he was disappointed. Kincaid's expression did not show shock or alarm; if anything, Kincaid simply looked disappointed himself.

"Do you want me to order your curricle, sir?" Wainwright asked. "Or your travelling coach?"

Kincaid sighed. He didn't believe the Gretna story for a minute, and he suspected Felicity had staged the entire affair for his benefit. "What for, Wainwright?"

"I thought you might want to go after them, sir," Wainwright said nervously. "It just seems rather suspicious that Miss Taylor thought she was going to Dover, but the coachman said they're going to Gretna."

"Perhaps they're going to Gretna Green by way of Dover," Kincaid said dryly.

"Er—perhaps," Wainwright said slowly. His knowledge of geography was rather vague, but he was fairly sure that Dover was not in the same direction as Scotland. "I just thought you would want to know."

"I didn't," Kincaid said tersely. "Miss Taylor is now of age, and she has made it clear that she wishes to manage her own affairs. Her whereabouts are no longer my business."

"I beg your pardon, sir," Wainwright said stiffly.

Kincaid realized he had been venting his anger on his butler, and he softened his tone. "You were right to inform me, Wainwright." After all, Wainwright didn't know Felicity like Kincaid did, and had no reason to suspect that the whole affair was a ruse.

Kincaid walked the short distance back to 29 Bentley, feeling betrayed. He knew Felicity had been disappointed that he hadn't let her join him on the search for her pearls, but he thought they had reached an understanding. The last thing he had expected was for her to stage another false elopement, simply to prove that he no longer had the right to control where she went. It was almost identical to the trick she had pulled the first time, except instead of a leaving a note, she had arranged for the coachman to drop the hint that they were heading to Gretna. He imagined she was looking forward to a confrontation with him, and he hoped she would be disappointed when he didn't chase after her.

Because one thing was clear to Lucas Kincaid: he was done chasing Felicity Taylor across the country. She had played him for a fool too many times, and he was determined not to let it happen again.

Nineteen

"I don't understand," Felicity said to Nethercott. "If we're not going to Dover, where are we going?"

"Gretna Green," Nethercott replied succinctly.

"Gretna Green!" Felicity exclaimed. All she knew of the Scottish village was that it was a common destination for eloping couples, but she still clung to the hope that her cousin hadn't deceived her. "Surely you don't think we'll find my necklace in Scotland?"

"I'm fairly certain we won't," Nethercott told her placidly. "But I'll buy you a new string of pearls after we're married."

Felicity gaped at him in disbelief, and her expression seemed to amuse him. "Don't look so surprised, Felicity," he admonished. "You must know I'm madly in love with you. I couldn't wait any longer to make you my wife."

For a moment, Felicity wondered if it could be true, and if he had truly tricked her into an elopement because he loved her. But as she stared at her cousin, lounging casually against the squabs of the coach, she realized she wasn't looking at a man in love. Nethercott appeared perfectly at ease, with his long legs stretched out in front of him and crossed negligently at the ankles. There was no madness in his pale blue eyes, and no passion either; his expression was one of cool calculation.

"I'm sorry, Mr. Nethercott, but I won't marry you," Felicity said firmly. "Please take me back to the inn. I would like to rejoin Lady Delphinia."

"I'm afraid I can't do that, Felicity."

"Then let me out of the carriage," she demanded. "I'll walk." She didn't think they were more than a mile from the inn, and although it would be awkward to arrive there on foot, without luggage or money, it would be better than remaining with her cousin.

"I'm afraid I can't do that either." Although Nethercott's tone was apologetic, there was no remorse in his eyes.

"So this is an abduction," Felicity said bluntly. "And the story about going to Dover to search for the necklace —that was all a lie?"

"Abduction is such an ugly word, Felicity," he said with a sigh. "But you're right that your necklace isn't in Dover, and that I mean to marry you. I need your fortune, you see."

Felicity had reached that conclusion at the same time she realized he wasn't in love with her, but it still hurt to hear it confirmed. "I suppose you think this is the only way you'll win a wife," she said waspishly.

"I think it's the only way I'll win an heiress within the next week," he replied. "I'm in debt to some very impatient people."

"Moneylenders?"

"Yes," he admitted, surveying her curiously. "What do you know of moneylenders?"

"Only that Mr. Kincaid warned me to avoid them."

"I wondered how long it would be before we reached the subject of Mr. Kincaid," Nethercott drawled. "I suppose I'm fortunate that he took such good care of your money."

Felicity looked at him contemptuously. "Much better care than you would have taken, had you been appointed my guardian. You seem to have a very poor notion of management. How did you fall into debt?"

"I'm afraid I have expensive tastes," he said with a shrug, as though this was a characteristic he couldn't control. "My mother does too, and my father's fortune was sadly insufficient for our needs."

"And your mother knew that you planned to abduct me," Felicity said slowly.

Nethercott nodded. "She's in debt too."

"I'll give you the money," she offered. "Take me home now and you can have it all."

Nethercott chuckled softly. "But it's not up to you, is it?" he asked smoothly. "Even if I trusted you to keep your word, Mr. Kincaid has control of your fortune until you marry. He might not like the idea."

"He'll give you the money if I ask him to," Felicity insisted.

"I doubt it." Nethercott was fairly certain that if he took Felicity back to Kincaid, the only thing he would win was an invitation to a duel.

Felicity realized she had no hope of reasoning with him, and her only hope was to escape. She rapped smartly on the roof of the coach in an effort to signal the coachman, but the pace of the coach didn't slacken. "Stop!" she shouted at the top of her voice. "Help!"

Nethercott didn't try to silence her, and if anything, her efforts seemed to amuse him.

"My coachman is conveniently deaf," he explained. "He knows it's a condition of his employment."

"But it will take several days to get to Gretna Green," Felicity pointed out. "We'll have to stop to eat and sleep. Surely someone at an inn will help me, and—"

"I'm not sure they will," Nethercott interrupted. "Not if I explain to the innkeeper that you're my wife, and you're unwell." He smirked. "I'm taking you to Scotland to consult with a physician who specializes in mental disorders."

Felicity's heart sank as she realized he was right. "And once we get to Gretna Green? How do you plan to force me to marry you?"

"I rather think, Felicity, that by the time we reach Gretna you'll be begging me to marry you." Although Nethercott's words were ugly, his voice was smoother than silk. "One night in my company will be enough to compromise you. Hell, I imagine the damage has already been done. My mother is on her way back to London, where she'll lose no time in telling her friends about our elopement."

"I would rather be ruined than marry you," Felicity retorted.

"Would you, though?" he mused. "I've always thought you were an intelligent girl, Felicity. Too outspoken for my taste, but certainly not stupid."

"I will never marry you," she repeated.

"I suppose that's your choice," Nethercott said gently, "but I'm afraid life is difficult for fallen women. You'll have your money, of course, but will it be enough? Society will cast you out, which will be quite a change, since I understand you've been moving in exalted circles. I hardly think the Marchioness of Ashingham or the Countess of Langley would recognize you after a scandal like this."

"My friends would stand by me," Felicity said staunchly.

Nethercott raised a skeptical eyebrow. "They might," he agreed. "If you wanted to involve them in your disgrace."

Felicity realized he was right about that, too. If she were ruined, she wouldn't want to drag her friends down with her. Amelia and Isabelle would be lost to her, as would the rest of polite society.

"And there's always the question of what Mr. Kincaid will think," Nethercott said thoughtfully.

Felicity had been thinking about that too, and she flushed. "I imagine he would think you were a scoundrel," she said scornfully.

"Oh, I'm sure he thinks so already," Nethercott said easily. "And I imagine he can think of worse names than that. But I expect he would also feel guilty."

Felicity looked at him in confusion. "Why would he feel guilty?"

"Because he didn't warn you that I was a scoundrel, and that I was desperate," Nethercott explained. "He came to see me this morning, to ask me where to find your necklace."

It took Felicity a moment to put it together, but when she did, she felt like a fool for not having seen it sooner. "You stole my necklace," she said flatly.

"I did," Nethercott confirmed. "Rather, my groom did, but he did so on my instructions. I'm afraid Mr. Kincaid suspected me from the start. He was rather unpleasant about it this morning."

"Did you give it back to him?"

"Oh, I'd already sold it. But I gave Kincaid the name of the pawn shop, and I imagine he's redeemed it by now. Assuming, of course, that it hasn't already been sold to someone else."

"How kind of you," Felicity said sarcastically.

"It was, wasn't it?" Nethercott agreed. "I had no objection to Kincaid buying it back. But you can understand why I had to act quickly this morning. After Kincaid told you about the necklace, I'd have had a far more difficult time tricking you into my carriage."

Felicity turned her face towards the side of the carriage and silently cursed her stupidity. In retrospect, it was obvious: Nethercott had told her the clasp was broken and watched her put the necklace in her reticule. Then, at the intermission, he had gone to instruct his groom to steal it as they left the theatre. Mr. Kincaid had evidently put it together without difficulty, but Felicity had been oblivious. To crown it all, she had believed her cousin's ridiculous story about chasing a gang of thieves to Dover.

"Mr. Kincaid will come after us," she said bravely, hoping that it was true. "When he reads your note and learns I've left with you and Lady Delphinia, he'll come after us."

Nethercott's soft chuckle told Felicity that she was still behaving like a fool.

"You didn't leave a note, did you?" she asked.

Nethercott shook his head. "Of course, there's always a chance that one of the servants recognized me, but it hardly matters. By the time Kincaid realizes what happened, it will be too late. And imagine how he'll feel when he learns of it, since he could have prevented it by telling you of his suspicions before he came to see me this morning."

"You can't blame Mr. Kincaid for this!" Felicity exclaimed. "That's absurd. This situation is entirely of your own making, and you have no one to blame but yourself."

"Now Felicity, that's hardly fair," Nethercott argued. "I think your father shares some of the blame, for writing such a ridiculous will. What did he think would happen when he wrote that the fortune would come to me if you married before you were of age?"

"Only if I married without Mr. Kincaid's consent," Felicity pointed out.

"If anything, I thought that improved my chances. Can you blame me for expecting you to marry to spite your guardian? You were a stubborn girl, and you always seemed to be at odds with Kincaid."

"I'm not foolish enough to marry just to spite Mr. Kincaid," Felicity said scornfully.

Nethercott chuckled. "As I learned, to my great disappointment. But I'm confident that our marriage will enrage him. In fact, I think I will enjoy telling him about it."

"I'm not going to marry you!" Felicity spat.

Nethercott shrugged. "As I was saying, if your father hadn't written such a will, I might never have dreamed that the money could be mine. As things stand, I've come to see it as my due."

"You always planned to steal my fortune," Felicity said slowly.

"I planned to have it," he admitted, "but I hoped I wouldn't have to steal it. I thought I might win your heart by fair means, you know. At your debut ball, I was insulted that you didn't fall for my charms, until I realized I never had a chance. You had already given your heart away."

"What do you mean?"

Nethercott's lips curled into a reptilian smile. "I mean, dear cousin, that you're in love with Kincaid."

Felicity was too surprised to deny it. "How did you know?" she blurted.

"I first suspected it at the ball," Nethercott explained. "When you leapt to his defence when I criticized him. And when I saw you at the opera, watching him and Miss Harris, I was sure of it. You're very beautiful when you're jealous."

Felicity stared at him with a stricken expression, afraid that if her feelings had been so obvious to Nethercott, they had also been equally clear to Kincaid.

Nethercott seemed able to read her thoughts. "You can relax, Felicity," he said. "The good Mr. Kincaid was entirely oblivious to your feelings. If I hadn't had an interest in it, I would have found the whole affair amusing."

"You didn't have an interest in it," Felicity said defiantly.

"I certainly did," Nethercott told her. "As I said, I hoped to win you by fair means, but it was clear you'll never look at another man until Kincaid is married. Unfortunately, I can't afford to wait that long."

"I don't know what you're talking about," Felicity protested. "Mr. Kincaid is betrothed to Miss Harris."

"But you're hoping something will happen to end their engagement," Nethercott said. "If you're not already plotting to bring it to an end."

Felicity's expression only changed for an instant, but it was enough for Nethercott to notice. "You were planning something," he said with a smirk. "What was it, I wonder? Were you trying to arrange for Kincaid to find Miss Harris in a compromising position with another man?"

"Of course not," Felicity retorted. "I would never do that."

"No?"

She could tell he didn't believe her, and Felicity felt obliged to explain. "Yes, I hoped Miss Harris would end the engagement, but only because she and Mr. Kincaid are so poorly suited! I thought their marriage would make them both miserable, so I was trying to promote a match between Miss Harris and a more compatible man." She decided not to tell him about her plan to play the role of a vulgar young woman to deter Jane from being her chaperone.

Nethercott raised an eyebrow. "I see. You knew what was best for them, and you decided to save them from themselves?"

"Yes, I suppose I did."

"And your motives were, of course, entirely selfless?" Nethercott asked dryly.

"No," Felicity admitted. "But I wasn't trying to hurt anyone."

"I think, my dear, that you and I have a great deal in common," Nethercott said with a grin. "We both have elastic morals, and we're not afraid to fight for what we want."

"You and I are nothing alike!" Felicity exclaimed in disgust.

"But we are," Nethercott said pleasantly. "Really, Felicity, you must see that this little trip to Gretna Green is for your benefit? I saw the men you danced with at your ball, and I knew none of them could make you happy. So I decided to save you from yourself."

Felicity could see the parallel, and it stung. "I wasn't considering marriage to any of the men I danced with at the ball," she snapped.

"With the notable exception of Mr. Kincaid, of course," Nethercott said with a chuckle. "I suppose you were assessing the others as potential suitors for Jane?"

Felicity nodded.

"You might as well give it up, Felicity. The Honourable Lucas Kincaid will never break an engagement, and Miss Harris will never cry off. She isn't as clever as you, but she has enough sense to know she won't get a better offer."

Felicity stared at the floor of the carriage and refused to meet his eye.

"So if you refuse to marry me," Nethercott continued, "Mr. Kincaid won't be able to marry you to save your reputation, but I imagine he'll feel guilty about your predicament."

"He has nothing to feel guilty about!" Felicity retorted.

Nethercott raised an eyebrow. "No? Even though this unfortunate situation might have been prevented if he'd warned you about me this morning?"

Felicity was silent for a moment. Nethercott had lit upon the one argument that might persuade her to marry him, and the smirk on his face told her he knew it.

"There is an alternative, you know," he suggested. "You could pretend we fell in love, and you convinced me to run away with you."

Felicity's eyes widened. "Mr. Kincaid would never believe that," she scoffed.

"He might," Nethercott said with a shrug. "I'm sure he will want to believe it, when the alternative is that I abducted you and forced you to marry me."

"You think he would believe I'm such a poor judge of character? That I fell in love with you?"

"You trusted me enough to get in my carriage, Felicity," Nethercott pointed out. "But perhaps we could say that I have reformed. My character has been redeemed by the love of a worthy young lady."

"You are beyond redemption," Felicity said scathingly.

"My darling—"

"If you call me darling again, I'll make you regret it!" she said hotly.

"Oh?" Nethercott asked curiously. "How exactly will you do that?"

"I will . . ." Felicity fell silent as she realized that she was completely within his power. She was athletic, but he was too, and he was a full foot taller than she was; if it came to a physical fight, she wouldn't stand a chance. The carriage, which had once seemed so comfortably spacious, now felt impossibly small. There was a predator lounging on the opposite seat, and Felicity was well and truly trapped.

"How disappointing," Nethercott murmured. "I was looking forward to hearing how you would punish me."

"Have you no shame?" Felicity cried.

"I'm in a great deal of debt, Felicity," Nethercott said unapologetically. "Shame is a luxury for the rich."

"And after we're married?" she asked. "What happens then?"

"Oh, you won't find me a difficult husband," he assured her. "And I'll make you a generous allowance."

"A generous allowance!" Felicity exclaimed. "Of my own money!"

"Well, it will become my money after we marry," Nethercott pointed out. "But yes, your allowance will come from your fortune. If I had my own money, I wouldn't have to marry such a shrew."

Felicity decided that the best thing she could do was pretend he wasn't there. She leaned her head back against the side of the carriage and closed her eyes.

"As heiresses go, you're not so bad," Nethercott mused. "In profile you're actually rather attractive. You were such a tall and skinny child that I didn't have high hopes for you, but you've turned out better than I dared expect."

Felicity heard him moving closer to her, and she opened her eyes to find him leaning in to kiss her. She received his kiss passively at first, then surprised him by biting his lip until she tasted blood.

The surprise caused Nethercott to release her, and she scrambled back against the side of the carriage. He raised a hand to his mouth, and when he took it away, Felicity was gratified to see blood on his chin.

"You little spitfire," he said appreciatively.

Felicity drew her legs up on the seat, preparing to kick him if he dared to approach her again. Her heart was hammering so hard she could feel her pulse in her throat, and her underarms were damp with nervous sweat. She fought to meet Nethercott's eye and keep her breathing even so he wouldn't see she was afraid.

"Relax, Felicity," he told her. "I can be patient. I'm even willing to wait until we're married."

Felicity didn't reply, but her fierce expression made it clear she wouldn't let him touch her without a fight. To her relief, he moved back to the opposite side of the carriage and seemed content to stay there. They travelled in silence for a while, and when Felicity was reasonably confident that Nethercott wasn't going to molest her, she turned away from him and pretended to sleep. Before long, she sensed that the carriage was slowing, and she looked out the window to see they had arrived at a posting inn.

"Did you have pleasant dreams?" Nethercott asked, in a tone that told her he knew she hadn't been asleep.

"Very pleasant," Felicity replied. "Where are we?"

"Welwyn," Nethercott replied. "We're only stopping to change the horses."

"I'm surprised you can afford the cost of the journey,

if you mean to change horses every time we pass a posting inn," she said tartly.

"It's fortunate I sold your pearls this morning," Nethercott remarked with a nod. "Otherwise, we would have to share a bedchamber tonight. As things stand, I can afford to pay for two rooms."

The carriage had stopped in the inn yard, and Felicity saw the ostlers leading out a fresh team of horses.

"I need to use the retiring room," she announced, and she moved towards the carriage door without waiting for Nethercott's permission.

"I'll accompany you," Nethercott said easily. "I hope you won't do anything foolish. I would hate to have to tell the innkeeper about your mental disorder."

He stepped out first and reached out to help Felicity down, but she ignored him and leapt down on her own. As soon as her feet reached the ground, she went for Nethercott's face with the pin of her horseshoe brooch, which she had removed from her dress while he was stepping out of the coach.

Surprise was on her side, for although Nethercott had expected her to try to escape, he hadn't expected an attack. She couldn't bring herself to aim for his eye, but she managed to land a deep scratch along his left cheek, and he howled in pain. His cries drew the attention of the ostlers and caused one of them to drop the reins of a magnificent black horse.

Seeing her opportunity, Felicity ran over and grabbed the horse's reins before the ostler could gather his wits. She looked around the yard, searching for a tree stump or fence post that could serve as a mounting block, but nothing appeared to be suitable. She knew she had only seconds before Nethercott recovered, and in desperation, she turned to one of the ostlers.

"Boost me up!" she commanded, as though she had every right to ride the horse. To her relief, the boy was in the habit of obeying orders, and he laced his fingers together to hold her foot. Felicity hitched up her skirts, the ostler threw her up into the saddle, and she gave the horse the signal to go.

Twenty

Felicity had ridden several miles before her heart rate slowed and she was able to take stock of her situation. She had intercepted the horse on his way to the stables, and she knew he had probably already travelled a considerable distance that day. It was clear he was tired, and Felicity felt guilty for pushing him, but she had no alternative. She expected Nethercott to come after her, but she hoped her stolen horse could outpace his carriage for another few miles.

She passed a stagecoach travelling in the opposite direction and received several lewd comments from the passengers on the roof. Felicity knew her appearance was scandalous; she was riding astride, with her skirts and petticoats bunched around her waist and her stockings in full view. No reputable inn would give her a room if she arrived in such a state, and she tried not to think about where she would sleep if she couldn't reach London by nightfall. She hoped she was headed towards London, but she wasn't even sure of that; she had been so focused on escaping from Nethercott that she hadn't stopped to think about her direction.

The horse slackened his speed, and Felicity didn't have the heart to urge him on. She realized she wouldn't be able to stay ahead of Nethercott for much longer, and her only hope was to get off the main road. The first crossroad she reached was little more than a path, and she was debating whether to take it when she heard hoof-beats behind her. With a sinking heart, she turned and saw a single horse and rider galloping towards her.

Felicity assumed that Nethercott had hired a horse to pursue her, and she knew she had no chance of escape. Her borrowed horse was spent, and her conscience wouldn't allow her to push him any farther, so she took a deep breath and prepared to confront her cousin. But as the rider drew closer, Felicity realized her pursuer wasn't Nethercott, and as he reined in his horse, she recognized the Marquess of Willingdon.

"Miss Taylor!" Willingdon exclaimed, drawing his horse to a stop several feet from Felicity. He seemed to be as surprised to see Felicity as she was to see him.

"Lord Willingdon," Felicity replied with a nod. She could feel his eyes move down her body, taking in her raised skirts and exposed stockings, before returning to her face.

"I was told my horse had been stolen by a young lady, but I never expected it to be you," the marquess said stiffly.

"I'm sorry, Lord Willingdon," Felicity said nervously. She racked her brain for an explanation for her circumstances, but couldn't think of anything better than the truth. "I was abducted by my cousin, Mr. Martin Nethercott," she explained. "He planned to take me to Gretna Green and marry me for my fortune."

She paused and looked at Willingdon, waiting for him to say something, but he seemed to have been stunned into silence.

"I apologize for stealing your horse," Felicity continued bravely. "And you have every right to be angry, but as you can imagine, my situation was desperate."

Willingdon seemed to collect himself. "Of course. Yes. Of course," he said awkwardly. "Er—are you all right, Miss Taylor?"

It was all she could do not to laugh. Not only was she hungry, tired, and humiliated, she was fairly certain her reputation was ruined. However, she hadn't been physically harmed, and she supposed she should be thankful for that. "I'm fine," she said briskly. "Although I would be grateful if you could help me get back to London."

"Certainly," Willingdon agreed. "Do you think you can ride a little farther? I won't be able to hire a chaise until we reach Barnet."

"Oh, yes," Felicity replied. "I'm more concerned about your horse, who I think is overdue for a rest."

"Caesar will be all right, so long as we keep an easy pace."

"Caesar's a good name for him," Felicity remarked, leaning down to pat the horse's neck. "He's a lovely animal."

"Thank you." The marquess's expression was stern, and he appeared to be deep in thought. They rode in silence for several minutes before Felicity spoke again.

"I know I've inconvenienced you, Lord Willingdon, and I'm really very grateful for your help."

"It's no matter," he told her. "I have an estate near Welwyn, and had been seeing to some business there, but I was planning to return to London tomorrow."

A heavy silence fell again, but this time Willingdon was the one to break it.

"I suppose it's fortunate I came after you," he remarked. "The landlord at Welwyn offered to send a boy, but I decided to hire a horse and come myself. You must see, Miss Taylor, that if word gets out, your reputation will be compromised."

"Yes," Felicity said simply.

"Who else knows about this—er—incident?"

"Mr. Nethercott's mother, Lady Delphinia. She was with us for the start of the journey, but left the carriage at Barnet."

Willingdon nodded thoughtfully. "And do you think Lady Delphinia can be trusted to keep quiet?"

"No," Felicity said bitterly. "I'm afraid she means to spread the tale."

Willingdon appeared to reach a decision. "Miss Taylor, I know I am in your debt," he began. "My son would have drowned without your intervention, and I'll never be able to repay you for what you did. But given your unfortunate circumstances, I think it is my duty to offer you my hand in marriage."

Felicity didn't reply immediately. She had always vowed that she wouldn't marry unless she was in love, and she wasn't in love with the Marquess of Willingdon. Willingdon certainly hadn't claimed to love her; he had made his offer out of duty, nothing more. Although she didn't know the marquess well, she didn't think they were particularly well-suited, and there was certainly no spark of attraction between them. The marquess didn't seem like a man who laughed easily or often, and Felicity feared he would think her frivolous.

But Felicity was realistic enough to know that she had lost her chance to marry for love. Only a fortune hunter would overlook a scandal like the one she was currently facing, and she thought Willingdon would be preferable to a man who only wanted her money. If she didn't marry, she would be exiled from polite society, and marriage to Willingdon might be preferable to that too. The marquess was reputed to be an honourable man, and his offer of marriage was chivalrous. Perhaps he only seemed austere because he was still mourning the loss of his first wife, who had died scarcely more than a year before. Her parents' deaths had taught Felicity a hard lesson about grief, and she knew it didn't respect society's timelines.

As they so often did, Felicity's thoughts turned to Mr. Kincaid. As Nethercott had shrewdly pointed out, when Kincaid learned of her abduction, he would blame himself for not having warned her about her cousin's true character. She knew the guilt would weigh heavily on Kincaid, and Willingdon was offering her a means to relieve it. It would be far better to return betrothed to a wealthy marquess than as a lady with a ruined reputation.

She took a deep breath and turned to face the marquess. "Thank you, Lord Willingdon," she replied. "I accept. I would like to marry you."

As soon as Felicity had given her answer, she heard a carriage approaching from behind. It swept past them at considerable speed before slowing to a stop a short distance ahead of them. Martin Nethercott sprang down from the carriage and started towards them, and Felicity met his eye with a look of disdain.

Nethercott stopped in front of Lord Willingdon and bowed deeply. "I owe you an apology, my lord," he began. "You can imagine my dismay when the staff at the inn told me my cousin stole your horse. I'm afraid I'm partly to blame; I told Miss Taylor I didn't think she could do it, and she set out to prove me wrong. It was a silly prank, but I hope you'll forgive us."

When Willingdon didn't reply, Nethercott turned to Felicity. "You've made your point, cousin, but it's time to get back in the carriage. You're making quite a spectacle of yourself."

"You should know, Nethercott, that Miss Taylor has just agreed to marry me," Willingdon said gravely.

Felicity saw a flicker of anger in Nethercott's eyes, but he collected himself quickly. "Congratulations, Miss Taylor," he said smoothly. He turned to the marquess expectantly, wondering if he was about to be challenged to a duel. If Willingdon had offered Felicity marriage, he must have heard the story of her abduction.

"But I agree that Miss Taylor shouldn't ride any farther today," Willingdon said. "You have behaved dishonourably, Nethercott, and I think the least you can do is allow her to ride in your carriage until we reach Barnet. I will ride Caesar, and you may ride the hired horse."

"Certainly," Nethercott agreed, with a quirk of his mouth that showed he found the situation amusing.

Felicity wasn't keen to get back into Nethercott's carriage, but she found the vehicle was actually quite tolerable when Nethercott was no longer in it. Nonetheless, she was relieved to reach the posting inn at Barnet, where she and Willingdon could part company with her cousin. After the marquess had made arrangements for the stabling of Caesar and the hired horse, he and Felicity set off for London in a post-chaise.

It was dark by the time Willingdon escorted Felicity to the door of 23 Bentley St. They were met in the entrance hall by Mr. Kincaid, who looked almost as exhausted as she felt. Kincaid had started to worry that Felicity's trip wasn't simply a stunt to annoy him, and there was some truth to the story about Gretna Green. He had spent the past hour pacing the hall, wishing he had gone after her, and he was greatly relieved that she had returned.

"Another prank, Felicity?" he inquired curtly. As well as relieved, Kincaid was tired and frustrated, and his expression showed it. "I wouldn't have expected you to draw Willingdon into one of your schemes."

Willingdon gave Kincaid a look of disapproval. "I'm afraid this wasn't a prank, Mr. Kincaid," he said severely. "Miss Taylor was abducted by her cousin, Mr. Nethercott. I understand he planned to compel her to marry him to gain control of her fortune."

Kincaid stared at Felicity in disbelief. She refused to meet his gaze, but she looked so wretched that he realized it must be true.

"Did he hurt you?" Kincaid asked softly.

"I understand that Miss Taylor's virtue is intact," Willingdon said awkwardly.

"Did he hurt you?" Kincaid asked again, as though the marquess hadn't spoken.

Felicity finally raised her eyes to look at Kincaid, and

was surprised by the hard expression on his face. "N-not really," she stammered. "He tried to kiss me in the carriage, but I bit his lip and he left me alone. That was all."

"I see," Kincaid said, in a deceptively calm tone of voice. "I think you should tell me the story from the beginning."

"I think we should let Miss Taylor sit down," Willingdon suggested. "And perhaps find her something to eat and drink."

Kincaid was ashamed to realize he had been interrogating Felicity in the entrance hall, with Wainwright hovering a short distance away. "Have refreshments sent to the drawing room," he told Wainwright, before turning to offer Felicity his arm. He was annoyed to see that Willingdon had beaten him to it, and Felicity's hand was already resting comfortably on the marquess's elbow.

When they reached the drawing room, Willingdon settled Felicity on the sofa and took the seat next to her, while Kincaid went to the sideboard to pour a glass of brandy.

"Shall I send for Miss Flint?" Kincaid asked, handing Felicity the drink.

"No," Felicity said. "She had a terrible cold this morning, and I expect she's already asleep."

"All right." Kincaid took the seat opposite her and studied her face. "What happened, Felicity?"

Felicity took a deep breath and began the story. "And you don't need to tell me I was foolish," she said miserably, after explaining how Lady Delphinia and Mr. Nethercott had persuaded her to get in the carriage. "I know the story about searching for the necklace in Dover wouldn't have deceived a child."

"I wasn't going to say you were foolish," Kincaid said gently. "They're your cousins, Felicity. You had no reason to mistrust them."

Felicity didn't agree, but she decided to continue with the tale before she lost momentum. "When we reached the inn at Barnet, Lady Delphinia left the carriage, and I realized we weren't going to Dover. Mr. Nethercott admitted he was taking me to Gretna Green, where we could be married without banns or a licence. Lady Delphinia planned to tell everyone in London that I had eloped with him, and if I refused to marry him, my reputation would be ruined."

A muscle ticked in Kincaid's jaw, but he didn't say anything.

"I managed to escape when we stopped in Welwyn to change horses," Felicity continued. "I was wearing the horseshoe brooch you gave me for my birthday, and I scratched Mr. Nethercott's face with it. I'm afraid I dropped the brooch," she said apologetically. "And I didn't stop to look for it."

"It doesn't matter," Kincaid said quickly. "I'll buy you another. How did you end up in Willingdon's company?"

"After I escaped from Mr. Nethercott, I saw an ostler leading a horse to the stables," Felicity explained. "It belonged to Lord Willingdon, although I didn't know it at the time. Nethercott was yelling about the scratch on his cheek, and the ostler was so distracted that I was able to take the horse and ride away. When Lord Willingdon learned that his horse had been stolen, he hired a horse from the inn and caught up to me. I explained what

Nethercott had done, and Lord Willingdon was very kind."

"The situation was unfortunate, but I don't think it was Miss Taylor's fault," Willingdon said. "And I haven't forgotten what she did for my son."

"It was good of you to escort her home, Willingdon," Kincaid said, hoping the marquess would take it as his signal to leave. He was grateful to Willingdon, of course, but he wished to speak to Felicity privately.

Willingdon, however, showed no intention of moving from his position next to Felicity on the sofa. "I'm afraid this affair has the potential to compromise Miss Taylor's reputation," he remarked gravely.

"I'll deal with the Nethercotts," Kincaid interrupted. "Lady Delphinia may not have spread the story yet, and if she has, she can tell her friends she was mistaken."

Willingdon cleared his throat. "I'm afraid I don't share your optimism, Mr. Kincaid," he said gravely. "I'm afraid you don't appreciate how difficult it is to stop rumours once they start."

At that moment, Kincaid was thinking that he didn't appreciate the marquess. He knew that despite his efforts with the Nethercotts the story would likely get out, but there was no need for the marquess to point out the obvious. Kincaid was irked by Willingdon's condescending tone, his closeness to Felicity on the sofa, and even his habit of starting his sentences with 'I'm afraid.'

But much as it galled him, he was indebted to Willingdon for escorting Felicity safely home. Kincaid swallowed the retort that had risen to his lips and forced himself to smile at the marquess. "We'll deal with that problem if it arises."

"I've always thought it's better to forestall a problem before it occurs," Willingdon said, frowning at Kincaid. "Which is why I made Miss Taylor an offer of marriage."

Kincaid fought to keep his expression neutral. "I see," he said lightly. He turned to Felicity, who was staring intently at the floor. "Did Miss Taylor accept?"

Felicity didn't reply immediately, so Willingdon answered for her. "She did." His tone of voice suggested that he had never doubted the outcome of his proposal.

"Then allow me to congratulate you both," Kincaid said. He looked at Felicity, who still refused to meet his eye. "I think Miss Taylor is tired," he said, rising to stand.

Willingdon finally recognized the signal to leave. He stood and kissed Felicity's hand, promising to call on her the next day to discuss the plans for their wedding.

"I don't suppose you saw Nethercott?" Kincaid asked casually, as he escorted the marquess to the door. "Do you know if he planned to spend the night at Welwyn?"

Willingdon shook his head. "I imagine he's back in London by now." His lips curved in a smile of satisfaction. "He caught up to us on the road, and I think he was quite surprised to learn of our engagement."

Kincaid's eyes widened. "Did you call him out?"

"Certainly not," Willingdon said with a frown. "I don't believe in gratuitous violence. But I persuaded Nethercott to let Felicity ride in his carriage."

"How did you do that?" Although Kincaid was relieved the marquess wasn't planning to fight a duel with Felicity's cousin, he would have been pleased to hear that Willingdon had taken the carriage by force.

"I told him that since he had behaved so dishonourably, the least he could do was to allow Miss Taylor to ride in his carriage," Willingdon said matter-of-factly.

"Indeed," Kincaid murmured. "How clever of you."

Willingdon nodded. "I wasn't aware Miss Taylor still lived with you," he remarked. "I understood that your guardianship had ended, now that she is of age?"

"Oh, I don't live here," Kincaid said quickly. "I own this house, but I live down the street."

This appeared to confuse Willingdon, but Kincaid spoke again before the marquess could question the arrangement. "I am still the trustee of Miss Taylor's fortune, and I'll call upon you later this week to discuss the marriage settlement."

Willingdon departed and Kincaid returned to the drawing room, where he found Felicity absently stroking Cleopatra. A maid had brought a tray of bread and cheese, but it sat untouched on the table.

"You might feel better if you eat something," Kincaid suggested.

"I'm not hungry," Felicity replied, but she forced herself to meet his eyes and smile.

"I'm sorry, Felicity."

"It isn't your fault. I was a fool to get in the carriage."

"You couldn't have known, Felicity. If anyone is to blame, it's me." He moved a chair closer to Felicity and sat facing her. "Nethercott took your necklace. I suspected him from the start, and when I went to see him this morning, he admitted it." He took a black velvet pouch from the pocket of his waistcoat and handed it to Felicity. "Nethercott had already sold it, but I was able to redeem it from the pawnbroker."

Felicity opened the pouch and pulled out her pearl

necklace. "Thank you, Mr. Kincaid. What did you have to pay to redeem it?"

"It doesn't signify."

"Of course it does," Felicity insisted. "The money should come from my fortune. We'll explain it to Mr. Battersby, and—"

"I don't want you to reimburse me, Felicity," Kincaid said tersely. "I said it doesn't signify."

"All right," she agreed. "Thank you."

"You shouldn't thank me, Felicity," he said bitterly. "If I had told you of my suspicions this morning, you would never have agreed to get into that carriage. When I think that I could have prevented this . . ." He trailed off and raked his fingers through his hair.

Felicity shook her head. "I should have known that my cousin took the necklace. That's why he said the clasp was loose and told me to put it in my reticule. And when he left at intermission, he went to instruct his groom."

"You had no reason to suspect him, Felicity."

"You seem to have figured it out easily enough."

"I knew Nethercott was desperate for money," Kincaid said with a sigh. "But I never thought he would try to abduct you. I wish I had told you about the necklace when you came to see me this morning, but—"

"You shouldn't blame yourself," Felicity interrupted, with more energy than she had displayed all evening. "The only person to blame is Nethercott himself. Well, I suppose Lady Delphinia, too, since she helped him."

Kincaid nodded but didn't reply. It was impossible for him not to blame himself; he had not only failed to tell Felicity of his suspicions, but he had ignored his servants' warning that Felicity had departed in a carriage bound for Gretna Green. If he had pursued them, he might have had the satisfaction of rescuing Felicity himself.

He looked so despondent that Felicity briefly forgot about her own misery. "If you had warned me about my cousin, he might have been forced to try a different method," she said lightly. "He might have crept into my bedchamber in the night, knocked me on the head, and smuggled me out through the window. I really think that would have been worse."

"You shouldn't joke about such things, Felicity," Kincaid said quietly. He leaned closer to Felicity, studying her face as though to convince himself she was truly unharmed. "You don't have to marry Willingdon, you know. The story may not get out, and even if it does, the consequences may not be as bad as you think. Some men will be put off by the rumours, but I think a good man would understand."

"My fortune might help him understand the circumstances," Felicity said wryly.

"I didn't say that."

"I know." Kincaid had never seen her as simply an heiress; it was one of the reasons she loved him. His face was only inches from hers, close enough for her to smell the familiar spice of his shaving soap, and she fought the temptation to bury her face in his chest and let herself cry.

But crying wouldn't help either of them, so there was nothing for Felicity to do but pretend.

"I think I would like to marry Lord Willingdon," she said, forcing another smile.

Kincaid nodded. "I'll call upon him later this week to discuss the terms of your marriage settlement."

"Just think, you'll soon be relieved of your responsibility for my affairs," Felicity remarked lightly. "I imagine it will be a weight off your shoulders."

"I won't know what to do with all my spare time," Kincaid said dryly. "I have to leave you now; shall I ring for your maid?"

"You're leaving?" Felicity asked. "I was hoping you might stay a little longer, or maybe even spend the night in your old bedchamber?"

Kincaid knew it hadn't been easy for Felicity to ask him to stay, and he hesitated for a moment before shaking his head. "I wish I could stay, Felicity, but I have an appointment this evening."

"And it can't be rescheduled?" Felicity couldn't imagine what sort of appointment he could have at that hour of the night.

Kincaid's expression hardened. "No, it can't be rescheduled. But you're safe here, Felicity. I'll tell Wainwright that if he lets anyone else into the house tonight, he'll be demoted to a footman."

Felicity managed a chuckle, and Kincaid rang the bell for her maid.

Twenty-One

The following morning, Martin Nethercott left for Dover on the stagecoach, the only means of travel he could afford. In a rare act of selflessness, he had left his horse and carriage behind so his mother would have something to sell to pay her bills. Since he had been paying her rent, Lady Delphinia would soon be forced to leave her townhouse, but he wasn't worried about where his mother would go. Lady Delphinia was the type to land on her feet, and he imagined she would soon find a gentleman to support her.

Nethercott's battered body felt every bump on the road, and his black eye and scratched cheek attracted curious stares from the other passengers. He had been ignominiously beaten in a fistfight the previous evening, and his opponent had persuaded him that a long trip abroad would be good for his health. He planned to sail from Dover to Calais, and to continue to Paris after that.

All in all, Nethercott wasn't sorry to leave England,

where he had nothing but debts to his name. Perhaps his luck would be better in France.

"What happened to your lip?" Felicity asked Kincaid when he joined her and Miss Flint in the breakfast parlour.

Kincaid ran his fingers over his swollen lower lip and the small cut that extended into the skin below it. "It's nothing," he said dismissively. "The razor slipped while I was being shaved this morning. How are you feeling, Felicity?"

"Much better," Felicity said truthfully. A good night's sleep had done a great deal to restore her spirits.

Kincaid cast a questioning look at Miss Flint, and Felicity hastened to reassure him. "I told Miss Flint the whole story this morning."

"I've never heard of such a villain!" Miss Flint declared, with a militant look in her eye. "The next time I encounter Mr. Nethercott, I mean to tell him what I think of his behaviour."

Felicity sighed. "For my part, I hope I never encounter him again, but . . ." She trailed off when Jane Harris strode into the room.

"Good morning, Miss Harris," Kincaid said, standing to greet her. "What a lovely surprise."

"Your butler was going to ask if you would receive me at the breakfast table, but I explained that I'm practically family," Jane said with a laugh.

"Of course." Kincaid pulled out a chair for his

betrothed. "I don't know what Wainwright was thinking. Will you join us for breakfast?"

"I've already eaten." Jane took a step towards him and stared at his lower lip curiously. "My goodness, Mr. Kincaid," she said in a disapproving tone. "You look as though you've been in a brawl."

"It was a shaving accident," Felicity put in helpfully.

Jane continued to frown at Kincaid's cut. "You might have been seriously injured," she remarked. "If your valet is as careless as that, you should replace him."

"It's only a scratch," Kincaid said impatiently.

Jane pursed her lips. "I came to ask if you had made any progress in the search for Felicity's necklace."

"Mr. Kincaid recovered it yesterday," Felicity said cheerfully.

"Really?" Jane asked. "How fortunate. Where did you find it?"

"At a pawn shop in the East End," Kincaid explained.

"It was clever of you to find it so quickly," Jane said, looking at him with admiration.

"It was luck," Kincaid said curtly.

Jane had opened her mouth to argue the point when Wainwright appeared in the doorway.

"Lord Willingdon has arrived, and is waiting in the drawing room," the butler announced. "Although, if you would prefer, I can show him in here?"

Jane sprang to her feet. "We will go to the drawing room," she declared, as though she was already the mistress of the house. "We are certainly not going to receive Lord Willingdon in the breakfast parlour."

Felicity swallowed a bite of toast and gave Jane an impish smile. "I don't see why we couldn't," she said thoughtfully. "After all, the marquess is practically family."

Jane's eyes widened. "Practically family?"

"Felicity is engaged to marry Lord Willingdon," Kincaid explained.

"Engaged to Lord Willingdon?" Jane repeated in disbelief.

"Yes," Felicity confirmed. "Is it really so shocking?"

"Not shocking," Jane said quickly, recovering her composure. "Merely unexpected. But I congratulate you, Felicity. When did this happen?"

"Yesterday," Felicity explained. "The marquess and I were riding together, and he made me an offer of marriage."

"We shouldn't keep Lord Willingdon waiting," Kincaid said, hoping to forestall further questioning from Jane. He hoped to keep the true story of Felicity's engagement a secret, and it was bad luck that the marquess had called while Jane was there.

They found Lord Willingdon pacing in front of the drawing room window. After bowing punctiliously to the ladies, the marquess announced he wished to speak to Felicity about the plans for their marriage. Kincaid led Jane and Miss Flint to the opposite end of the room to give the newly engaged couple some privacy.

"I wanted to tell you, Miss Taylor, that I have sent a notice to the papers and obtained a special licence," Willingdon began. "Given the circumstances, I think we should be married as quickly as possible."

Jane was staring at them with barely concealed interest, and Felicity was afraid their conversation could be heard across the room. She rushed to speak before the marquess could explain why he thought a hasty marriage was necessary. "I am certainly eager to marry you, Lord Willingdon, but I will need time to prepare."

"Certainly," Willingdon agreed. "I thought we could wait until next Saturday."

"Next Saturday!" Felicity blurted. "So soon!" Kincaid, who was also listening to their conversation, thought she looked terrified.

"Yes, next Saturday," Willingdon repeated, looking at her strangely.

"Oh, Lord Willingdon," Felicity began. "You must understand, I have dreamed of my wedding since I was a little girl. I have a vision of the dress I want to wear, but it can't be made in under a month."

Now Lord Willingdon looked surprised. "A month! I don't see how it could take a month to make a dress."

"Oh, at least a month," Felicity insisted. "And that's if the fabric is readily available. The lace may need to be ordered from France, which will take several weeks more."

"I don't see why you need such an elaborate dress," Willingdon said with a frown. "It's not as though we're going to have a big ceremony."

"The size of the ceremony doesn't matter," Felicity insisted. "What's important is that you will see the dress, and I want to look beautiful for you."

"I'm sure you will look beautiful, Miss Taylor," Willingdon said, looking embarrassed. "But since money isn't an object, I'm sure the modiste could hire additional seamstresses to complete the work quickly. And perhaps you could make do with English lace?"

Felicity's brow furrowed. "I suppose," she conceded.

"But if the seamstresses are in a rush, they may make mistakes, and the process may take longer."

There was a beat of silence as Willingdon considered this, and Felicity pressed her advantage. "I think it would be bad luck to wear a wedding dress that had been sewn in a rush," she said. "And if the seamstresses rush, they'll be unhappy, and a wedding dress sewn by unhappy seamstresses is likely to lead to an unhappy marriage."

"An unhappy marriage?" Willingdon said dubiously. "Because the seamstresses were rushed?"

"Yes," Felicity said, as though it was a perfectly natural concern.

"Miss Taylor, you must see that such an idea isn't rational," the marquess said gently. "The feelings of the women who sew your dress won't affect your happiness. That's like thinking it's unlucky to have thirteen people to dinner."

Felicity's eyes widened. "But of course it's unlucky to have thirteen people to dinner," she told him. "Surely you've heard that, Lord Willingdon. If you have thirteen people to dinner, one of them is likely to suffer a great misfortune within a year!"

"But there is no reason why someone is more likely to suffer a misfortune if you have dinner with thirteen people than with twelve," Willingdon said. "It's a superstition, Felicity, and we must deal in facts."

"But if you invite more people, you increase the odds that one of them will suffer a misfortune," Felicity pointed out.

"Well, yes," Willingdon admitted, unable to argue with that logic. "But it has nothing to do with the number thirteen."

Jane could no longer resist the temptation to join the debate, and she crossed the room to sit opposite Felicity. "My governess used to say that superstition was a refuge for the uneducated," she remarked.

Willingdon gave her an approving look. "I quite agree, Miss Harris."

Felicity looked at him thoughtfully before turning to Jane. "That's a very interesting idea, Jane. I think I would be wise to improve my education before I marry."

Kincaid walked over to take a chair next to Jane. "I'm sure Jane didn't mean to imply that there was anything lacking in your education, Felicity," he said kindly.

"Oh, I'm sure she didn't," Felicity said quickly, turning back to Lord Willingdon. "But I want to be a credit to you, Lord Willingdon. Perhaps you could suggest a course of study for me to pursue while we wait for the dress to be finished."

"I would be pleased to do so," Willingdon told her. "As you may know, I have made a study of educational methods."

"Perhaps you could help me too, Jane," Felicity said earnestly. "With four younger sisters, you must have a great deal of teaching experience."

When Jane hesitated, Willingdon spoke. "That's an excellent idea," he agreed. "I'm sure your help would be invaluable, Miss Harris."

Jane's cheeks reddened at his praise. "I would be happy to help."

"We could begin tomorrow afternoon," Felicity suggested. "Shall we meet here at two o'clock?"

"Very well," Willingdon agreed. "Is that convenient for you, Miss Harris?"

"Yes," Jane replied.

"I'll have to think about what books to bring," Willingdon said thoughtfully. "I have several that I think you'll appreciate."

"I look forward to it," Felicity replied.

"But about our wedding date, Miss Taylor . . ." Willingdon began.

"I think we should wait at least two months, so I'll have time to complete my studies," Felicity said thoughtfully. "And if we wait until June, it will be less likely to rain. I've heard that rain at a wedding is a bad omen."

Willingdon and Jane left a short time later, and Miss Flint proved her worth as a chaperone by taking herself and her knitting to a chair in the corner. Kincaid turned to Felicity, who was staring out the window, apparently deep in thought.

"I thought we might call upon the Langleys tomorrow," Kincaid suggested casually. "Lady Langley might explain what to expect in a marriage. On your wedding night."

"If you like," Felicity said placidly. "Although I would think it would be an awkward conversation for you to have with Amelia. If you're ignorant of the subject, you might do better to ask Lord Langley."

"Felicity!" he exclaimed. "You know I meant for Lady Langley to explain it to you. I thought my mother would do it, but since she's still at Brentwood, I thought Lady Langley might."

"What brought this to mind?"

"I know you're not superstitious, Felicity," he said with a sigh. "I wondered if you were hoping to delay your wedding because you were nervous."

"I am nervous," Felicity admitted, with a mischievous smile. "But not about the wedding night, merely about the prospect of having an inferior dress." She rose to her feet. "I'm going to ask Miss Flint if she will accompany me to Madame Sylvie's."

Kincaid watched her cross the room, admiring the way her dark hair shone in the midday sun that was streaming through the drawing room window. He was tempted to tell her it didn't matter what she wore to her wedding; all anyone would see was the gleam of her hair, the light in her eyes, and the graceful way she moved.

He gave his head a shake and decided he would spend the afternoon reviewing Felicity's investments. He intended to call upon Willingdon the following day to discuss Felicity's marriage settlement, and he wanted to ensure that everything was in order.

When Felicity and Miss Flint arrived at Madame Sylvie's, they found the modiste in the midst of an argument with a haughty baroness. Upon seeing Felicity, Sylvie tried to hand her unhappy customer off to an assistant, but the baroness took offence and left in a huff.

"I'm sorry, Sylvie," Felicity apologized, as the modiste led them to the back room. "I'm afraid I've cost you a customer."

"That one is no loss," Sylvie said with a sniff. "The gown she wants me to make would only suit a young lady, and I've told her I won't do it. If she wants someone to make her look ridiculous, she can go elsewhere."

Felicity chuckled, but the humour didn't reach her eyes, and something about her expression troubled Sylvie. "How was your ball?" Sylvie asked. "Were you pleased with the red satin?"

"Oh, yes," Felicity replied matter-of-factly. "It turned out just as I hoped. And now I need a wedding dress, Sylvie. I'm going to be married."

"Congratulations, *chérie*," Sylvie said carefully. "Who is the fortunate gentleman?"

"The Marquess of Willingdon," Felicity replied woodenly. She didn't bother pretending she was overjoyed, since Sylvie knew her too well to be fooled.

"That happened quickly," Sylvie remarked.

Felicity nodded and told her the story, beginning with the day she rescued Willingdon's son Ernest from the Serpentine.

"You are a brave girl, Felicity," Sylvie said.

"Brave, but also very foolish," Felicity said ruefully. She went on to explain about Nethercott's abduction and her escape on Willingdon's horse.

"That doesn't sound foolish," Sylvie argued. "It was natural for you to trust your cousin."

Felicity shrugged. "When Lord Willingdon learned what had happened, he thought it was his duty to propose to me. Since I rescued his son, he thinks he is in my debt."

"I'm sure that's not the only reason he proposed to you," Madame Sylvie said kindly.

"Oh, he said it was."

"Even so, it may be a good basis for marriage," Sylvie

said philosophically. "You saved his son, and he will save your reputation."

"Maybe."

"If you don't want to marry Lord Willingdon, I don't see why you must," Sylvie said. "There may be rumours about the incident with Mr. Nethercott, but many people won't believe them. And your parents left you a great deal of money, did they not?"

"Yes," Felicity admitted.

"So you don't have to marry at all," Sylvie pointed out. "There are worse things than living alone."

"I know," Felicity agreed with a sigh. "But my parents left me the money in trust, under Mr. Kincaid's control. He promised to give me the income from it when I turned twenty-one, but there's nothing to stop him from changing his mind. I would never truly be independent, and all in all, I might as well marry Lord Willingdon."

"Ah," Sylvie said. "And Mr. Kincaid, is he still betrothed to the young lady who wanted to wear a green dress?"

"Miss Harris, yes," Felicity said, with a strange little smile. "She looked lovely in the blue dress you made her."

"Hmm." Sylvie still didn't understand why Felicity had been so determined to save Jane from a sartorial disaster.

"But marriage to Lord Willingdon won't be so bad," Felicity said, as though she was trying to convince herself. "He's a scholar, you know, and he's working to develop a new method of teaching Latin. So he will be occupied with that, and I can spend my time riding and sewing. Really, I think it will work out rather well."

"I see many young ladies who are convinced that marriage will make them happy," Sylvie said thoughtfully. "And I'm afraid most of them are disappointed. But you, Felicity, are planning to make your own happiness, and I think you will succeed."

Felicity hoped Sylvie was right. "I'll send you an invitation to the wedding, Sylvie."

"I can't attend a marquess's wedding, Felicity," Sylvie scoffed, although she was secretly touched. "But I will come and stand outside the church, and watch you and Lord Willingdon leave together."

Felicity nodded. "And I'll need a dress."

"Do you have a design in mind?" Sylvie asked. "Have you brought me any sketches?"

Felicity shook her head. Contrary to what she had told Lord Willingdon, she didn't care what she wore to her wedding. "I'll leave it in your hands, Sylvie."

"I will make you a magnificent dress," Sylvie assured her. "Every man in the church will wish he was marrying you."

"Thank you, Sylvie," Felicity replied, but she didn't look cheered by the prospect. She didn't care if every man in the church admired her; there was only one man whose admiration she sought, but unfortunately, he was not the man she was preparing to marry.

Twenty-Two

The following morning, Kincaid presented his visiting card to Lord Willingdon's sour-faced butler.

"I will ask if the marquess is receiving visitors, sir," the man said superciliously.

As he waited in the entrance hall, Kincaid wondered what Felicity would think of the butler. His own servants liked Felicity a great deal, and he imagined she would charm Willingdon's servants just as easily.

Ten minutes later, the butler returned with the news that Lord Willingdon would receive him. Kincaid was led to the study, where the marquess was seated behind a cluttered desk. There were several books open in front of him, and he was so engrossed in his work that the butler had to announce Kincaid twice before he looked up.

"I'm sorry to disturb you, Willingdon," Kincaid said, striding into the room.

"Not at all," Willingdon said politely, gesturing for him to take a chair on the opposite side of the desk. "I'm afraid I've been distracted by this translation, so I don't recall if we had an appointment?"

"Not exactly," Kincaid replied. "But I'm one of Miss Taylor's trustees, and I would like to discuss her marriage settlement. I imagine you know she inherited a large fortune?"

Willingdon bristled. "I can assure you, Mr. Kincaid, that I am not marrying Miss Taylor for her fortune." He paused. "How much money does she have?"

Kincaid named a figure that made Willingdon's eyes widen. "Almost half is in the Funds, but I've also invested in various stocks and a small shipping company," he explained. He had devoted considerable time and energy to managing Felicity's money, and now that he was reasonably confident she wouldn't waste it on fripperies or lose it at Newmarket, he could have happily given her the lot. He was having difficulty, however, with the thought of giving it to her husband.

"That is a handsome fortune," the marquess finally said. "But I have my own money, and I won't need to rely upon my wife's."

"I am aware of that." Kincaid knew Willingdon was a very wealthy man, and he hoped it would induce him to be generous with Felicity.

"I suppose you want to discuss the terms of her jointure," Willingdon said, referring to the income Felicity would receive if she were widowed. "If half of her money is in the Funds, I think it would be fair for her to receive the income from that."

"All right," Kincaid agreed. It wasn't a particularly generous offer, since the money in the Funds earned significantly less than the other investments, but it would allow Felicity to live very comfortably. "I also thought a portion of her money could be set aside for any children of your marriage."

Willingdon gave him a look of distaste. "You may rest assured that I will make suitable provisions for our children."

Kincaid tried not to show his frustration. "There is also the matter of her allowance—"

"Miss Taylor will never want for anything while she is my wife."

"Then you should not object to discussing the terms of her allowance," Kincaid persisted. "She will need money for her clothes—"

"I can assure you that I will make her an allowance that is sufficient for her needs," Willingdon interrupted.

"And as I'm sure you know, Miss Taylor loves horses," Kincaid continued. "Her mare, Sugarplum, will come with her. She drives very well, and she may wish to purchase a phaeton and pair."

Willingdon knitted his brows together and grimaced. "I have a carriage and a coachman, so my wife will have no reason to drive herself."

"No reason except that she would enjoy it."

"I can't see why she would," Willingdon remarked, looking genuinely perplexed by the suggestion that Felicity would enjoy driving. "But it is certainly not something that I would permit."

Kincaid took a deep breath and gritted his teeth. He knew he wasn't negotiating from a position of strength; after all, Felicity had essentially stolen Willingdon's horse after spending the day in a closed carriage with a fortune hunter. Although Felicity insisted that Nethercott hadn't done anything more than kiss her, there were many who wouldn't believe it. All Willingdon had to do was spread the story, and Felicity's reputation would be ruined.

"I thought I could explain how Miss Taylor's money is invested?" Kincaid tried. "It's made quite a good return over the past seven years. I could explain why I chose the investments I did, since you may want to keep some of them."

"Yes, yes, I'm sure you've done very well," Willingdon said dismissively. "But I have a man who manages my financial affairs, and I'm sure he'll sort it out."

"Certainly," Kincaid agreed. "Miss Taylor also owns a small estate in Hampshire, Fairleigh Manor. It's run by quite a capable land agent, but it may require your attention from time to time." He paused. "She likes to ride there in the summer."

Willingdon frowned. "We will spend most of our summers at Willingdon," he said, referring to his principal seat in Derbyshire.

"Of course," Kincaid said. "But she might like to go to Fairleigh on occasion."

"I'll keep it in mind," Willingdon replied. "If there's nothing else, I'll have my solicitor draw up a contract outlining the terms of the jointure."

"Thank you." Since it was clear that further discussion was pointless, Kincaid rose to leave. As the butler showed him to the door, he tried to convince himself that he had done all he could.

The following week, Kincaid called at 23 Bentley to ask Felicity if she wished to go riding.

"I'm afraid I've already made plans with Lord Willingdon," Felicity said regretfully.

"I suppose you're discussing the plans for your wedding?" Kincaid asked casually.

"Actually, Lord Willingdon is teaching me Latin."

"Teaching you Latin?" Kincaid repeated incredulously.

Felicity nodded. "Don't you remember? I would like to improve my education before I get married, and Lord Willingdon offered to help me."

"I didn't think you were serious." Kincaid had thought Felicity was simply trying to delay her wedding, although he still didn't understand her reasons for it.

"Well, I was," Felicity said with a shrug. "I never learned Latin, so Lord Willingdon is teaching me."

"No doubt you blame me for this deficiency in your education," Kincaid said dryly.

"Oh, no," Felicity replied. "Much as I would like to blame you, it wouldn't be fair. One of my governesses tried to teach me Latin, but I'm afraid I was a poor pupil. I didn't see the point of it."

"I see."

"Do you read Latin, Mr. Kincaid?"

"I used to," Kincaid said carefully. "I haven't had much use for it since I left Oxford. I'm afraid Lord Willingdon would be disappointed in my abilities."

"He probably would," Felicity agreed. "But he doesn't mind my ignorance, since it gives him an opportunity to test his method of Latin instruction on an untainted mind."

"Really?"

Felicity nodded. "He hopes his method will be adopted at Eton, and he also plans to start a charity school and teach the pupils Latin. He says I'm the perfect test subject for his method, since I'm at least as intelligent as the average schoolboy."

Kincaid looked at her skeptically. "Willingdon didn't really say that?"

"Oh, he certainly did," Felicity said with a grin. "You don't agree?"

"I think you're far more intelligent than the average schoolboy," Kincaid said truthfully. "That's why you caused me so much trouble. But I would think Willingdon's charity pupils would be better served by learning to read and write in English."

"Oh, they'll probably learn that too," Felicity said. "After Latin and Greek, of course. Lord Willingdon means to teach me Greek, but he doesn't want to begin until after we're married."

Kincaid chuckled. "Is he afraid it will lead to improprieties?"

"He would prefer to start Greek when I no longer need a chaperone," Felicity said earnestly. "It seems Miss Flint never learned it, and Lord Willingdon thinks she will find the lessons so interesting that she will want to participate. The marquess is interested in the results of one-on-one instruction, you see."

Kincaid gaped at her. "Felicity, you're not serious."

"I never joke about Greek, Mr. Kincaid," she replied, although there was a twinkle of mischief in her dark eyes. "Lord Willingdon thought we might put some of my fortune towards the charity school."

"Why doesn't he use his own fortune?" Kincaid asked with a frown.

"Oh, he'll put some of his own money towards it as well," Felicity explained. "But he thought I would like to contribute."

"Generous of him," Kincaid said, studying her expression carefully. "Are you happy, Felicity?"

Felicity knew he was really asking if she was happy with Willingdon, and she took a moment to consider her answer.

"Yes, I suppose I am," she finally replied. "I think Lord Willingdon and I will manage very well together."

Kincaid smiled in spite of himself. He had no doubt that when Felicity spoke of managing well, she intended to be the one managing Lord Willingdon. "Be careful, Felicity. Lord Willingdon may not appreciate your efforts to manage him."

"Oh, I know that. Lord Willingdon strikes me as the sort of man who likes to think he is in charge."

"Indeed," Kincaid said dryly.

"So I suppose something good came out of Mr. Nethercott's treachery," Felicity said thoughtfully. "That's not to say I forgive him, or that I ever want to see him again." The memory of Nethercott's behaviour in the carriage still made her shudder.

"You won't have to see Nethercott again," Kincaid assured her. "I heard he went abroad."

"Abroad!" Felicity exclaimed. "To escape from his debts?"

"I believe so." The ghost of a smile tugged at Kincaid's lips.

"You had something to do with it, didn't you?" Felicity asked suspiciously.

Kincaid didn't deny it. "I acquired one of Nethercott's more pressing debts and told him if he didn't leave England, I'd have him sent to a debtor's prison." He had bought the debt from a moneylender immediately after redeeming Felicity's necklace, intending to use it to persuade Nethercott to leave Felicity alone. "I spoke to Lady Delphinia, too. She's not leaving the country, but she won't bother you again."

Felicity remembered the cut on Kincaid's lip the day after the abduction. "Did you hurt Nethercott, Mr. Kincaid?"

"Maybe a little," Kincaid replied cautiously. He studied her face, wondering if it would upset her to learn that he had beaten her cousin. "I know he's your cousin, Felicity, but I couldn't help myself. He deserved far worse."

"He certainly did!" Felicity agreed, with a vengeful look in her eyes. "Thank you, Mr. Kincaid."

"Had I known you would feel that way, I would have told you sooner," Kincaid said with a chuckle.

"I wish I could have done it myself, but I never learned how to fight." Felicity paused and regarded him thoughtfully. "Do you think—"

"No," he interrupted firmly.

"You don't even know what I was going to ask you," she protested.

"Felicity, I will not teach you how to fight."

"What about how to fence? Or shoot a pistol?"

"No," he said firmly. "I will not instruct you in any form of physical violence."

"Why not?"

"My sense of self-preservation is too strong."

"That's not fair, Mr. Kincaid," Felicity protested. "Although we've had our differences of opinion, I've never resorted to violence. I've certainly been tempted, but I've managed to restrain myself."

Kincaid wasn't worried that she would lose control, but that he would. There was something very intimate about teaching a woman self-defence.

"Mr. Kincaid?"

He realized he had been staring at the wall, and he returned his gaze to Felicity. "If anyone's going to teach you those skills, it should be your husband," he said crisply. "You should ask Willingdon."

Felicity smiled. "Perhaps I will, but not today. Lord Willingdon wants to discuss one of Cicero's speeches, and Jane is going to join us."

"It sounds fascinating," Kincaid remarked. "Are they coming here?"

Felicity shook her head. "We meet at Lord Willingdon's house now, since his library is more extensive. He's sending his carriage to pick us up."

Kincaid frowned. "You're welcome to take my carriage, you know."

"I'll keep that in mind," Felicity said easily. "But we've already made arrangements for this afternoon."

"Of course," Kincaid said, rising to leave. "I'm pleased to hear that you're happy, Felicity."

"Oh, I am," Felicity assured him.

~

Kincaid was curious to see how Felicity was progressing with her Latin, and he found himself on Willingdon's doorstep later that afternoon. When the butler tried to tell him the marquess was occupied, Kincaid explained that he had come to join the Latin lesson.

He was shown to the marquess's study, where he found Willingdon and Jane sitting side by side with their heads bent over a book. Willingdon was reading aloud, and neither of them noticed Kincaid standing in the doorway. As Willingdon reached to turn the page, his hand brushed Jane's, and she met his eye and blushed.

Since the butler seemed reluctant to interrupt them, Kincaid strode into the room unannounced. "Good afternoon," he said, bowing to Jane. "I thought I would escort you home, to save Lord Willingdon's coachman the trouble."

Jane did not look ashamed to have been found in another man's study without a chaperone. "That was thoughtful, Mr. Kincaid," she said. "But do you think you could wait another quarter of an hour? Lord Willingdon and I have a difference of opinion on the meaning of this phrase."

"Perhaps you would care to give us your thoughts, Kincaid?" Willingdon asked.

"I wouldn't," Kincaid said succinctly. "Where is Miss Taylor?"

"Felicity and Miss Flint are upstairs in the nursery with Lord Ernest," Jane explained. "Felicity said her brain had absorbed all it could for one afternoon."

"I see," Kincaid said curtly. "Then I will take you home and return for Felicity, to give her a chance to become better acquainted with Lord Ernest."

Jane was clearly reluctant to leave, but something in Kincaid's eyes warned her not to argue with him. "Thank you for an enjoyable afternoon, Lord Willingdon," she said.

"The pleasure was entirely mine, Miss Harris," Willingdon said with a bow. "I hope you will join us again."

Jane beamed. "I would like that very much. I will try to accompany Miss Taylor the next time she visits."

When they were alone in his carriage, Kincaid faced Jane. "You seem to have become well acquainted with Lord Willingdon."

"Oh, yes," Jane agreed. "We share a great many interests, you know. Lord Willingdon is a Latin scholar, and he is working on a new instructional method."

"How fascinating."

"Yes, it is," Jane agreed, oblivious to the sarcasm in his tone. "While I wouldn't presume to call myself a scholar, I have always been interested in Latin, and I think I've been able to make some helpful suggestions."

"I'm pleased to hear it," Kincaid said abruptly. "I hope you shared all your ideas today, because I don't want you to go back to Lord Willingdon's house."

"Not go back to his house?" Jane asked in disbelief. "Why not?"

"You were alone with Willingdon in his study, and it isn't proper, Jane!" Kincaid exclaimed. "Willingdon is betrothed to Felicity."

"Yes, and I am betrothed to you!" Jane retorted. "But sometimes I think you've forgotten."

"I can assure you I haven't forgotten," Kincaid said curtly. "I apologize if I've been neglecting you."

"It seems unfair for you to accuse me of impropriety,"

Jane continued. "Lord Willingdon and I were merely reading a book."

"You were practically sitting in his pocket, Jane!"

To his surprise, Jane smiled at this. "Were you jealous, Mr. Kincaid?" she asked archly.

Kincaid realized he wouldn't care if Jane jilted him for another man, so long as that man wasn't Willingdon. The marquess was promised to Felicity, and she seemed to be happy in her engagement. Personally, Kincaid thought the man was a dead bore, but Willingdon was certainly eligible, and he meant to support Felicity's choice.

"Perhaps I was a little jealous," he lied. "I don't want you going back to Willingdon's house."

This answer seemed to please Jane a great deal. "I was starting to think you didn't care," she said happily. "You didn't seem eager to set a wedding date, and—"

"Let's set a date," Kincaid said recklessly. "In two weeks' time. I'll speak to the vicar tomorrow."

"Two weeks!" Jane exclaimed. "That won't be enough time for the reading of the banns, much less to organize a ceremony."

"I'll apply for a special licence, so we won't need to bother with the banns," Kincaid told her. "We won't need to have the ceremony in the church, either. My drawing room should accommodate our close friends and family, so there should be no impediment. Unless you were still hoping for a more elaborate affair?"

Jane realized that after complaining about his reluctance to set a date, she could hardly object to his wish to be married quickly. "I don't want a big wedding, Mr. Kincaid," she assured him. "I only want to be your wife."

"Then we agree," he said. "I'll arrange for the licence and let you know when the date is confirmed."

After walking Jane to her door, Kincaid returned to Lord Willingdon's, where he was told Felicity was still in the nursery. He found her and Ernest racing across the room on all fours, while Miss Flint and the nanny looked on. Neither of the racers noticed that another spectator had arrived, and Kincaid watched from the doorway as Ernest romped to victory.

"I won!" Ernest crowed as he touched the far wall.

"Fair and square," Felicity conceded. Her hair was coming loose from her coiffure, and she raised a hand to tuck a curl behind her ear.

Ernest turned and saw Kincaid in the doorway. "It was a horse race," he explained kindly.

"I could tell," Kincaid said with a grin.

Ernest nodded proudly. "I won, but Miss Felicity was close."

"I'll have to practise harder if I'm going to beat you," Felicity said with a laugh, before turning to Kincaid with a questioning look. "I didn't know you planned to visit Lord Willingdon today."

"Would you like to race too?" Ernest invited.

Kincaid smiled and shook his head. "I came to escort Miss Felicity home."

"Have Jane and Lord Willingdon finished their studies?" Felicity asked.

Kincaid nodded. "I've already driven Jane home."

Felicity frowned. "Already? You should have told us. Miss Flint and I would have come with you."

Kincaid winked at Ernest. "I didn't want to interrupt the horse races."

Felicity knelt to say goodbye to Ernest, who made a very proper bow and said he hoped to see her soon.

"You're a perfect gentleman," Felicity told him delightedly. "And I will see you soon, since Miss Harris and I intend to return tomorrow."

As they travelled back to Bentley Street, Kincaid considered telling Felicity that he had asked Jane not to return to the marquess's house, but he feared it would raise questions he didn't want to answer. He decided not to mention it, and hoped Jane would come up with an excuse for staying away.

When Felicity swept into the breakfast parlour at 29 Bentley the following morning, it was clear that Jane hadn't thought of an excuse.

"What have you done?" Felicity asked, waving a letter under Kincaid's nose. "Jane writes that you have forbidden her from joining me to study with Lord Willingdon!"

Kincaid sighed and set down his slice of buttered toast. "Have a seat, Felicity," he suggested. "Would you like some coffee?"

"Don't try to distract me," she said indignantly. "I want to know what this means."

"What exactly did Jane write?" Kincaid asked cautiously.

"Just that. That you don't want her to accompany me to Lord Willingdon's."

It was the truth, but Kincaid thought that in such circumstances, the unvarnished truth was overrated. He wished Jane had said she was too busy preparing for their wedding, or that she had to play nursemaid to a sick relative. Since she had so many sisters who could fall sick, the nursemaid excuse might have worked for a week.

"I don't think it's wise for Jane to spend too much time at Willingdon's," he said vaguely. "She needs to focus on preparing for our wedding, and—"

Felicity searched his face. "I don't think this has anything to do with your wedding!" she exclaimed. "I think you're jealous of Lord Willingdon's attentions to Jane!"

"I am not jealous of Lord Willingdon," he retorted.

"I don't see any other explanation," Felicity insisted. "I never took you for a man who would try to control his wife's activities, simply to prove he had the power to do so."

"Jane isn't my wife yet," Kincaid replied. "But I never took you for the sort of lady who would stand by and watch her betrothed fall in love with another woman!"

"Falling in love?" Felicity asked slowly. "Jane and Willingdon? Do you really think so?"

She was looking at him with a strange expression that made Kincaid wish he had held his tongue. "I'm sure they're not in love," he tried to reassure her. "But they looked very cozy in Willingdon's study this afternoon, and I think it would be best if Jane didn't join you in the future."

Felicity's brow furrowed. "If you don't think you can trust Jane, perhaps you should delay your marriage."

"On the contrary, I intend to hasten it," he told her. "Jane and I will be married in two weeks."

"Two weeks!" Felicity exclaimed. "But—"

"But?"

"But that's so soon," Felicity said weakly, wishing she could think of a better objection.

"The sooner the better," Kincaid said. "We've delayed long enough."

Twenty-Three

After Felicity had left, Kincaid wrote to his mother and brother to update them about his wedding plans. He assured his relatives that his wedding would be a small affair, and that he would understand if they didn't want to travel to London to attend.

When that chore was completed, he decided to visit Lord Langley and give him the news in person. He found Langley and Amelia in their drawing room, watching their infant son use the leg of the sofa to pull himself to a stand.

"Julian's almost walking," Kincaid said in surprise.

"He will be soon," Langley said proudly.

Since it was clear that Kincaid had a weight on his mind, Amelia excused herself to take Julian up for his nap, and Langley invited Kincaid to move to his study.

"How is Miss Taylor?" Langley asked, after he had closed his study door and poured his friend a drink. He was one of the few people Kincaid had told about Felicity's abduction and Willingdon's rescue.

"I think she's well," Kincaid replied. "She seems happy enough, although she's persuaded Willingdon to delay their wedding until June. She claims it will take at least two months to make her dress."

"I see," Langley said thoughtfully.

"But Miss Harris and I have set a wedding date," Kincaid continued. "We will be married the Saturday after next."

Langley frowned. "I thought Miss Harris also wanted to wait until June?"

"She did, but our plans have changed," Kincaid explained. "It seemed best to get it over with. It won't be a big affair, but I hope you and Amelia can attend?"

"We would be delighted," Langley replied. "Will you take Miss Harris on a wedding trip?"

Kincaid looked so dismayed that Langley would have laughed if he hadn't been so concerned for his friend. "I forgot about the wedding trip," Kincaid said glumly. "I suppose Jane will expect me to take her somewhere."

"She probably will," Langley agreed.

"Where did you take Amelia for your wedding trip?"

"We spent two weeks at the manor in Oxfordshire," Langley said, referring to one of his secondary estates. "We didn't tell a soul where we were going, apart from the servants, of course."

"Two weeks?" Kincaid couldn't imagine how he and Jane would occupy themselves in the country for two weeks. He supposed they could go for walks, and he knew Jane was a keen reader.

"It wasn't nearly long enough," Langley said, smiling at the memory.

"How did you fill the time?"

Langley raised an eyebrow. "You're not seriously asking me that?"

Kincaid chuckled ruefully. "No, I suppose I'm not." It was no secret that Langley was madly in love with his wife.

"You're welcome to use the manor, if you like," Langley offered. "It's quite pleasant in the springtime."

"Thank you, Robert. I don't suppose you and Amelia would like to join us?"

"I thought you and Miss Harris might want to take your wedding trip alone," Langley said gently.

"Yes, of course. I'll think about it and let you know."

Langley nodded and wished he could do more to help. It was clear that Kincaid didn't love Miss Harris, but a gentleman didn't cry off from a betrothal.

"I wonder if Willingdon will take Felicity on a wedding trip," Kincaid mused. "He's been teaching her Latin, you know, so perhaps they'll continue with their lessons."

"I didn't know Miss Taylor was interested in Latin."

"She wasn't, until she met Willingdon," Kincaid grumbled. "It isn't like her, and I can't understand it."

Langley leaned back in his chair and steepled his fingers together. "Perhaps Willingdon's been a good influence on her."

"I'd be ashamed if I couldn't think of anything better to do with a girl than study Latin," Kincaid muttered. "But Felicity says she's happy, and I suppose that's all that matters."

~

While Kincaid was with Langley, Felicity was walking in Hyde Park with Miss Flint. It was a glorious spring day, but since Felicity was in a dour mood, she felt as though the sunshine was mocking her. Fortunately, Miss Flint was content to walk in silence, and didn't subject her to inane observations about the colour of the sky or the beauty of the flowers.

Martin Nethercott had been right; Felicity had been clinging to the hope that something would happen to stop Jane from marrying Mr. Kincaid. She knew it was unlikely, but she had still dreamed that Jane would realize she and Kincaid weren't well-suited, or fall in love with someone else. But they were due to be married in two weeks, and what had once seemed unlikely now seemed impossible. Felicity supposed it wasn't surprising; if she were in Jane's place, nothing could have convinced her to cry off.

Felicity reminded herself that Kincaid had chosen Jane, and her belief that they weren't well-suited was probably only wishful thinking. They would likely be very happy together, and there was nothing for Felicity to do but be happy for them both.

"Beautiful day today," Miss Flint remarked, in her usual abrupt way.

"Yes, indeed," Felicity replied irritably. She resolved to ask Lord Willingdon to take her abroad for a wedding trip. She needed to get away from England, and away from Mr. Kincaid. Perhaps the marquess would take her to Italy to explore the Roman ruins. She would suggest they bring Ernest with them.

The park was crowded with pedestrians and riders, and Felicity barely noticed the girl walking furtively towards her until after her reticule had been ripped from her hand. There were only a few shillings in the reticule, but Felicity was determined she wouldn't be robbed again, so she hitched up her skirts and sprinted after the thief. The girl ran fast, with a speed borne of desperation, but Felicity was athletic and equally motivated.

With a final burst of speed, Felicity caught the girl's arm, but the girl stumbled and pulled Felicity down on top of her. Felicity was the first to recover, and she plucked the reticule from the girl's hand with a shout of satisfaction.

"Ha!" she said triumphantly, staring down at the would-be thief. The girl was slow to get up, and Felicity saw that her knee was scraped and bleeding.

"I'm sorry about your knee," Felicity said matter-of-factly. "But it was your own fault, you know. You shouldn't have taken my reticule."

The girl didn't reply, but her eyes darted nervously around the park as though she was looking for someone.

"What's your name?" Felicity asked briskly.

The girl looked at her warily but still didn't answer.

"If you don't tell me your name, I'll take you to the magistrate." Felicity wasn't sure how she would find a magistrate or transport the girl there, but fortunately her threat was effective.

"My name is Sarah Sullivan, Miss." It was the voice of a girl with some education, and it was at odds with her ragged appearance.

"And do you make a habit of stealing from people in the park, Sarah?"

The silence that followed answered Felicity's question.

"I should take you to the magistrate," Felicity told her, but to her surprise, Sarah no longer seemed concerned by the threat. A crowd of curious passersby had grown around them, and the girl seemed to be scanning the faces. Felicity noticed that Sarah was painfully skinny, and her brown eyes seemed enormous in her pale face.

"When did you last eat?" Felicity asked abruptly.

Sarah blinked at the unexpected question. "Yesterday."

"Are you all right, Felicity?" interrupted Miss Flint, who had finally caught up to them.

"Just fine," Felicity assured her, before turning back to Sarah. "Are you hungry? Is that why you took my reticule?"

Sarah didn't reply, and as Felicity watched, her wary expression was replaced by a look of abject terror. Felicity followed her line of sight and saw a middle-aged man standing at the edge of the crowd. He was dressed like a prosperous tradesman, in a black overcoat and trousers, but there was a mean look in his eyes.

Felicity knelt down and pretended to be examining Sarah's scraped knee. "Is it the man in the black coat and trousers?" she asked in a low voice.

"I—I—don't know what you mean," Sarah stammered. "I'll come with you to the magistrate."

"It's that man, isn't it?" Felicity asked again. "You're afraid of him. I'll help you if I can, but you must tell me the truth."

Sarah nodded miserably. "He's my Uncle Reginald," she admitted. "And my guardian."

"And does he mistreat you? I suppose he must, if you haven't eaten since yesterday."

Sarah cast an anxious glance at her uncle, who had backed away from the crowd and stood about a hundred yards away.

"He can't hear you," Felicity assured her.

Sarah took a deep breath. "He makes me steal," she confessed. "If I don't, he doesn't give me anything to eat. He'll be furious that I got caught."

"I see." Felicity surveyed the girl again, taking in her ragged gown, scrawny frame, and bleeding knee. "Well, Sarah," she said. "You have a choice to make. If you don't want to go back to your uncle, you can come home with us."

Sarah looked at Felicity in confusion. "Come with you where? I don't even know your name."

"I'm Felicity Taylor, and this is my companion, Miss Theodora Flint."

"What would you do with me?"

"Well, first we'll find you something to eat, and then we'll clean your knee," Felicity said practically. "And then, perhaps a bath and some clean clothes. After that— well, after that, I don't know, but I'm sure we'll figure something out. I suppose we'll have to consult Mr. Kincaid."

"What will he do with me?" Sarah asked suspiciously. Her experience with her uncle had given her a distrust of men.

"Oh, Mr. Kincaid's nothing like your uncle," Felicity assured her. "He was my guardian for seven years, and I trust him. But it's your choice. If you would rather go back to your uncle, I won't stop you."

For Sarah, there was no choice to make. "I'll come with you," she said resolutely.

"I'm glad," Felicity replied. "How is your knee? Do you think you'll be able to walk?"

Sarah nodded, and Felicity helped her to stand. Although the crowd had dispersed, Sarah's uncle hadn't moved, and Felicity made an impulsive decision. After instructing Sarah to wait with Miss Flint, she walked briskly towards Sarah's uncle.

The man saw her coming and hurried away. "Sir!" Felicity called, in her usual confident voice. "Sir! Are you that girl's uncle?"

"No," he called over his shoulder, without breaking stride.

"She tried to steal my reticule," Felicity persisted. "She claims you are her uncle and her guardian."

The man finally turned to face Felicity, but his shifty eyes didn't meet hers. "She's lying," he insisted. "I've never seen her before in my life."

Felicity raised an eyebrow. "Really?"

Sarah's uncle glared at Felicity. "If she's a thief, is it any surprise that she's a liar?"

"Well, I don't know," Felicity said. "In my experience, liars usually lie for a reason, and I don't see what she stands to gain by claiming a relationship with you. If you were my uncle, I wouldn't wish to advertise it, but it's no matter. My husband is waiting by the entrance to the park, and when I tell him the story, he will take her to the magistrate."

"It's no concern of mine," he said, turning away again.

"My husband is close friends with the magistrate, so I'm confident the matter will be taken seriously," Felicity called after him. "The girl will probably be transported to Australia."

The man didn't slow down, but Felicity was confident he had heard her. She rejoined Sarah and Miss Flint with a satisfied look on her face.

"What did he say to you?" Sarah asked nervously.

"He claimed he had never seen you before in his life," Felicity replied. "I didn't believe him for an instant. I told him I was taking you to the magistrate, and that you would probably be transported to Australia."

Sarah's eyes widened in horror. "Australia!" she exclaimed, looking at Felicity with a pitiful expression. "But I thought—you said—"

"Oh, you won't be transported," Felicity assured her. "I'm not taking you to the magistrate, I was just hoping to mislead your uncle a little. If he thinks you've been sent to Australia, he's less likely to come looking for you."

Sarah thought that seemed very clever, and she began to think she had been wise to put herself in Felicity's hands.

When they reached 23 Bentley, Felicity swept Sarah past a curious Wainwright and up the stairs to her bedchamber. A maid was dispatched to the kitchen for a tray of food, and a second was sent for water to bathe Sarah's scraped knee. Felicity waited until her guest had worked her way through a bowl of chicken stew before asking for more details about her life with her uncle. Sarah's answers were hesitant at first, but Felicity's kind eyes and matter-of-fact questions soon drew out the story.

Sarah Sullivan was a thirteen-year-old orphan. Her mother had died giving birth to her, but she had lived a comfortable life until her father, a moderately prosperous merchant, had died three years earlier. She thought her father had left her some money, but her Uncle Reginald, who had been appointed her guardian, claimed it wasn't nearly enough for her keep.

Reginald had also taken over her father's business, but he lacked her father's business acumen, and there was never enough money. Within a week of her father's funeral, Sarah's governess had been dismissed, and Sarah had been told that she would spend her afternoons picking pockets. She was young and quick, and her uncle would rather risk her neck than his own.

"I've been chased many times, but I've never been caught," Sarah admitted, looking at Felicity with admiration. "You looked so distracted, I didn't expect you to react so quickly, and most ladies don't run as fast as you do."

By this time, Felicity was convinced that Sarah was more a victim than a criminal, and she was determined to find a way to help the girl. After entrusting Sarah to Miss Flint's care, she walked to 29 Bentley to confer with Mr. Kincaid.

The butler showed her to the study, where Kincaid was reviewing a set of accounts. "I need to talk to you," Felicity told him, before glancing down at the ledger that was open on his desk. "That is, if you're not busy."

"I'm not busy, Felicity." Kincaid stood and moved a chair so she could sit facing him.

"Miss Flint and I were walking in Hyde Park today, and a girl tried to steal my reticule," Felicity began.

Kincaid's eyes widened. "Was there anything of value in it?"

"Only a few shillings, and I have recovered it," Felicity assured him. "I caught up with the girl and got the reticule back."

"You shouldn't have chased a thief over a few shillings," Kincaid remonstrated. "It wasn't worth the risk, Felicity. You might have been hurt—"

"Not by this scrap of a girl," Felicity interrupted. "She's only thirteen, and she's so underfed that I'm surprised she had the strength to run away from me. She's been living with her uncle, and the scoundrel forces her to pick pockets. If she's unsuccessful, she doesn't eat."

"I see," Kincaid said slowly. "How do you know all this?"

"Her uncle was at the park, and I could see that she was afraid of him," Felicity explained. "So I brought her home with me. Her name's Sarah Sullivan."

"So she's at 23 Bentley now?"

Felicity nodded. She studied Kincaid's face, hoping for a clue to his thoughts, but his expression was inscrutable.

"What do you mean to do with her?"

"I don't know," Felicity confessed. "I wanted to consult you about it." It was a relief to bring the problem to someone she trusted. "I thought we might find a respectable lady to live with her, or send her away to school. Surely some of my fortune could be used to cover the school fees."

Kincaid pressed his lips together. "I'm afraid you'll have to consult Lord Willingdon about it."

Felicity's face fell. "I don't see why we need to involve Lord Willingdon," she said slowly. "I won't be marrying him for nearly two months."

Kincaid nodded. "But you're proposing to use your fortune to support the girl, perhaps for years. You would need Willingdon's approval."

"But you still have control of the money," Felicity pointed out. "Is there no way to set some aside before the marriage?"

"Not legally, no." If there had been a way to set some of Felicity's fortune aside for her own use, Kincaid would have already done it.

"Perhaps I could tell the marquess that Sarah's a distant cousin, and I have an obligation to help her," Felicity mused.

"You could try," Kincaid said dubiously. "But is that really the sort of marriage you want, Felicity? Willingdon's likely to learn the truth, and when he does, you'll lose his trust."

"You're right." Although Felicity wasn't keen to tell the marquess about her new protégée, she knew there was no alternative. "I'm sure Lord Willingdon will understand the circumstances."

Kincaid nodded, although he didn't share her confidence in Willingdon's understanding. "I think that's the right decision."

"And do I have your permission to let Sarah stay at 23 Bentley for a few days? Just until I can find a better solution?"

"I suppose," Kincaid agreed with a sigh. "But you must talk to Willingdon about it soon." He knew that if Willingdon refused to help Sarah, he would find himself stuck with the problem, but he didn't have the heart to send the girl back to her uncle.

Felicity's face lit up with a smile of gratitude. "Thank you, Mr. Kincaid. If you'll lend me your pen and some paper, I'll write to Lord Willingdon now."

Pen, paper, and inkwell were passed across the desk,

and Felicity scrawled a note asking Lord Willingdon to call upon her at his earliest convenience. "I'll give it to one of the footmen," she told Kincaid. "Do you want to come back with me, so you can meet Sarah?"

"I guess I could," Kincaid said, rising to his feet. Although he hoped to avoid the upcoming discussion with the marquess, he couldn't say no to Felicity.

Twenty-Four

When Felicity and Kincaid reached 23 Bentley St., they were told that Felicity's maid had taken charge of Sarah and was giving her a bath. Felicity persuaded Kincaid to stay for tea, with the promise that Cook's new recipe for lemon tarts was superior to the original. Kincaid expressed a preference for the old recipe, and a spirited debate ensued. They appealed to Miss Flint for her opinion, but since she said the tarts were all delicious, the matter remained unsettled.

As they were finishing their tea, Wainwright announced the Marquess of Willingdon.

"Miss Taylor," the marquess said ponderously. "I came as soon as I received your note." He cast a critical eye over Felicity's dress. She hadn't bothered to change out of the walking dress she had worn to the park, and her struggle with Sarah had left grass stains on her skirt. "Have you been in an accident?"

"Oh, no, nothing like that," Felicity assured him. "But

an important matter has arisen that I would like to discuss with you."

Willingdon nodded. "I am at your disposal, Miss Taylor."

"I met a young girl in Hyde Park this afternoon," Felicity began. She decided not to share the details of how she and Sarah had met. "Her name is Sarah, and she's thirteen years old. Her parents died three years ago, and she's been under her uncle's guardianship ever since."

Willingdon's forehead pleated in confusion. "And what has this to do with you?"

"Well, Sarah was hungry, so I brought her here to feed her," Felicity said carefully. "Her uncle mistreats her, so I don't think she should go back to him."

"If her uncle's her guardian, you have no right to remove her from his care," Willingdon said sternly.

"No legal right, perhaps, but a moral one," Felicity retorted. "He was forcing her to steal from people in the park! If she was unsuccessful, her uncle wouldn't give her anything to eat. I met her when she tried to steal my reticule."

"So the girl's a thief!" Willingdon exclaimed. "And you have no way of knowing if anything she tells you is true. For all we know, this uncle doesn't even exist, and she simply uses him as an excuse."

"I saw her uncle, and Sarah was terrified of him," Felicity said. "Before I knew the circumstances, I threatened to take her to the magistrate, and that didn't frighten her in the slightest. She would much rather be taken to the magistrate than go back to her Uncle Reginald."

"And what if this uncle comes looking for her?" Willingdon asked. "You have no proof that he forced her to steal."

"I don't think he will look for her," Felicity said. "I confronted him in the park, and it was clear the man's a coward. I explained that Sarah tried to steal my reticule and I was taking her to the magistrate, and he said he had never seen her before."

"And you should have taken her to the magistrate," Willingdon remarked sternly. "We should do so now. Where is the girl?"

"We will do no such thing," Felicity said firmly, with a fire in her eyes that Willingdon had never seen before. "Sarah is only thirteen, and she is not to blame for her situation." She took a deep breath. "Under different circumstances, I might have been in Sarah's position. Had my parents been foolish enough to appoint Mr. Nethercott as my guardian, he might have forced me to pick pockets after he squandered my fortune. I'm truly fortunate that my father had the sense to appoint Mr. Kincaid instead."

"You still have only her word that the story is true," Willingdon said thoughtfully. "But if you don't want to involve the magistrate, I suppose we could take her to an orphanage."

"I don't want to take her to an orphanage," Felicity said stubbornly. "I hoped she could stay with me until we can find a home for her."

"She can't stay with you!" Willingdon exclaimed, looking at Felicity as though she had gone mad. "Miss Taylor, you've just said the girl's a thief. Nothing in the house would be safe."

"She stole so she could eat," Felicity retorted. "If we feed her, she will no longer need to steal."

"And what sort of home do you propose to find for her?"

"Well, I don't know," Felicity admitted. "I was hoping you could help with that."

"I can assure you, Miss Taylor, that I have no experience finding homes for young girls of the criminal class," Willingdon said stiffly.

"I thought we might send her to school," Felicity suggested.

"And who would pay the fees?" Willingdon asked.

"I would."

"I'm afraid I couldn't allow you to do that," Willingdon said tersely.

"I would use my own money," Felicity said, before she remembered that when she married Lord Willingdon, all of her money would pass to his control.

"But I could not allow you to do so," Willingdon said again. "As your husband, it will be my responsibility to ensure that our money is wisely spent."

Felicity looked at him through narrowed eyes. "But the amount of the school fees is trivial compared to the money that I will bring to our marriage. I imagine I could pay it out of my clothing allowance."

"I would not allow it, Miss Taylor," Willingdon said curtly. "It is the principle of the matter."

"I agree," Felicity said. "I knew you would control my fortune when we marry, but I didn't think you would deny a reasonable request."

"I beg your pardon, Miss Taylor," Willingdon said tightly. "But this is hardly a reasonable request."

At this inauspicious moment, Wainwright announced Miss Jane Harris.

"Good afternoon, Miss Harris," Kincaid said warily, as he and Willingdon stood and bowed.

"Good afternoon," Jane said brightly, seemingly oblivious to the tension in the room. She made a pretty curtsy to Lord Willingdon before turning to Mr. Kincaid.

"I was hoping to discuss the music for our wedding, Mr. Kincaid, and the butler at 29 Bentley St. said I would find you here." She glanced at Lord Willingdon. "I wasn't aware you had company. Perhaps it would be more convenient for me to call upon you tomorrow?"

"It is not inconvenient," Willingdon said quickly. "I would hate for you to leave on my account."

Jane smiled at the marquess before taking a seat on the sofa opposite Kincaid. "I know our wedding won't be grand, but you have a lovely pianoforte, and my sister Mary plays very well. I thought she could play before and after the ceremony, and I wanted to ask if you had any favourite pieces?"

"I'm sure I'll be happy with whatever you and Mary choose," Kincaid replied.

Jane looked disappointed. "I thought perhaps one of Handel's concertos, but I wondered if you wanted something different?"

"Handel will be fine," Kincaid said quickly.

"I've always liked Handel's Water Music," Willingdon put in. "I think it would be lovely."

Jane looked at him gratefully. "Thank you, Lord Willingdon."

"A pleasure, Miss Harris," Willingdon replied. "I should be going."

Felicity stared at him in disbelief. "But we haven't finished our conversation."

"I don't think there is anything more to be said," Willingdon declared.

"I think there is a great deal more to be said," Felicity argued. "We haven't decided what to do with Sarah, and—"

"Perhaps you would give us your opinion on the matter, Miss Harris," Willingdon interrupted. "Miss Taylor was walking in the park earlier today, and a girl tried to steal her reticule. Miss Taylor brought the girl home with her and proposes to pay to send her to school. I have said no."

Jane's eyes widened. "What a peculiar idea, Felicity," she began.

"There's nothing peculiar about it," Felicity said. "And I'm afraid Lord Willingdon hasn't given you the whole story. The girl is an orphan, and her uncle is taking advantage of her." She gave Willingdon a look of entreaty, but his eyes held no sympathy, so she turned to Kincaid. "You understand, don't you, Mr. Kincaid?"

Kincaid understood, and he found it exceedingly difficult to listen to Felicity and Willingdon debate the point. He also knew it wasn't his business, and that his interference in the argument wouldn't help Felicity.

He looked at Felicity with an apology in his eyes. "It isn't my concern," he said gently. "And Miss Harris and I should leave you to discuss it with Lord Willingdon in private."

Kincaid rose to leave, but Jane didn't follow him. "I think I should stay," she said primly. "I may be able to help Lord Willingdon explain things to Miss Taylor."

"I don't think—" Kincaid began, but Willingdon interrupted him.

"That's an excellent idea," the marquess declared, looking at Jane with approval. "Perhaps the counsel of another lady will help Miss Taylor understand the situation."

Kincaid decided to leave the room before he lost his temper. Miss Flint followed him out, leaving Felicity alone with Jane and Lord Willingdon.

"I understand that the girl's circumstances are unfortunate," Willingdon told Felicity. "But there are many unfortunate children in our city, and you can't take responsibility for them all."

"I don't want to take responsibility for them all," Felicity argued. "At the moment, I'm only concerned with Miss Sarah Sullivan, and we certainly have the means to help her."

"But where will it end?" Willingdon asked, apparently concerned that Felicity would make a habit of adopting orphans.

"I don't know," Felicity admitted. "But that isn't a reason not to do it. It's only one girl."

"And what would people think?" Willingdon questioned. "I'm sure you don't realize the sort of rumours that would start, if people knew I was paying school fees for a young girl—"

"Are you worried people will think you have an illegitimate daughter?" Felicity asked matter-of-factly.

Willingdon and Jane gaped at her. "Felicity!" Jane blurted. "How can you suggest such a thing?"

"Lord Willingdon alluded to it first," Felicity said, without a hint of remorse. "I'm not sure if he expected me to grasp his meaning, or if he was simply trying to convince me I'm too ignorant to understand him. And I'm sorry if I shocked you, Jane, but if you had left when Mr. Kincaid asked you to go, you wouldn't have heard it."

"Miss Taylor," Willingdon said reproachfully, "I must advise you that I will not tolerate this sort of language from the lady I am planning to marry."

Felicity took a deep breath and met his eye. "Lord Willingdon, I'm afraid I won't be able to marry you," she said calmly. "I must ask you to release me from our engagement." She glanced at Jane before turning back to the marquess. "I had hoped to inform you of this privately, but I wasn't given the opportunity."

There was a beat of silence as Willingdon and Jane stared at Felicity in shock.

The marquess found his voice first. "I appreciate your honesty, Miss Taylor," he said curtly. "I will send a notice to the papers that our engagement is at an end."

"Thank you, Lord Willingdon. You are very kind."

"Felicity, are you sure?" Jane asked in disbelief.

"Don't worry, Jane," Felicity assured her. "I won't be in your way. I intend to move out of this house as soon as I can make arrangements to do so."

"Where will you go?"

"I don't think that concerns you," Felicity said pleasantly. "Suffice it to say that I don't intend to live with you and Mr. Kincaid." She smiled serenely at Jane before moving to the tea tray. "Can I offer you tea, Jane? I'm afraid it may have cooled a little, but I think it should still be tolerable. One milk and one sugar, is that right?"

She poured out the tea and carried it towards Jane, who watched her approach with a frown.

"I think I have a duty to inform Mr. Kincaid of your behaviour," Jane announced, rising to her feet. As she stood, she collided with Felicity, who had reached out to hand her the tea. The teacup fell on the floor with a thud, spilling tea down Jane's gown in the process.

Jane let out a very unladylike screech. "You—you did that deliberately," she cried.

"It was an accident," Felicity said truthfully. "I'm very sorry. If you'd like to come upstairs, I can lend you another dress."

Jane glared at Felicity. "You've ruined my best dress, you vulgar, unprincipled—"

"I'm sure it was an accident, my dear Miss Harris," Willingdon said, rushing over with a handkerchief. "I doubt the dress is ruined, and if it is, it can be easily replaced. If you would allow me . . ." The marquess dabbed at the wet spot on the front of her gown.

"I'll go fetch another towel," Felicity said, slipping quietly out of the room. In the doorway, she encountered Mr. Kincaid, who had heard Jane scream and come to investigate.

"Are you all right, Felicity?" he asked anxiously.

"Oh, yes," Felicity assured him. "It was Jane who screamed. I think she's all right, but I'll let her explain it to you herself. I promised to go fetch a towel."

Kincaid strode into the drawing room and beheld Lord Willingdon dabbing at Jane's gown with a handkerchief. "What is the meaning of this?" he asked incredulously.

Jane blanched at the sight of Kincaid, and crossed her arms awkwardly across her chest. "It is all Felicity's fault!" she blurted. "She threw her tea at me."

"Threw her tea at you?" Kincaid repeated in disbelief. "Was it hot?"

"No," Jane admitted. "But nonetheless—"

"I believe it was an accident," Willingdon put in. "When Miss Harris stood up, she struck Miss Taylor's arm and knocked the teacup off the saucer."

This interpretation did little to placate Jane. "That was no accident," she insisted. "Miss Taylor knew exactly what she was doing. It grieves me to say it, but I've never met such a poorly behaved young woman in my life!" She took a deep breath in an effort to compose herself. "I'm sorry, Mr. Kincaid, but I cannot marry you so long as Felicity is welcome in your house!"

"Very well, Miss Harris," Kincaid said. "Thank you for making your sentiments clear. I will send a notice to the papers that our engagement is at an end."

"Of course you would choose Felicity over me!" Jane cried. "That girl has you so bewitched that you're blind to the impropriety of her behaviour. It's my belief that she is either mentally unhinged or morally depraved!"

A muscle ticked in Kincaid's jaw. "I might point out, Miss Harris, that I just found you unchaperoned in my drawing room, with a gentleman pawing at your gown. You didn't appear to be resisting his attentions."

"Lord Willingdon wasn't *pawing* at me," Jane protested. "He was merely helping to dry my dress."

Willingdon drew himself up to his full height and glared at Mr. Kincaid. "I find you offensive, sir," he exclaimed. "To suggest that Miss Harris is guilty of improper behaviour—"

"I don't think I made such a suggestion," Kincaid said

calmly. "I merely observed that I found Miss Harris unchaperoned in my drawing room, with a gentleman pawing at her gown. Any suggestion of impropriety came from you."

Willingdon's face turned a deep shade of red as he realized the implications of the situation. After a moment's reflection, he dropped to one knee in front of Jane.

"Miss Harris, since your prior engagement is at an end, I wonder if you would do me the honour of marrying me?"

"Oh, Lord Willingdon!" Jane breathed. "I would like it more than anything."

Felicity, who had returned with the towel and been watching from the doorway, decided she had heard enough. She handed the towel off to Wainwright, who was hovering a step behind her, and walked away with a smile on her lips.

Kincaid stared at Lord Willingdon in disbelief. "Have you forgotten, Willingdon, that you're already betrothed?"

Willingdon glared at him. "Miss Taylor has asked me to release her from our engagement."

"I see," Kincaid said. "In that case, Lord Willingdon, Miss Harris, let me be the first to wish you joy. I'll leave you to discuss the particulars."

Lord Willingdon and Jane had no wish to remain under Kincaid's roof any longer, so they departed together immediately. Kincaid walked to his study, poured himself a glass of cognac, and tried to make sense of his emotions.

Jane's decision to end their engagement had lifted a weight from his shoulders, and his relief turned to elation as he realized he was free to marry another lady. From there, his thoughts turned to a question of etiquette; namely, how long a jilted gentleman should wait before making an offer of marriage to another lady. Lord Willingdon had evidently thought that fifteen minutes was an adequate interval, and although Kincaid had no wish to emulate any other aspect of the marquess's behaviour, he thought he was probably right on that point. He swallowed the rest of his cognac and went to look for Felicity.

He didn't find her in the drawing room or the library, and he was about to climb the stairs to her bedchamber when he remembered the girl she had brought home from the park. The last he had heard of Sarah was that she was being given a bath, and since he had no wish to walk in on that, he rang for his housekeeper.

"Please send Miss Taylor to my study," he asked Mrs. Sutherland.

"She's not here, sir," Mrs. Sutherland informed him.

"What do you mean?"

"She's gone out, sir. With Miss Flint and Miss Sarah."

"Out!" Kincaid exclaimed. He had thought Felicity might want to see him, to discuss what she would do now that her betrothal had ended. He had a great deal to say on the subject, and he could hardly believe she had left. "Did they say where they were going?"

"I believe, sir," Miss Sutherland said slowly, "that they have gone to the modiste's."

Kincaid laughed at the absurdity of it. He should have

known that Felicity wasn't the type to sit at home and lament the fact that her betrothal had ended.

"If you intend to return to 29 Bentley St., sir, I can send someone to inform you when Miss Taylor returns," Mrs. Sutherland suggested.

Kincaid shook his head. "There's no need, Mrs. Sutherland. But you can tell Miss Taylor I will call upon her tomorrow morning." He remembered Felicity's remark that a gentleman who could successfully make an offer of marriage in an unromantic location must have a marvellous way with words or a lady who loved him very much. He wasn't sure he had a marvellous way with words, but he hoped the strength of his feelings would give him eloquence, and he resolved to propose to Felicity at the breakfast table.

Twenty-Five

Kincaid rose early the following morning, but he forced himself to wait until a civilized hour to present himself at 23 Bentley St.

Wainwright answered the door with a nervous expression. "Good morning, sir."

"Morning, Wainwright," Kincaid said briskly. "Is Miss Taylor in the breakfast parlour?"

"Not exactly," Wainwright replied, drawing a letter from his pocket. "She left you a letter, sir. I was just on my way to 29 Bentley to give it to you."

Kincaid snatched the letter from his butler and read it in the entrance hall.

Dear Mr. Kincaid,

Since my engagement to Lord Willingdon has ended, I have decided to marry someone else. I can't tell you the gentleman's name yet, but I think you will approve of him. I've always wanted to see Scotland, and since I would rather not be

308

troubled by banns and marriage licences, I have left for Gretna Green.

Yours affectionately,
Felicity

Kincaid cursed softly and speared his butler with a glare. "How long ago did she leave?"

"Perhaps an hour, sir."

"And did you see the vehicle?"

"I believe it was a post-chaise and four."

"Send a message to the stables to saddle Apollo," Kincaid instructed grimly.

"Yes, sir." Wainwright scurried off to deliver the message himself.

After hurrying back to 23 Bentley St. to fetch a roll of banknotes, Kincaid went to the stables and waited impatiently for the grooms to ready his horse. Ten minutes later, he was navigating the busy roads out of London and cursing the traffic. By the time he reached Finchley Common, the congestion had eased, and his mind drifted to the problem of who could have eloped with Felicity. He remembered the name of every man she had danced with at her debut ball, and aside from Martin Nethercott, they had all been eminently respectable. He certainly couldn't imagine any of those men participating in an elopement, and for an awful moment, he wondered if Nethercott had returned to England and abducted Felicity a second time.

Kincaid reminded himself that Felicity wouldn't have gone with Nethercott willingly, and if he had taken her by force, she wouldn't have left such a maddening note. Nethercott might have compelled her to write a letter, but

Kincaid trusted that Felicity would have found a way to let him know if she was under duress. He took comfort from the fact that the note was in Felicity's own hand, and in her typical provoking style. She even had the gall to suggest that Kincaid would approve of the gentleman she planned to marry, which was patently ridiculous.

He stopped to investigate a post-chaise that was changing horses at Potter's Bar, and was disappointed to find its only occupant was an elderly gentleman. After muttering an apology to the traveller, Kincaid realized that Apollo was exhausted and arranged to hire a fresh horse from the posting inn. To his relief, the hired horse was a spirited animal, and he reached Hatfield in under an hour.

Kincaid had hoped to catch Felicity by Hatfield, and his heart sped up when he spotted a post-chaise drawn up in front of the posting-inn. After handing his reins to an ostler, he threw open the door to the chaise and was greatly relieved to see Felicity smiling back at him. He turned his gaze to the opposite seat, expecting to confront the man who was trying to elope with the woman he loved. To his disbelief, he found himself staring at Miss Flint.

Kincaid couldn't understand why Miss Flint had accompanied Felicity on her elopement, but he didn't dwell on that puzzle. "Felicity," he said in a deceptively calm voice. "Where is he?"

"Mr. Kincaid," she said placidly. "How nice to see you."

"Where is he, Felicity?" Kincaid repeated. "And who is he?"

"I don't know whom you're talking about," Felicity said innocently.

"The scoundrel you've eloped with," Kincaid bit out. "I don't know what's gone on between you, but since you're nowhere close to Scotland yet, I assume you're not married. You're not going to be, Felicity, do you hear me? Whoever he is, he isn't good enough for you, and I won't let you throw yourself away like this."

Felicity's brow furrowed. "Don't you think you should wait to learn his name before you decide he's not good enough for me?"

"No!" Kincaid said roughly. "If he were a decent man, he wouldn't be spiriting you away to Scotland."

"But I think, Mr. Kincaid—" Felicity began.

"Don't argue with me, Felicity. I know you're upset about Willingdon, and you have every right to be, but in time you'll see that it was for the best. Willingdon didn't appreciate you and he doesn't deserve you, but in time you'll find someone who does." He turned towards the inn, searching for Felicity's prospective husband. "But it won't be the villain who tried to lure you to Scotland while you were in a vulnerable state."

"You shouldn't judge him too harshly, Mr. Kincaid," Felicity said. "If you must know, I tricked him into it."

He stared at her suspiciously. "You expect me to believe that you tricked a man into eloping with you?"

"Yes," Felicity said calmly. "At least, I think I did."

"Felicity, any man foolish enough to be tricked into an elopement would bore you within a week."

Felicity smiled. "I don't think this man will," she said simply. "But it's a risk I'm willing to take."

The look in her eyes gave him pause. "You love him," he said quietly.

Felicity nodded. "Very much."

Kincaid still didn't understand how Felicity had managed to fall in love without his knowledge, or where her man had been when Nethercott had abducted her, but she spoke with such certainty that he couldn't doubt her feelings. "And he cares for you?"

"I think he does," she replied. "I hope so, at least. We haven't had a chance to discuss it yet."

"When did you think you might discuss it?" he asked incredulously. "At Gretna Green?"

"I hoped I wouldn't have to wait that long," Felicity replied. "It will take us three days to reach Scotland, and I don't want to wait any longer."

"Who is it, Felicity?" Kincaid asked again. "Is he in the inn? Shall I go look for him?"

"Lucas, there is no other man," Felicity confessed. "There has only ever been you."

He stared at her in disbelief. "But your note—Gretna Green—" he said inarticulately.

"I'm trying to elope with you, Lucas," Felicity explained simply. "But you're not making it easy."

"Felicity, I—" he broke off, at a loss for words.

"I think I will go into the inn for refreshments," Miss Flint announced tactfully. Kincaid helped her down from the carriage before climbing up to take the seat opposite Felicity.

"So there was no other man?" he asked, still struggling to make sense of the situation.

"No," Felicity admitted. "There's never been any man but you."

It took Kincaid a minute to absorb this. "And you set this up," he said slowly, "knowing I would come after you?"

"Yes," she confessed. "That is, I hoped you would come after me." Felicity's voice was steady, and only the look in her eyes betrayed her nerves. "After everything that happened, I wouldn't have blamed you if you hadn't, but I had to know."

"To be clear, Felicity, are you asking me to marry you?"

"Well, I rather hoped you would ask me," Felicity said. "I think that's how it's conventionally done."

Kincaid was struck by a paroxysm of laughter. When he finally collected himself, he dropped to one knee on the floor of the carriage and took her hands in his. "Will you marry me, Felicity Taylor?"

"Yes, but only if you like the idea. You do want to marry me, don't you?"

"At the moment, there are a great number of things I want to do to you," Kincaid retorted. "But most of them are frowned upon outside of marriage, so I suppose there's no alternative for us."

Some ladies might have been insulted by this unromantic declaration, but Felicity wasn't one of them. "I knew I could rely on you to take a practical view of the matter," she replied. "I think, Lucas—"

But Mr. Kincaid decided he had listened to enough nonsense, and he silenced her with a kiss. Her wide-brimmed hat limited his access to her face, but he solved that problem by tearing the ribbon and tossing the hat to the floor of the carriage. Restraint was impossible; Kincaid kissed Felicity with the emotion of a man who had loved a woman for a very long time, but hadn't let himself dream she would ever be his. To his relief, Felicity returned his kiss with all the desperation he felt.

When they finally broke apart, Felicity looked down and saw her hat on the floor. "That was one of my favourite hats," she said reproachfully. "I'm afraid it's ruined now."

"You can buy yourself another one," Kincaid said unrepentantly. He moved next to her on the seat and took her in his arms.

"It's not like you to be such a spendthrift," she teased.

Kincaid paused. "Felicity, you know I don't have as much money as Willingdon," he said awkwardly.

Felicity shifted in his arms so she could look into his eyes. "Very few men do, Lucas," she replied. "But I don't think we should let it trouble us."

"And my position as your guardian, and now the trustee of your fortune—Felicity, I don't want to take advantage of you. You might think you want to marry me because I'm familiar to you, or because it's convenient."

Felicity's eyes widened. "Lucas, there was nothing convenient about it!" she exclaimed. "Your position as my guardian made everything much more complicated."

"It did?" Kincaid was surprised to hear that Felicity shared his opinion on the subject.

"Oh, yes," she told him. "I think I fell in love with you before I even knew what love was."

It was the first time Kincaid had seen her with her guard down. The veneer of confidence was gone, and Felicity was speaking the truth from her heart.

"Felicity," he said softly. "I had no idea."

"I realized it when I was eighteen," she confessed,

"but I had to hide my feelings, because I didn't want to scare you."

"You wouldn't have scared me, Felicity," he scoffed.

"Lucas, I was eighteen, and you were my guardian," Felicity pointed out. "To make things worse, you had control of my fortune, and I couldn't marry without your permission or I'd lose the money. If I told you I loved you then, you would have tried to send me back to Miss Archer's seminary, or to live with your brother and his wife."

"I suppose I probably would have," Kincaid admitted.

"So I was planning to tell you when I turned twenty-one," Felicity explained. "I hoped that by then, you wouldn't dismiss it as a schoolgirl's infatuation. If I was of age, and free to marry where I chose, I might have been able to convince you that you weren't taking advantage of me."

Understanding dawned on Kincaid. "Is that why you didn't want a Season until this year?"

"Of course," Felicity said, as though it was the most obvious thing in the world. "I was waiting for you."

"You were waiting for me?" Kincaid repeated with a laugh.

"It's always been you, Lucas," Felicity explained. "I was waiting for the guardianship to end, so that you could offer for me without feeling guilty about it. So I chose to delay my debut, since I had no interest in marrying anyone else. But then, a month before my twenty-first birthday, you came and told me you had decided to get married, and I wouldn't need to find a chaperone. I was foolish enough to think you were going to propose to me."

Kincaid's eyes widened. "Felicity, I never dreamed that you thought—"

"I know you didn't," Felicity said. "You made that quite clear. But I suppose I had my revenge today, when I let you think I'd eloped with someone else. There's a certain justice in that, don't you think?"

"No, I don't," Kincaid retorted. "When I think of what I suffered today, thinking I had missed my chance—"

"But that's exactly what I mean," Felicity interrupted. "Now you understand how I felt when you told me you were betrothed to Jane. I think understanding is very important in a marriage, Lucas."

Kincaid muttered something inaudible.

"In any case," Felicity continued, "I was terribly jealous, but I vowed to try to like Jane, and to be happy for you. But then I saw the way you looked at her when she came for tea, and I couldn't believe you loved each other."

Kincaid's brow furrowed. "Why not?"

"You pressed her hands in a perfectly polite way, and she seemed happy with such an insipid display of affection!" Felicity smiled mischievously. "I'll have you know, Mr. Kincaid, that if my betrothed greeted me with so little passion I wouldn't tolerate it as meekly as Jane did."

"What would you do, Felicity?"

"You should hope that you never find out," Felicity said, with a roguish gleam in her eyes.

"So you realized Jane and I didn't love each other, and decided to try to scare her off?"

"Not exactly," Felicity said carefully. "Although I did hope to dissuade her from acting as my chaperone. She smiled at me in such a condescending way, and spoke as though I was a child to be pitied! She seemed to expect me to behave badly, and I couldn't resist the temptation to meet her expectations."

"I imagine you exceeded them," Kincaid said, chuckling at the memory of the things Felicity had said when she first met Jane.

"I know my behaviour was atrocious," Felicity admitted. "I'm ashamed to think of the things I said. And then when I ran off with Adrian, and let you think I had eloped . . ." She sighed. "I let myself be ruled by my emotions, and I've resolved not to let it happen again."

"Your behaviour was atrocious," Kincaid agreed. "But I can't argue with the outcome. And I must say, Felicity, that I like the idea of marriage to a lady of strong emotions. I think Jane will be happy with Willingdon, so it's not as though you've wronged her."

"Oh, yes," Felicity said. "I was hoping that Jane would form an attachment to someone else."

Kincaid's eyes narrowed as he thought of the men Felicity had danced with at her debut ball. "In fact, you were scheming to promote a match between Jane and someone else."

"I wouldn't call it scheming, exactly," Felicity said. "But it struck me that another man might appreciate Jane's virtues more than you would. I knew she had to be the one to end the engagement, and I wanted her to be happy too."

"So you had Madame Sylvie make her a dress," Kincaid said slowly. "And all the scholarly men you danced with were potential suitors for Jane?"

Felicity nodded. "But it's a funny thing, Lucas. Many studious men aren't looking for studious wives. And then

Mr. Nethercott abducted me, and Lord Willingdon proposed, and I thought the situation was hopeless."

"Until you had the idea to pair Jane off with Willingdon."

"Yes," Felicity admitted. "And things were looking promising until you forbade Jane from joining me when I visited him. You can imagine my frustration when I heard about that."

"Forgive me for not having guessed that you were trying to promote a match between your betrothed and mine," Kincaid said sarcastically.

"Well, I think you might have figured it out," Felicity said matter-of-factly. "It was the only logical solution to the problem. Willingdon and Jane seemed ideally suited, and by then I had started to hope that you cared for me. I hardly trusted my judgment because I was desperate for it to be true, but I didn't think I was imagining it. There were several times when I caught you looking at me in a way that was—well—unbefitting of a guardian."

"You weren't imagining it," Kincaid told her with a chuckle. "And I suppose that explains why you wanted to delay your wedding to Willingdon. Here I thought you were nervous about the wedding night, and you wanted time to get to know him. But all the while, you were hoping to arrange his marriage to someone else!"

"I was nervous about the idea of the wedding night," Felicity replied. "To have a wedding night with Lord Willingdon, I would have had to marry him, and then I wouldn't have been able to marry you. But it all worked out in the end, and I think Jane and Lord Willingdon will suit each other very well. So I can marry you with a clear conscience."

"I'm relieved to hear you have a conscience," Kincaid remarked.

"Oh, yes," Felicity assured him. "My only regret is about Willingdon's son. I like Ernest, and I was looking forward to being his stepmother." She chewed her lip contemplatively. "I wonder if I should offer to help Willingdon find a tutor for the boy. He kept threatening to hire one, but I have very little confidence that he'll find someone Ernest will like."

Kincaid laughed. "I think you should leave that to Jane," he told her. "I doubt she or Willingdon will appreciate your interference."

"I imagine you're right," Felicity agreed reluctantly.

"And I expect Jane will be a good stepmother to Ernest," Kincaid said optimistically. His opinion of Jane had improved considerably since his engagement to her had ended. "I don't think you saw her at her best, Felicity."

"Perhaps not," Felicity replied. "She seemed to recognize your value, at least. There was a time when I feared she would never consider another suitor. And I suppose I can't blame her, because if I were in her place, nothing would have induced me to give you up. You may not have realized it, Mr. Kincaid, but you're a very eligible gentleman."

He laughed ruefully. "I'm not very eligible, Felicity. I don't have a title, and although I have some money, it's nothing compared to your fortune—"

"I thought you might still be concerned about that," Felicity remarked. "It's why I decided we should elope. If I hadn't forced the issue, you might have dithered—"

"I would not have *dithered*, Felicity!" Kincaid protested.

"You might have," Felicity insisted. "You might have convinced yourself that your position as my trustee made it improper, or that you shouldn't propose to me so soon after your betrothal to Jane had ended, or—"

"I'll have you know, Felicity, that I would have asked you to marry me yesterday evening," Kincaid interrupted. "But when I went to look for you, I was told you had gone to the modiste's!"

"I had to take Sarah to Madame Sylvie's," Felicity explained. "I didn't want to bring her to Scotland with us, so she needed somewhere to stay until we return to town."

"You left Sarah with the modiste?"

"Madame Sylvie was my mother's dressmaker, and I've known her for years," Felicity explained. "She's like family to me."

"I see," Kincaid said. "And that's why you visit her so often?"

Felicity nodded.

"Here I thought you were ordering new dresses every week!" Kincaid exclaimed. "I didn't understand how you could afford it, on the allowance I made you."

Felicity smiled. "Sylvie insists on sewing my gowns for free. We've had several arguments about it, and I do pay for the cost of the fabric. But I wasn't ordering new dresses nearly as often as you thought, you know. I like to sew, and I make over a lot of my old dresses to keep them in fashion. I often visit Sylvie to discuss ideas for designs."

"Why didn't you tell me, Felicity?"

"I should have," she admitted. "It was silly of me. But I knew you were confused by how I could afford all the dresses, and I suppose I enjoyed having a secret."

"I see," he said. "And so you left Sarah with Madame Sylvie."

"Sylvie was happy to have her," Felicity said with a nod. "And Sarah's uncle is unlikely to look for her there, so I think it will work out well. If they get along, I think Sylvie might offer to let her stay on as an apprentice."

"It's a good solution," Kincaid admitted.

"But if Sarah doesn't want to be Sylvie's apprentice, could we use some of my fortune to send her to school?" Felicity asked.

"Of course," he agreed. "It's your money, Felicity."

"It's our money," Felicity corrected. "I'm a very fortunate woman, Lucas. I doubt there are many men who think as you do."

"I hope you remember this the next time we quarrel," he teased. "And I should warn you, Felicity, that in some ways I'm still very traditional. When we are married, I'll expect you to take greater care for your safety. No more jaunting about the country with only the postilions for protection, like you did today."

"I knew you would join us soon," Felicity told him. "And I wasn't unprotected. Besides the postilions, I had Miss Flint."

"Of course, Miss Flint," Kincaid remarked dryly. "I'm sure she could defend you if you were set upon by highwaymen."

"Well, I hoped she could, but I didn't want to depend on it," Felicity told him. "That's why I brought a pistol."

Kincaid watched in astonishment as she reached

inside her reticule and produced a delicate weapon. "You brought a pistol?" he exclaimed. "Do you even know how to use it?"

"I think so," she replied. "But I think it's almost as effective when people believe I don't."

"Give it to me," he said nervously.

"I don't think I will," Felicity said, with a teasing look in her eyes. "You see, Lucas, you might still have an attack of conscience, and decide you shouldn't marry me after all. If I must, I can hold the pistol to your head, so you can tell your friends I forced you into it."

"Give me the pistol, Felicity."

"Do you still feel guilty, Lucas?" she asked, waving the pistol in the air.

"Hardly," he said roughly. "My friends are sure to pity me, since I've just become engaged to a madwoman who's waving a pistol in my face."

Felicity did not appear offended by this remark. "That's excellent news," she said cheerfully. "I hoped to convince you that this won't be an unequal marriage."

"You don't have to convince me of anything," Kincaid replied. "I love you, Felicity, and I no longer care if it's honourable or dishonourable. Right or wrong, sane or mad, I love you, and since you say you feel the same way, I mean to have you. I've fought this thing long enough."

"You've fought it too, Lucas?" Felicity asked hopefully. "For how long?"

"I'm not going to tell you that," he said with a laugh.

"I told you when I fell in love with you," Felicity pointed out reasonably. "I think it's only fair that you reciprocate."

"Give me the pistol first. I can't concentrate when you're pointing it at my shoulder."

"Relax, Lucas, it isn't loaded."

Kincaid's heartbeat slowed a fraction. He took the pistol from her hand and examined it carefully to satisfy himself that it was, indeed, unloaded. "Where did you get it?"

"Adrian Stone lent it to me," Felicity explained. "I went to see him yesterday, after I took Sarah to Madame Sylvie's. I needed his help to hire a post-chaise, since I was afraid the posting-inn wouldn't want to deal with a lady."

"What a valuable acquaintance Adrian has been," Kincaid remarked.

"Oh, he didn't want to at first, but I reminded him that he owed me a favour, for giving Cleopatra a good home."

Kincaid placed the pistol carefully in the pocket of his greatcoat and resolved to give Adrian a piece of his mind when he returned to town. "Did you tell Adrian what you were planning?" he asked, wondering if his friends had already heard about his elopement.

"I just told him I wanted to go to Scotland with Miss Flint," Felicity said. "And that I would be more comfortable on the journey if I had a pistol."

Kincaid nodded. "I think I'll be more comfortable on the journey if I hold on to it."

"If you like," Felicity agreed generously. "Now, you were going to tell me when you realized you loved me."

"When you returned from the seminary three years ago," he admitted with a sigh. "I missed you, Felicity, but I didn't realize how much until you came back. I had gone to balls and met other young ladies, but none of them had your spirit, your wit, or your heart. I knew I loved you then, but I couldn't say anything without abusing my position as your guardian."

"But if that was the case, Lucas, why didn't you wait and propose to me when I came of age?" Felicity asked.

"I thought you deserved a man with a fortune and a title," he explained. "And then Lady Delphinia offered to act as your chaperone and suggested that you live with her. I didn't trust her or Nethercott, and I hated the idea of you living with them. And then I ran into Jane, and I thought that if I married her, she could act as your chaperone—"

"You were willing to marry, just to provide me with a chaperone?" Felicity asked in amazement. "Of all the mad ideas! You would have been tied to Jane for the rest of your life!"

Kincaid nodded. "I didn't think I could have you, Felicity, and if I couldn't—well, it didn't seem to matter whom I married."

A short while later, Felicity sighed and disentangled herself from Kincaid's arms. "I suppose we should find Miss Flint," she said reluctantly. "And I can only imagine what the postilions are thinking."

"The postilions have probably found the taproom," Kincaid said dismissively. "And as for Miss Flint—you don't think she would like to spend the night at this excellent inn? I could arrange for a post-chaise to take her back to London tomorrow, while we continue to Scotland."

"Lucas Kincaid!" Felicity admonished. "You aren't suggesting we make the journey to Scotland without a chaperone?"

"Er—well—yes," he said hopefully. "I don't have much experience with runaway marriages, Felicity, but I don't think a chaperone is required. And it seems rather inconsiderate to ask Miss Flint to travel all the way to Gretna Green."

"Oh, no, Lucas," Felicity told him. "We're not going to Gretna Green."

"We're not?" he asked in confusion. "But your letter said you were going to Gretna. And I don't have a marriage licence, so if we're not going to Scotland we'll have to return to London—"

"Oh, we are going to Scotland, and we'll have to pass through Gretna," Felicity said. "And I suppose we could get married there, if that's your preference. But there's something distasteful about a Gretna Green marriage, so I thought it would be better to join Miss Flint on a visit to her half-brother."

"Miss Flint's half-brother?" Kincaid asked, looking bemused. "I didn't know she had one."

"Well, she does," Felicity replied, "and it seems he's a Scottish laird. He recently inherited the title, along with an estate near Lockerbie, and he's invited Miss Flint to live with him and his wife."

"Oh." Kincaid was having difficulty wrapping his mind around the news that Miss Flint's half-brother was a Scottish laird.

"Miss Flint intended to turn him down," Felicity said. "She wasn't even going to tell me about it, but I came across the letter she wrote to her brother. She said that although she would have liked to accept his invitation, she didn't want to abandon me while I still needed a chaperone."

"I see."

"So you see, Lucas, we can tell people we accompanied Miss Flint to Scotland and stayed at her brother's estate for a week. While we were there, we realized we were madly in love and got married. I'm sure we can find a minister in the village to perform the ceremony, so it will be entirely respectable."

"Entirely respectable, Felicity?" Kincaid asked, his eyes crinkling with amusement.

"Well, more respectable than a Gretna Green marriage," she amended. "And we won't need to fuss about invitations, or betrothal parties, or wedding breakfasts."

"It's brilliant," Kincaid agreed, reaching over to play with a lock of her hair. "Did you know, Felicity, that I've been longing to run my hands through your hair for months?"

"Then we shouldn't waste any more time," Felicity said, pulling the pins from her chignon and shaking her dark curls free. "Did you know, Lucas, that since Miss Flint will be staying in Scotland, we'll be travelling back to London alone? We could think of it as a wedding trip."

"It seems there's nothing for me to plan," Kincaid remarked. "Although I didn't bring any clothes, which will be rather inconvenient."

"Oh, I had your valet pack some things for you."

"You had my valet pack some things?" he repeated.

"Well, I remembered that you forgot to pack when you followed Adrian and me to Ashingham, and you had to borrow dinner clothes from Oliver. I thought you might forget again, and it might be awkward for you to borrow from Miss Flint's brother. I thought of asking your valet to come with us, but I thought you could probably manage without him. You will be able to dress yourself, won't you?"

"I imagine I'll make do," Kincaid agreed. "I expect that by now, the staff all know that you've run off with me?"

"I'm afraid it's likely," Felicity acknowledged. "I couldn't think of a reason to speak to your valet, so I had to send Wainwright to do it. I also spoke to him about Cleopatra, and he will make sure she's looked after while we're away."

"What a relief," Kincaid said dryly.

Felicity nodded. "I asked Wainwright not to tell anyone where we were going, but he doesn't strike me as the sort of man who can keep a secret. And I knew some of the servants would see me leaving this morning, and I thought they would be less likely to worry if they knew what I was planning."

"You didn't want them to worry about you?" Kincaid asked wryly. "Felicity, sweetheart, you've shown far more consideration for my servants than you have for me."

Instead of trying to defend her behaviour, Felicity decided to distract him, which she did very effectively by playing with the knot of his cravat. A moment later the cravat was on the floor of the coach, Felicity had started on the buttons of his waistcoat, and Mr. Kincaid had forgotten his grievance.

Epilogue

"Look Lucas, it's Jane!" Felicity exclaimed. "Up there, walking with Ernest." She and Kincaid were enjoying a ride through Hyde Park on a warm autumn afternoon.

Kincaid, who had been admiring Felicity's new riding habit, turned his head to follow his wife's gaze. "She's Lady Willingdon now," he corrected. "Should we turn off the path?"

"Of course not," Felicity replied. "I have no reason to avoid a meeting with Lady Willingdon."

Kincaid arched an eyebrow and looked at his wife skeptically.

"If she has any sense, she will realize that she is in my debt," Felicity said confidently. "In yours too, really."

"Do you think so?"

"Well, certainly. If you hadn't proposed to her, she might never have become acquainted with Lord Willingdon," Felicity explained. "And if I hadn't—er—encouraged her acquaintance with the marquess, she would have ended up married to you!"

Kincaid's laughter attracted Jane's attention, and Felicity frowned. "She's staring at us now, Lucas," she reported. "Perhaps we should have turned off the path after all."

Kincaid made an effort to compose himself, and he and Felicity fell silent as they approached Jane and Ernest. Since Jane now outranked the Kincaids, it fell to her to address them first, and for a moment it looked as though she wasn't going to acknowledge them. Ernest, however, prevented the snub by rushing towards Felicity.

"Miss Taylor!" he exclaimed happily.

"It's Mrs. Kincaid now," Jane corrected him stiffly.

"Good afternoon, Lady Willingdon," Felicity said cheerfully.

"Can I pet your horse?" Ernest asked eagerly, reaching up to stroke Sugarplum's flank.

Felicity smiled down at him, then caught the look in Jane's eye. "Just for a minute, Ernest, then Sugarplum and I must be on our way."

Ernest had only a nebulous grasp on the concept of time, but it seemed as though no time at all had passed before his stepmama was leading him away.

"Lady Willingdon didn't act as though she was in your debt, Felicity," Kincaid remarked.

"Perhaps she was embarrassed," Felicity suggested with a shrug.

"I'll never forget your performance when she first came to tea," Kincaid said with a laugh. "When I think of the things you said! I'll never forget the look on her face when you told her I didn't receive love letters from other young ladies!"

"I didn't think you did, Lucas," Felicity said innocently. "Are you telling me I was wrong?"

"I'm telling you that you're incorrigible," he said with a chuckle. "Even if I had wanted to correspond with other young ladies, Felicity, I wouldn't have had the time or the energy; I was too distracted by you."

"Do you know, Lucas, I think that's one of the nicest things you've ever said to me?"

"Is that so, Felicity?" Kincaid asked, with a look of feigned confusion. "If I recall, you told me that many people think it's perfectly acceptable for a man to keep a mistress. It was one of the things you learned from the French young ladies at Miss Archer's seminary."

Felicity sighed. "I said a lot of foolish things, Lucas, because I didn't want you to see me as an ingenue."

Kincaid's brow furrowed. "So what are you saying, Felicity? You no longer think an honourable man can keep a mistress?"

"I really don't care what other men do," Felicity replied. "I'm saying that you can't. I wouldn't put up with it."

"Do you think it would be improper?" Kincaid asked with a frown. "Because you also said you hoped I was capable of improper behaviour. Or something to that effect."

"What I think, Mr. Kincaid, is that if you want to misbehave, you can do so with me."

Kincaid abruptly decided that he had seen enough of Hyde Park, and convinced his wife it was time to go home.

About the Author

Emma Melbourne lives in Toronto with her family. She loves Regency fiction (along with many other genres). *The Honourable Lucas Kincaid* is her third novel.

Contact her at emmamelbournewrites@gmail.com
Website: emmamelbourne.com

Acknowledgments

Thanks to my family for all their support, and to Mary Matthews for help with the editing.

Thanks to all the readers who have told me they enjoyed my books; you have encouraged me to keep writing.

Made in United States
Orlando, FL
26 December 2024

56551947R00202